ARMY GIRLS REPORTING FOR DUTY

FENELLA J. MILLER

Boldwood

First published in Great Britain in 2023 by Boldwood Books Ltd

Copyright © Fenella J. Miller, 2023

Cover Design by Colin Thomas

Cover Photography: Colin Thomas and Alamy

The moral right of Fenella J. Miller to be identified as the author of this work has been asserted in accordance with the Copyright, Designs and Patents Act 1988.

A CIP catalogue record for this book is available from the British Library.

Paperback ISBN 978-1-80549-262-7

Large Print ISBN 978-1-80549-258-0

Hardback ISBN 978-1-80549-257-3

Ebook ISBN 978-1-80549-255-9

Kindle ISBN 978-1-80549-256-6

Audio CD ISBN 978-1-80549-263-4

MP3 CD ISBN 978-1-80549-260-3

Digital audio download ISBN 978-1-80549-254-2

Boldwood Books Ltd
23 Bowerdean Street
London SW6 3TN
www.boldwoodbooks.com

For Peter Miller 1927–2023

1

APRIL 1942

Minnie Wolton slipped out of the front door at dawn, clutching her battered cardboard suitcase in one hand. The narrow street was quiet but there were lights on in the downstairs windows of two of the terraced houses she had to creep past. Aggie, next door, would be straight down to tell her mum and dad what was happening, and then there'd be a tearful goodbye and the little ones would wake up. She'd left them a note – Dad couldn't read but Mum would do it for him – telling them she'd got her papers and was now a volunteer in the Auxiliary Territorial Service, the women's army; the ATS.

Girls like her didn't join the WRNS or the WAAF so, when conscription had come in, the only option she had was to work in a munitions factory or join the women's army. She didn't fancy making bombs and bullets, so the ATS it was.

'Here, Minnie, where you sneaking off to?'

The suitcase fell on the road. It wasn't Aggie who'd seen her but the old biddy with half a dozen cats who lived opposite.

'Shush, I don't want to wake me family. Had enough tears last night. I'm off to join the army. TTFN.'

'Good for you, I reckon you'll do well. Better than sewing uniforms for soldiers for a living. Where you being posted to?'

'I ain't being posted anywhere until I've been trained. That takes four weeks. I've got to go, or I'll miss me train.'

Minnie recovered her suitcase, glad it wasn't raining or the cardboard might have fallen to bits. With her blooming gas mask dangling around her neck getting in the way, she resumed her walk. There was no need for her to spend any of her precious pennies on a ticket for the underground as it was only twenty minutes from her home in Mansford Street, just off Bethnal Green Road, to Liverpool Street station where she had to catch the train.

London didn't seem the same since the Yanks had

arrived in January, and the local girls flocked to the West End in order to pair up with one. They came back with chocolate – candy, the Yanks called it – and chewing gum. If they were lucky, they also got nylons – flimsy stockings a bit like silk but stronger and a lot nicer than the lisle ones.

Stockings were a luxury in Minnie's family – it was socks in the winter and bare legs in the summer. It didn't seem right that the Americans were swanning about the place, money in their pockets and no rationing on their bases, when folk around here had to do without and couldn't afford to pay the rent some weeks.

There'd not been a raid last night and not for a while, so there was no new rubble to walk over. London had been hammered last year and there were two gaps, like missing teeth, where houses had once stood, in their road alone. Fortunately, both families had been in the shelter down the end of the street, so nobody had died.

There'd been a permanent smell of smoke and damp bricks in the air everywhere you went in the East End until the Blitz had more or less ended a year ago. Hundreds of homes had been bombed by them Nazis and the homeless had been sent all over the shop. Minnie reckoned the East End wouldn't be the same even when the war was over.

Working as a seamstress alongside her mum had been all right, but now all women had to do essential work and the army was for her. Sewing uniforms was essential but she was ready for a change. It'd be grand to get away from the bombing, the sirens wailing and the crush and smell of the communal shelters. Lots of families still went down the underground every night, even though the Germans didn't come very much now.

And Chelmsford wasn't far. She'd miss her family, the noisy heap of little ones she shared the back bedroom with, and her mum and dad, but she'd come back for a visit if she got any leave. She was nineteen, old enough to be on her own, and she couldn't wait to make a fresh start in the army.

By the time she arrived at the station, the city was waking up; blokes with barrows piled high with veg and that were trundling to their daytime positions. A big red bus rumbled past as she turned into the station and ran down the steps.

She wasn't fond of trains – much preferred the underground – they weren't noisy and smelly like them steam engines. Despite the early hour, there were already people coming and going at this busy station.

The air was thick with smoke, steam billowed upwards and the rattling clank of these metal monsters set Minnie's teeth on edge.

There was a porter having a fag and she approached him with a smile. 'Mister, where do I catch this train?' She held out the crumpled travel warrant, and he nodded.

'You're the third girl what's shown me one of them. Platform nine, plenty of time, it don't go for another ten minutes.'

'Ta ever so.'

Minnie dashed across and held her paper in front of the ticket collector. He waved her through and she made her way along the train looking for the two girls who must be new recruits like her. She was halfway down the snake of carriages when she spotted them.

She might not be God's gift when it came to looks but Mum had said that her nice curly hair made up for her face. It was meant to be a compliment. No bloke looked twice, not that that bothered her, as they were more trouble than they were worth in her opinion, and people warmed to her, although she didn't have any real close friends.

The carriage door was heavy, but Minnie opened it easily. The travel warrant was for third class – couldn't expect the army to pay for anything better. She might be only a smidgen over five feet tall and light as a feather, but she could take care of herself. She'd learned the hard way that being seen as weak just led to bullying. Dad had been a decent lightweight boxer in the past and he taught her everything he knew. She might be small, but she was tough and strong and could throw a mean left hook.

After sidling down the narrow passageway, she reached the compartment where she'd spotted the two other girls. She slid the door open and they both looked up, but neither looked particularly pleased to see her.

'Morning, ladies, I'm Minnie Wolton and I reckon we're all going for training in the ATS.'

The girl sitting in the window seat facing for-wards, a cracking natural blonde with bright blue eyes and who seemed petite like Minnie, exchanged a glance with her companion.

'Actually, Clara and I have something personal to discuss. Would you mind very much sitting elsewhere?'

She was a posh bird, looking down her nose at someone she thought her inferior. Minnie ignored the request, stepped in and closed the door loudly behind her. 'I can sit where I bloody well like. You carry on – I'll read me book.'

If she'd said she was going to do a handstand they couldn't have looked more surprised. Did they think everyone from the East End was illiterate? She pulled out her well-thumbed copy of *Pride and Prejudice*. This had been written by some historical lady called Jane Austen. She'd picked it up in the market and had read it four times already.

She'd sat on the far end of the seat, the one that the other snooty girl was sitting on. Deliberately, Minnie put her suitcase in the space between them. A heavy silence filled the compartment, but she wasn't going to be the one to break it. Dealing with bullies of any sort was something she was good at. She smiled, hoping she didn't have to give either of them a black eye to make her point.

There was a lot of whistleblowing and shouting going on outside; doors were slamming, and the carriage rocked a bit. The train was just about to leave the station when a tall, plump girl with hair the colour of conkers appeared at the door.

Minnie, who was closest, jumped up and slid it open. 'Are you a new recruit like us?' She'd recognised the arrival was holding a paper like hers.

'Golly, that was a close thing. I'm Eileen Ruffel, and yes, I'm on my way to be bashed into shape.'

Silence still from the other two but that didn't matter. Minnie knew she'd made a friend.

She introduced herself and Eileen followed her lead and put her own much less scruffy suitcase in the space beside her. 'I'm not good at early mornings and I'm surprised I got here at all.'

Minnie closed her book and was about to put it back in her coat pocket. To her surprise, one of the silent girls spoke to her. She was tall, her dark hair pinned up in a posh sort of arrangement at the back of her head, and had a lovely set of pearly whites.

'*Pride and Prejudice* is my absolute favourite. Have you read all Jane Austen's books? I'm Clara Felgate, the rude one sitting opposite me is Grace Sinclair. She's not a particular pal of mine as I only met her five minutes ago.'

The one called Grace stared out of the window as if she hadn't heard what Clara had said.

Minnie moved the suitcase and Clara deliberately shuffled into the empty space. The other girl glowered in the corner. Who'd pulled her chain?

'I've only read this one. I found it on a market stall and ain't found any of the others. I've looked.'

'Have you tried Boots subscription library? I'm sure all the public libraries would have copies you could borrow.'

Eileen nodded. 'I get ever so many books from the library. I love to read.'

'Hey, what's up? Is your hubby overseas?' Minnie asked. She'd seen a wedding ring on the girl's plump finger.

'He is, Danny was in the Territorials and got called up that first September. He didn't enjoy being up to his waist in snow over the winter but until then he'd had a jolly time. He was one of the lucky ones evacuated from Dunkirk last year. Then a few weeks ago he was posted overseas but I don't know where.'

She smiled and Minnie thought she'd misjudged the situation. Eileen wasn't upset at all.

'Actually, he didn't come home even though he could have done, so I've not seen him for eighteen months. I'm beginning to enjoy my independence. There's no need to worry about me, Minnie, I've almost forgotten what he looks like.' She pulled a face. 'I made a mistake marrying him, and the longer I've been away from him constantly criticising me, the happier I am.'

The train lurched and shuddered as it went over a set of points and Minnie's case fell off the seat, the catches sprung free, and the lid flew open at Grace's feet.

Her grey underwear and scruffy nightdress, along

with several other personal items, were now on full view. Minnie wasn't ashamed of who she was. She was more concerned that the sharp metal catch had caught Grace's ankle and her leg was bleeding.

'Blimey, I'm ever so sorry.' She slammed the lid shut and pushed the case to one side and then dropped down in front of the girl. 'It ain't too bad. I've got me first-aid certificate – I'll see to it for you.'

There was no answer from the girl and when Minnie looked up, she saw that Grace had fainted. She was slumped to one side and her face was deathly white. A little cut like this shouldn't have caused her to pass out.

'Quick, I need to check it's only a faint.' She took the girl's pulse and it was steady. 'Right, if you'll give us a hand, we'll sit her up and then put her head between her legs. If she don't come round smartish, one of you will have to pull the emergency handle.'

The other two followed her instructions without question. 'Right, you hold her steady and I'll clean up the cut. I reckon she'll be right aggravated about the hole in her silk stocking.'

There was a rudimentary first-aid kit in her case – she always carried it with her –and she cleaned the cut and put a sticking plaster over it. She sat back on her heels and took Grace's pulse again.

'I reckon she's coming round. Let's sit her up. She might be sick. Do either of you have a towel in your suitcase?'

Eileen flicked hers open and produced one that had been freshly laundered. It was newish and it would be a shame to spoil it.

Slowly, Grace recovered her senses and looked around as if not sure where she was. Minnie had initially been worried the girl was having a fit, but she was pretty sure it was just a common or garden faint.

Grace opened and closed her eyes a few times. Eileen had spread the towel on her lap just in case.

'I'm not going to be ill, but thank you for thinking of me. I'm terribly sorry for scaring you. It's blood, you know – I just pass out if I see it.'

'Crikey, you won't last long in the army,' Minnie said.

'Oh, it's only my own blood – I'm absolutely spiffing with anybody else's.'

This was such a strange thing to say that Minnie laughed and then Eileen and Clara joined in. It hung in the balance for a few seconds but eventually Grace smiled, her colour fully restored, and then she too was laughing.

This incident broke the ice and although it didn't explain why Grace had been so snotty earlier, Minnie was happy that at least on the surface they were all getting along. The ticket inspector didn't bother to come in when they held up their warrants, he just smiled and waved and continued on his journey down the train to clip the tickets of the other passengers.

'Why did you volunteer for the ATS, Clara? I'd've thought you'd prefer to be in the WAAF as that's where the posh girls go,' Minnie asked.

'I don't like aeroplanes and I think being so close to them would be most unpleasant. I didn't apply to the WRNS as I'm not fond of the sea either, so that only left the army. So here I am. What about you, Eileen?'

'As my husband's in the army, I already know quite a lot about it so it made sense to join the ATS. Danny won't be happy that I've joined up but he's not here, so I've done it anyway.'

'It's the ATS what's advertising for volunteers and me folks were only too happy to have one less mouth to feed. Mum wouldn't hear of sending me little brothers and sisters away and reckoned they would be safer with her, and she were right. There's been no bombs dropped on our house and the bombings are more or less over now,' Minnie said.

This just left Grace to explain her reasons. They looked expectantly in her direction, but she was steadfastly staring out of the window, refusing to catch anyone's eye.

'Go on then, Grace, tell us why you're here,' Minnie asked, as no one else seemed prepared to do so. 'I thought posh birds like you and Clara could evade the conscription.'

'Oh, very well then, not that it's your business why I volunteered. Mater wanted me to marry a silly young man, the son of my godmother, but I couldn't stand him. I couldn't avoid doing war work indefinitely so joined the ATS and killed two birds with one stone. I expect they'll be sending out search parties but it's too late for them to do anything as I'm already signed up and no longer their responsibility.'

'No one can make you marry a bloke you don't want to. Still, best to scarper, I suppose,' Minnie said. 'Me, I wouldn't do nothing I don't want to do.'

The train began to slow, and Minnie checked her old case was securely fastened. This was their stop. She'd never been further down the line than Romford and here she was arriving at Chelmsford. She reckoned before the war was over, she'd have been all over the shop. When she'd signed up, the recruitment lady had said she could be posted anywhere in the country.

'I'm going to wait at the door. Don't want to be left

on board. It never stopped for more than a minute at Romford, did it?' Minnie slid back the door and rocked her way along the narrow passage, not waiting to see if the others followed her lead.

Eileen was right behind her when she reached the doors. 'Are them two coming or what?' Minnie asked.

'Grace has changed her mind and has decided to return home. I don't think she wants to be with us, we're too common for her. Clara's trying to persuade her to come as she's signed the papers, she can't just slope off. She'll be a deserter or something like that.'

'Daft cow. She's got to get off this train and cross the lines if she wants to go back to London.' Minnie grinned. 'She never thought this through. Being an army girl isn't right for someone as posh as her. She'd have been better being an ARP or an ambulance driver.'

She was poked in the small of the back by something hard. She turned and nodded. The sharp object had been the corner of Grace's very expensive leather case. 'Are you coming with us or what?'

'I'm coming. I might be posh but I'm not stupid. Clara's just explained it to me. With my background, I might be an officer in no time and that makes things seem a little more interesting.'

Minnie had no chance to answer this challenge as

the train ground to a noisy halt. There were no name signs on stations any more, but she'd been counting the stops and was certain this was where they had to get off. Eileen let down the window and then leaned out and turned the knob. The door swung open, almost taking her with it.

'Look, there's loads of other girls getting off. They must have all sat together at the front so we didn't see them,' Eileen said as she jumped out onto the platform.

'Jolly good show,' Clara said. 'I was thinking that we couldn't be the only ones in this intake.'

Grace said nothing and if Minnie had allowed her, she would have pushed past and got out next. However, despite making it clear she didn't want to be with them, Grace didn't rush off to join the throng of noisy girls milling about talking loudly further up the platform.

'Right, ladies, we're closer to the exit. Looks as if we've got a load of stairs to go down. I reckon there'll be transport waiting outside for us.'

Minnie was right. A large canvas-covered lorry was standing outside the station and a soldier was leaning against the side smoking a fag. He had no stripes so wasn't anyone they had to salute or nothing.

He saw them emerge, took a last puff and pinched

out his cigarette then dropped it into his battledress pocket.

'Right, ladies, in the back.' He leered at Minnie. 'I'll give you a bunk up, love, you'll not get in on your own.'

'No, thanks.' She threw her case up and, putting one hand on the tailgate, vaulted easily inside. She was small, but not useless. There were narrow, shiny wooden benches running down each side of the lorry. She grabbed her case, relieved it hadn't fallen apart, and made her way to the back.

Eileen hopped in easy enough as she was tall, then made her way to the back, too. Next Clara scrambled in, and, from the raucous catcalls, must have shown her knickers in the process.

'Golly, I suppose I've got to get used to that sort of thing,' Clara said as she slid along the bench and joined the two of them.

To Minnie's surprise, Grace arrived next and sat next to Clara and almost smiled. 'I thought I might abandon you three and find someone else to be rude to, but I think we're the best of the bunch. Therefore, I'm afraid you're stuck with me.'

'That's fine by me. I've just realised it might have been a bad idea to get on first as we'll have to get off last. That means them others will get first dibs on everything.'

'I think we're allocated a billet, Minnie, and no one has any choice in the matter,' Clara said as the remainder of the intake jumped, scrambled, or were shoved into the rapidly filling lorry.

The driver, whistling cheerfully, pulled up the tailgate and secured it and was about to drop the canvas cover so they'd be in stuffy darkness. Minnie was going to yell at him to leave it open but the girl sitting closest did it for her.

The bloke shrugged and left it as it was. The lorry rocked a bit as he got into the cab and then, with a hideous grinding of gears, it moved off. The noise from the engine and the rattle of the canvas cover against the metal hoops that it went over made conversation difficult.

A girl sitting opposite nudged her companion and then they started singing 'It's a Long Way to Tipperary' and soon everyone joined in. There was nothing Minnie liked better than a sing-song and a knees-up. She decided she was going to like this ATS lark.

2

Eileen was crammed between Minnie and Clara on the narrow bench; they were packed like sardines with their luggage dumped in the space between them. Even if the lorry swerved, it was unlikely any of them would slide off.

'If we stop suddenly, the girls sitting by the open end might be catapulted into the road. We should have had the canvas put down like the driver wanted to do,' Eileen said at the top of her voice. The only way to be heard was to shout as the noise from the rattling vehicle and the engine was so loud.

'You could be right, so let's hope it ain't going to happen. Look, both them girls sitting on the end of the benches are hanging on like grim death to the tail-gate. That should be enough.'

'At least we won't fall off the bench – in fact, I'm hoping it won't be a long journey as I'm already feeling breathless from being cooped up in here.'

'Blimey, are you claustrophobic?' Minnie asked.

'No, I don't think so, but I'm finding breathing difficult being squashed like this.' Eileen shifted uncomfortably, hoping to find herself a few inches of extra space.

Her movement had a ripple effect and the small push she'd given Clara became exaggerated as it went down the line and the penultimate girl was ejected from her place like a pea from a pod and landed face first in the luggage, whilst the very last girl continued to hang desperately onto the tailgate.

She sat up, giggling. Her skirt was rucked up, showing her knickers, suspenders and stockings. She was just lifting her bottom to pull her skirt down when the lorry braked sharply and began to turn left. The suit-cases cascaded down the centre space and she disappeared beneath them with just her legs waving in the air.

By the time she was extricated, thankfully un-harmed, everybody was laughing, and the ice had been broken. The singing continued and when, twenty minutes later, they pulled up outside the barracks that was to be their home for the next four weeks at least, they were the best of friends.

The lorry was waved through by the guards and shuddered to a standstill. The jolly driver appeared at the rear of the vehicle and let down the tailgate.

'Crikey, I can't find my case,' one of the girls who had to get out first wailed.

'You lot at the front get out and me and my mates will throw them out after. It'll be easier to sort out what's what doing it that way,' Minnie yelled.

There was a chorus of agreement, and the girls began to tumble out. Minnie got the four of them organised and in no time the muddled suitcases were flying through the air. Most were caught and none of them so far had fallen apart.

'These are ours,' Clara said, holding one up. 'I think we might as well carry these as I don't think Minnie's would survive being thrown out.'

When Eileen jumped to the ground clutching her own luggage, she saw they were parked in front of a large two-storey brick building. It didn't look very welcoming but at least the windows were sparkling, and the paintwork gleamed in the mid-morning sunshine.

The girls were milling about chatting, gazing with

interest at what was to be their home for the next month at least.

'Don't look too bad, do it? Blooming well cleaner than where I live. Look at them stones what edge the path – all of them are painted white. I reckon that's so we can find our way about the barracks in the dark,' Minnie said.

Eileen agreed – everything looked spick-and-span, exactly how she liked things. There were soldiers marching smartly about the place and the group received several appreciative grins but fortunately no catcalls or rude remarks. It was going to be interesting living cheek by jowl with the men, but she hoped none of them were actually billeted in the same depressing block they were standing outside. She dreaded to think what might happen if temptation was put so close to some of these girls.

'Cor, here comes someone in uniform. I need the lav, let's hope she can tell us where to go,' a peroxide blonde said as she hopped anxiously from foot to foot.

There was no need to ask. 'Line up in threes. Be quick. We haven't got all day. It's latrine parade first,' the woman barked at them, and they began to shuffle about. Eileen knew what the order meant but some of

the girls lined up one behind another in threes instead of three abreast.

It took the unfortunate woman five minutes to get
them in some sort of order. They were marched
around the back of the barracks and taken towards a
group of four brick-built buildings. These were the
latrines and ablutions. They were sent in sixes to use
the facilities and were only allowed a minute.

Grace, Clara, Minnie and Eileen were in and out
in the allotted time, as were all but one of the girls.
This poor soul exceeded this and was fetched out, red
with embarrassment.

'Excuse me,' Grace asked politely. 'Where do we
wash our hands?'

'No hand washing. This isn't an ablutions parade,'
she was told smartly.

About half the assembled group of twenty-four
volunteers were unhappy about the lack of hygiene
but the rest seemed unbothered.

'Do you think we have to get permission to spend
a penny?' Clara whispered, not wishing to be overheard by the fierce corporal who'd yet to identify
herself.

'I shouldn't think so,' Eileen said. 'Danny certainly
doesn't have to – mind you, things are different over-

seas and I expect they just nip behind the nearest bush, which is something we can't do.'

Next, they were marched to another building where they were told they were to have a medical.

'Remove everything apart from your knickers and jacket or coat and line up in alphabetical order,' a corporal barked.

'Crikey, are we supposed to strip off in front of him?' Eileen wasn't the only one bothered by the lack of privacy and the fact that the medical was going to be conducted with men in attendance.

'We ain't got a choice, we better get on with it, but that bugger's got to go,' Minnie said. 'Excuse me, Corporal, we ain't undressing with you in here. It's not right or decent.'

'I'll wait outside. You've got three minutes.'

Eileen couldn't believe that so many women could remove their clothes so fast. There was no time for worrying about any of the squad seeing their bits and bobs – their main concern was that they wouldn't be stared at by strange men. She was glad she'd been wearing a raincoat, which meant she was respectably covered. A lot of the girls just had cardigans or jackets and although their top half was covered, their knickers were on full view.

They were more or less decent, when the corporal

came back but it took a few more minutes to get themselves into order. The first in the line was a tall, thin, dark-haired girl with the surname Adams.

'I had a medical when I signed up,' one of these next in line said. 'What's this all about then?'

'FFI inspection. Free from infection,' another said helpfully.

She gave her name, the soldier ticked her off on a list, and then she stepped through the closed door. Moments later she was out and the next unfortunate went in.

'I had to pull down me knickers. I never been so embarrassed in me life,' Adams said. 'Checking for scabies or something worse, I reckon. He looked at everything, under your arms, down below. I nearly died.' The girl was in tears and rushed into a corner to get dressed as quickly as she'd stripped.

'Here, Adams,' Minnie called across the room. 'How many men in there?'

'Just the doctor, he don't look old enough to be qualified. If I'd known what was going to happen, then I'd never have joined up but gone into the munitions factory where me sister works. I like to keep me privates private.'

They filed in and out, and by the time it was Eileen's turn, she was resigned. Being in the army meant no privacy and she'd known this when she signed up. Marriage to Danny hadn't been happy and now she was in the army too and he couldn't do anything about it.

Once this hideous experience was over, they regrouped in the same order and then in their threes were marched across the concrete and back to the barracks. They trooped upstairs and into a long room. The iron bedsteads were lined up in the centre, head to tail, and the woman in charge allocated the beds. Eileen and her friends were at the head of the queue so they were sent to the far end. This meant they could stay together. Minnie took the end bed, Eileen was next, then Clara and finally Grace.

On the beds were three square straw-filled objects, three fiercely folded dark-coloured blankets and a pillow. Corporal Rigby – someone had asked her name and it had been passed down the line like wildfire – waited until they were all standing by a bed and then called them to attention.

'About turn. Eyes forward. Watch and learn.' She held up one of the square things. 'These are called biscuits – every morning you will return your bed to the state it's in now. Is that understood?' Everybody nodded but nobody spoke, and she seemed happy enough with that. 'You will be issued with two sheets and two pillow slips. You will then be shown how to make your bed correctly.' She snapped to attention, swivelled and took two steps towards the exit. 'Fall in, in threes. Quick march. Follow me to the stores.'

Eileen had no idea what they were supposed to do with their suitcases so pushed hers under the bed and, from the rattling and banging down the long room, all the girls were doing the same.

This time, the four of them were at the rear of the shambolic group. Grace managed to persuade the two girls ahead of her in the row of beds to stand on either side, so she was in a three as she was supposed to be.

'Here, Grace, let them others go ahead of us. We'll show them there's six of us what can march like what we're supposed to,' Minnie said.

This was where Eileen could help. 'Right, when someone says, "By the left, quick march," you have to move off on your left foot with the right arm up. The idea is for your arms to swing forward alternately to your legs. You've got to step out like a man if it's going to work.'

She demonstrated what she was telling them. She'd gone along to watch the Territorials a few times and had learned from that.

The rest of the group were already out of the room and halfway down the stairs but the six of them wanted to get it right and make a good impression. 'We'll soon catch them up as they're hopeless at marching in time,' Eileen said, and the others agreed.

'Right, I think we've got it. Will you go in front of us, Eileen, then we can follow your lead,' Grace said and was actually smiling when she spoke.

'Happy to. Ready? By the left – quick march.'

In perfect step, they marched briskly out of the room, down the steps and as expected the others were stumbling about, being shouted at by the irate corporal.

'We'll keep a couple of yards behind. Eyes front,' Eileen said with a smile. She was proud of her new friends and determined to make sure all of them were the best recruits in this cohort.

By the time they reached the stores, the remaining girls were more or less in lines of three and a few of them were in time – the rest were doing the best they could. It didn't go unnoticed that Eileen and her friends were in good order.

'Blooming silly, if you ask me, marching like this in our civvies,' Minnie said without turning her head. 'Some of them poor buggers are trying to do it with high heels.'

'They shouldn't have come inappropriately attired,' Grace said from directly behind Eileen.

'That big building ahead is the stores. I hope this doesn't take too long, I'm absolutely starving,' Clara added.

Rigby slammed to a halt in the mistaken belief that the girls would do the same. The front row, seeing their leader stationary, stopped abruptly. Inevitably the row behind walked into them and Eileen watched half with horror and half with enjoyment at the chaos that ensued.

Of course, the six of them remained outside the mêlée of tangled girls and stood at ease, waiting to be told what to do next.

'Shouldn't we help?' Clara asked.

'No, better to stay where we are and let them sort themselves out,' Eileen replied.

It was difficult not to laugh as the girls rearranged themselves, some laughing, some crying and others swearing. The unfortunate red-faced NCO struggled to regain control. Shouting at the girls was just making it worse and she told them all to queue for their kit in alphabetical order, which caused further milling about.

'Crikey, we'd better find our places,' Minnie said. 'Makes sense to be in order so they give us the right stuff and all that.'

A male sergeant, hearing the racket outside the

door, came out to see what the fuss was. He saw the six of them standing tidily and beckoned them over.

'Right, you six, let's get you kitted out.'

'Excuse me, Sarge, but we're not in alphabetical order. Won't that mean we're issued with the wrong uniform?' Eileen said.

He laughed, a sudden barking sound. 'You get whatever looks as if it fits. Did you think it was tailor made for you?'

Embarrassed, Eileen hung her head. Then Minnie spoke up.

'What about for everything else? I ain't getting no one else's jabs and that.'

He nodded and stared at her. 'Good girl. Obviously being in name order is essential for medical things – and for pay parade.' He gestured towards the waiting orderlies and the six of them ventured forwards nervously.

The stores was a huge room with a long polished wooden counter running from one end to the other. Behind it stood half a dozen orderlies, both male and female, and behind them shelves and shelves of khaki waiting to be issued.

They obediently began to travel down the counter, collecting everything they would need. Goodness knows how they were going to get anything that actually fitted them as nobody had asked for their measurements. It seemed it was done by eye.

Jackets, skirts, and shirts, two of each, were flung at them first. These were quickly followed by vests, hideous khaki knickers, matching stockings, suspender belt, ties, greatcoat, woollen gloves and jumper, as well as pyjamas, waterproof groundsheet-cape and overalls. A heavy canvas cylindrical kitbag was added to this bundle.

'Over there, pack everything away and then line up again for the rest,' one of the orderlies said with a smile.

As they queued a second time, the correctly arranged column of sixteen girls arrived at the uniform counter. The next issue was lighter and more interesting.

Badge, button sticks, shoes, shoe brushes, shoelaces, gym shoes, field dressing, cutlery, mugs, towels, brass cleaner, hairbrush, toothbrush, and what they called a housewife – pronounced 'hussif' – a little rollup mending kit which even had a thimble included. All in dreary khaki, of course. Eileen thought this an unbecoming colour for women.

They then headed to a separate table where the sergeant who'd called them in was now seated. After they'd given their names, he handed them each their identity discs, for which they signed.

He smiled kindly at them. 'Right, ladies, take your kit back to your billet, then return to collect your bedding and then go to the PAD store. It's in the next building along. Don't worry about being out of order – it's going to take hours to sort out this shower. God knows where they got this lot. I can't see Corporal Rigby making them into soldiers – she has enough difficulty with good recruits.'

They marched to their barracks, put the bulging kitbags neatly against the end of their beds and then headed off to collect their bedding. They arranged themselves correctly before they exited the building.

'Do you think we've got to wait for the other girls before we can get something to eat?' Clara said plaintively.

'Let's get our bedding and whatever else we're going to be issued from the PAD store back to the billet and then I reckon we can go in search of the cookhouse. Me belly thinks me throat's been cut,' Minnie said cheerfully.

'What on earth does PAD stand for?' Grace asked.

'I've no idea,' Eileen said, 'but we'll find out when we get there.'

'Did you notice that every single item is stamped?'

Grace said. 'We don't own any of it, it all belongs to the king.'

'He's welcome to it when I leave.' Clara laughed. 'I sincerely hope that won't be until the end of the war, but you never know – any of us could be dismissed from the service.'

'I ain't going anywhere. I'm here for the duration, as if I've got any choice in the matter.'

There was still no sign of the other sixteen members of their troop as they marched three abreast in the correct fashion past the open door to the stores. From the racket going on inside, the orderlies were having no better luck.

In the next store – they'd discovered that the initials stood for Passive Air Defence – they were given a service gas mask, eye shields – anti-dim, and the case to put them in as well as anti-gas ointment, pots, and earplugs. All these fitted neatly into the haversack which they were told to wear over one shoulder at all times.

'Golly, I hope we don't have to use any of this,' Clara said as they doubled back to their billet. The other sixteen girls had returned and none of them were looking particularly happy.

'Everything's a parade and we have to march back and forth like soldiers,' a tall thin girl complained.

'Blimey, girl, that's what we signed up for – what we're going to be when they've finished with us.'

'We've got to make our beds when we get the bedding,' one of them said. 'Then can we finally go to the mess hall for something to eat?'

'No, you can't, you've got to get this lot as well,' Eileen told them and the other girls wandered out to get their remaining kit.

Eileen had a rough idea how the uncomfortable-looking mattresses worked and set about making up her bed. 'We put them end to end on the bed. Then one of the blankets over the top to hold them in place, then the sheets and so on. I'm sure there's a proper way to do it but as we haven't been shown, we'll just have to hope what we do is good enough.'

'I ain't hanging about to find out,' Minnie said as she deftly arranged the biscuits.

Less than five minutes later, the beds were neatly made, the top blanket smooth as you like, and they were ready to empty the kit bags.

They had the room to themselves again, which gave them a small degree of privacy. 'Shall we unpack and put on the uniform?' Eileen wasn't sure if they should and wanted the others to agree before they did so.

'We can't swan about in ordinary clothes, can we? I

expect the NCO will be along in a mo and give the order. Can't see it matters if we've already done it,' Clara said as she began to remove her civvies.

They were all giggling as they held up each item.

'Bleedin' Nora – me knickers will come down past me knees,' Minnie said, laughing.

'I can see why they're called passion killers,' Eileen said as she stepped into hers. 'I'm keeping my own drawers on underneath.'

'I'm not wearing this brassiere,' Grace said as she waved it in the air in disgust. 'I'm going to keep my own camisole on underneath this ghastly uniform. Are you quite sure we should be putting it on now, Eileen? Shouldn't we wait until someone demonstrates the correct way of wearing it?'

'It's common sense, really. Badge goes on the cap, and everything else is obvious, don't you think?' Clara said.

By the time they'd changed, put away the rest of their folded kit in the lockers and hung the coats on the pegs, the room was no longer their own. The remaining sixteen girls had now got their bedding and were assembling to parade to the PAD store. Even they seemed to be getting the hang of things.

Eileen led the others down the stairs, all clutching

their cutlery and mugs, but paused at the door. 'Right, ladies, let's show them how smart we are.'

'Don't matter how smart we are if we ain't got a clue where we're going,' Minnie said.

'Follow our nose, perhaps?' Clara suggested.

'Actually, ladies, I'm not sure we should be galivanting about without our NCO. We've changed into our uniforms without being instructed to as well,' Grace said.

She had a point. 'Shall we wait here until Rigby returns and issues orders? Grace is right. We've been charging around...'

Minnie interrupted Eileen. 'The sergeant what told us to collect everything might still be in the stores. I'll go and ask him.'

She didn't wait for confirmation from them and marched off. Minnie might be small, but she looked every inch a soldier.

3

Minnie thought this Rigby attached to their lot was useless. Their corporal should have been there to issue orders and then she wouldn't have to brave the dragon in his den. She'd volunteered to go, but wished she hadn't.

She hesitated outside the now closed door of the stores, not sure if knocking was against regulations.

'Attention,' a man barked from right behind her.

Her feet left the ground and she stumbled forward. If a strong hand hadn't grabbed her arm, she'd have fallen on her face.

'Sorry, couldn't resist. Didn't mean to startle you.'

Minnie wrenched her arm from his grip and spun round, ready to give whoever was playing silly buggers a piece of her mind. Facing her was a young, fair-haired officer, a head taller than her, with lovely grey eyes.

She jumped to attention and saluted. He returned the gesture.

'No need for that. Are you missing some vital piece of kit?' He nodded towards the door.

'No, sir, I wanted to know if we're allowed to go in search of the mess without our NCO?'

His friendly smile slipped, and his expression became serious. 'Is your NCO Rigby by any chance?'

She nodded. 'Yes, sir, we seem to have lost her.'

'How many of your cohort are correctly dressed?'

'Six of us, sir.'

He shook his head. 'I take it the others are in a state of disarray in your billet?'

This time she just nodded, and his friendly smile returned.

'Right. Fetch those that are ready, and I'll escort you there myself.'

Blimey, what would the girls say when they saw her with this handsome officer in tow? Eileen must have been watching, because when she returned, the five girls stepped out and all saluted perfectly. Eileen had taught them it was long way up, short way down, so they had it down pat.

The officer saluted back and nodded. 'Excellent. When did you arrive?'

Minnie answered for them. 'An hour and a half ago, sir.'

'Good God! Despite Rigby, you six have triumphed. Come with me. You deserve to eat first.'

Minnie nodded at the others, and they fell in as before and marched behind him. What was his name? He was a lieutenant – she knew that from his stripes, but she could hardly ask him. He didn't look behind and strolled, but in a marching kind of way, to the end of the road.

'The mess hall for ATS is the smaller building on the left. Well done. Cheering to think at least some of the today's intake will make decent soldiers.' He looked them all over a second time. 'You're the fourth lot in today. God help us all.' With a nod, he strolled off and they watched until he turned a corner and was out of sight.

'Gosh, where did you find that gorgeous gentleman?' Grace asked, seeming interested in her surroundings for the first time.

'I didn't, he found me. I'll tell you over dinner,' Minnie said.

They had sorted themselves into alphabetical order just in case they were grilled. This meant that

Clara was first, being a Felgate, and Minnie was last, being a Wolton.

The mess was half-full and everybody was in uniform, which was a relief. Minnie had been half-expecting them to be the only ones that had changed. An orderly greeted them at the door.

'Where's the rest of your lot?'

Clara, being at the front, answered for them. 'An officer escorted us here because we were ready and no one else in our intake was.'

The orderly frowned and pointed them to a table laid up for eight. 'Sit there, seeing as you've come on your own. Supposed to be eight of you at a time but can't be helped, I suppose.'

They did as instructed. 'I thought we'd have to queue up at a hatch and fetch our own dinner. Didn't expect to be waited on,' Minnie said.

'Maybe it's just because this is our first day. From their appearance, I think we're all in the same boat. I can't see anybody who looks as if they've been here more than five minutes,' Eileen replied.

There was a general clatter as the cutlery and mugs were put out on the table. Minnie was almost as thirsty as she was hungry and couldn't see a teapot anywhere.

'Do you reckon they bring round the tea? I ain't seeing any place we can go and fill these mugs.'

'It's coming now – there's an orderly with an enormous teapot on her way over,' Clara said happily.

What was tipped into the mugs was brown and wet but wasn't like any brew Minnie had ever had. 'Fancy putting the milk in with the tea – it tastes ever so strange, but I reckon we'll get used to it. Good thing I don't like sugar in me tea.'

'I prefer sugar but can't be helped with there being a war on and it being rationed. And we are in the army now,' Eileen said as she drank down half her mug in one swallow.

Next their dinner arrived, and it was a tasty stew with potatoes and a slice of bread. Much better than Minnie had expected, and she wolfed it down with enjoyment, as did the rest of them.

'Blimey, that was a bit of all right. No gristle and stringy bits in the meat and a lovely big portion. Almost as good as me mum makes on high days and holidays.'

'I'm impressed,' Clara said as she wiped the last of the gravy up with her slice of bread. 'I didn't expect to get anything as palatable. Shall I pass the plates so you can stack them at your end, Minnie?'

The orderlies returned with jam roly-poly and

custard and the girl with the huge teapot filled their mugs up a second time. None of the women had anything to complain about as far as the food was concerned.

They were just finishing their afters when the rest of their troop arrived. Rigby seemed to have got them in order as they all looked ever so smart. The same orderly sent them to the empty tables next to their one. They got a lot of snarky looks, including from Rigby.

Minnie wasn't bothered – no one was going to bully her or her friends or they'd feel the weight of her left hook. She could take care of herself.

There'd been no time for talking and she'd yet to tell them about the officer. 'I reckon we'd best wait until them others have finished. Then we can fit in the right place after. We won't be together no more if we go everywhere in order.'

'I notice there's a bucket of hot water by the door. I presume we have to rinse our cutlery and mug on the way out,' Clara told them.

'They'll need more than a rinse. I hope we can visit the ablutions without being paraded, then we can do it properly there,' Eileen said.

While they waited, Minnie explained how she'd met the officer and even Grace laughed. 'I'm going to ask an orderly if they know who it was. I'll take the plates back to the hatch.'

The girl behind the counter was friendly and knew the officer when she described him. 'Oh, that'll be Lieutenant Sawyer. He's a bit of all right, isn't he?'

'I never noticed. Why's he here? Shouldn't he be with his regiment somewhere?'

'I was told he had a motorbike accident and broke his leg and is only just fit for duty.'

'Right, ta ever so. Is this where we come for all our meals?'

'You do. I warn you that you'll get stew and steamed pudding most days for dinner.'

'Can't complain about that. Ta for the information.'

She returned to the others and passed on what she'd been told. The two tables with the rest of their group were now finishing their afters so they'd all be on the move soon.

'I need the lav,' Minnie said. 'I ain't happy about being told like kiddies when we can go. Lieutenant Sawyer knows what's what where our NCO's concerned, I reckon our officers do too.'

Eileen stood up. 'I'm going to go across and ask one of the girls if they know what we've got to do next.'

Minnie had been about to do so herself but was happy to let Eileen do it. It must be hard for her friend to be married and not have seen her husband since September two years ago, not know how he was or when she'd see him again. Not that Eileen seemed too attached to this Danny bloke of hers, clearly the marriage wasn't a happy one.

Eileen returned with a grin. 'Rigby said when they'd finished eating, they were to go to the latrines and ablutions and then report to her outside our billet for a demonstration of something – they weren't quite sure what.'

Minnie was on her feet immediately. 'I'll see you at the billet. Can't hang about or I might wet me pants.'

* * *

Eileen wasn't in such a hurry and paused to rinse her eating-irons and mug in a somewhat grubby jug of hot water before heading in the same direction. She'd learned *irons* were what the cutlery and mug were called. The other four at her table followed. At least the loos were spotless and she remembered Danny telling her that when a soldier was put on a charge he was given fatigues and this meant they would sometimes have to clean the ablutions and latrines for a week as a punishment. They might also have to run around the parade ground wearing their heavy packs, but she doubted that punishment would be applied to the ATS girls.

When she emerged from the ablutions with her irons sparkling, Minnie was waiting for her.

'I've just had a gander to see what Rigby's got planned for us. There's a long trestle table set out in the road, and it looks as if it's a sample of all the kit we've been given laid out in order. I ain't sure why it's being done outside.'

'I don't suppose many of the other beds are made up or the kit properly unpacked. Perhaps it makes sense to do it where we can all gather round without falling over each other.'

'I reckon it'd be more sensible to do it in the billet where we could follow what was being done. I won't be the only one who's forgotten by the time we have to do it upstairs.'

Eileen waited with Minnie for everybody to gather and then the six of them slotted into their correct places in the line. 'Keep eyes front, no talking, and lovely straight backs. Let's show Rigby that we can be the best intake.'

Eileen knew all their surnames and noticed all but the four of them were using those and not first names.

Being addressed as Ruffel sounded silly but she was in the army now and had to lump it. Danny had told her he and his mates used nicknames. He was called Frilly because of his name. His best friend Freddie Bell was known as Dinger. She prayed they would both come home safe and sound one day.

The group marched off smart as paint and she was pleased the rest of the squad weren't as hopeless as she'd thought. From the corner of her eye, she noticed several soldiers stop to watch and so did some of the other girls. This would be good for morale. She wondered if the various groups of twenty-four would be competing against each other? If so, from a poor start, no fault of the girls, they were now looking first class.

Rigby glared. Shouldn't their NCO be pleased by their improvement? Why wasn't she proud of them?

'Get your beds made up and be outside in ten minutes,' she snapped.

As Eileen's bed was made, as were those of the other five she'd eaten lunch with, she was tempted to remain behind. However, Clara, ahead of them all, continued into the barracks so that's what Eileen did too.

The six of them helped the others and in less than ten minutes, all the beds were done. 'Did you see that absolutely everything we were issued is laid out in a certain way on that table?' Clara said. 'I'm never going to remember where it all has to go.'

Minnie made a sensible suggestion. 'If we each concentrate on a sixth of the table, we can then put the information together after. I'm the last of us so I'll do the last sixth.' This was a good idea and Eileen could hear some of the others arranging to do the same. As long as at least one set of kit was laid out as it should be, it should be simple for the rest of the girls to copy.

They hurried out to stand in their threes around the long table. Eileen was aware this strange occurrence was drawing embarrassing attention from passing soldiers.

Rigby then proceeded to hold up each item in turn and explain its use, even the intimate ones. 'If your brassiere doesn't fit, use your hussif to alter it. Have it done by morning parade tomorrow.'

She seemed to be enjoying their embarrassment. The woman spoke even louder. 'Turn your stocking tops over when you attach them to the suspenders, as if you don't do it your stockings will ladder and you have to mend them.'

With relish, she waved a stocking and suspender about in the air. Eileen wasn't the only one feeling uncomfortable, but their corporal seemed to be relishing this. What a particularly unpleasant person Rigby was – being trained by her was going to be horrible, even for those like herself who knew a little of what they were doing.

They were then obliged to listen to a detailed explanation of how to lace a pair of shoes and there surely couldn't be a single girl who didn't know how to do that. And so it went on until triumphantly their tormentor held up in full view of all and sundry two packets of sanitary towels. She yelled, just in case those across the road couldn't hear, that these were issued monthly and if they didn't want size two, they had to speak to her.

Eileen was a married woman, more knowledgeable than most of the girls, but even she was horrified. These items weren't displayed in chemist shops, you had to wait until there were no male customers or children and then quietly ask the sales assistant to fetch them from a cupboard somewhere out of sight.

There was a stunned silence from her squad. Those standing close to her were as scarlet faced as she was. They were then dismissed and fled up the stairs to the billet.

'How could she do that when there were men in earshot?' Clara said, shaking her head in disgust. 'One just doesn't talk about such things in public. I knew things were going to be different, but I never expected to be publicly humiliated.'

'The cow did it on purpose,' Minnie said. 'But she won't get me down. That officer don't think much of her and you can be sure them blokes watching will be talking about it and word will get back to someone in charge.'

Grace had collapsed on her bed. 'I don't think I can take any more. I wish we were volunteers and could leave if we want to. It was a dreadful mistake coming and now I've just got to lump it.'

'Anyway, if you could go home with your tail between your legs, your parents would have forced you to marry that man you don't like.'

Minnie snorted. 'No one can make you marry someone you don't like as you ain't a prisoner – you should have stood up for yourself. If they'd thrown you out, you could have got a job. A posh bird like you could work at Harrods or Fortnum & Mason's as all the assistants in there are toffee-nosed.'

'You could always have been a land girl – not so many rules and regulations for them.'

'The uniform's much nicer than ours too,' Clara said.

Grace's eyebrows rose. If Eileen had suggested Grace dance naked down the room, she couldn't have looked more shocked. 'A farm labourer? I should think not. You're right, I have no option but to stay here, however appalling it is. After all, one must hope that it can only get better.'

Eileen stood up and clapped her hands. A startled silence fell. 'Before you put everything away, why don't we practise setting it all out? The six of us at this end can do Minnie's and then you can have a look.'

A murmur of agreement rippled around the long room. The scheme they'd come up with to remember the order worked wonderfully and in no time Minnie's kit was beautifully set out.

'Blooming heck, that's a turn-up for the books,' one of girls said admiringly. 'I'd never have thought of that.'

Then Clara, Grace, Mabel and Barbara, the two girls who'd made up their six, copied. Then each girl did the same and in twenty minutes they'd all got an immaculate kit display. Eileen and Minnie had wandered down their sides of the room and helped those that needed it.

Suddenly a female voice shouted, 'Attention. Officer present.'

Eileen ran back to her bed and jumped to attention, facing the end of the room. Minnie did the same and then seconds later the entire squad were eyes front, standing as they should.

It wasn't Rigby who'd given the order but another woman with two stripes on her arm. Standing next to her was a very important officer, as she had three pips on her epaulette. It was confusing that the ATS had different names for the officers. Eileen thought Danny had told her that three pips were the same as a captain, but she'd no idea what the name of the equivalent rank in the ATS was.

'Stand at ease,' the officer ordered.

You had to be at attention before you could stand at ease. Why hadn't she shown the girls this too? Eileen relaxed her stance and linked her hands behind her back. Minnie copied her and then Clara, after a quick glance over her shoulder, did the same. Surprisingly quickly, all twenty-four of them were standing at ease. Watching Danny's training was proving useful.

'The privates who were away from their beds, step forward and identify yourselves.'

Eileen's knees were trembling. She did as instructed. 'Private Ruffel, ma'am.'

Minnie did the same. 'Private Wolton, ma'am.'

'I came expecting to find chaos but have found the reverse and am certain it's down to the leadership of you two. Corporal Rigby is unwell, therefore Corporal Endean will be your instructor from now on. I'll leave you in her capable hands.'

She nodded, smiled and vanished as silently as she'd appeared. Eileen was relieved they now had someone better to train them. After all, she couldn't be worse.

'Right, ladies, I can see you've mastered the tricky task of setting out your kit. Can you now put it away as efficiently? Then stack your bedding. Beds are only made up to sleep on or for a kit inspection. When that's done, I'll direct you to the rec room where you can meet the rest of the new intake.' Corporal Endean smiled. 'You are Platoon C. You'll have an hour to mingle, then supper, and this evening you must do any alterations to your uniform that are needed. Make the most of these few hours as from reveille tomorrow at six you'll have no free time until next week.'

4

Minnie didn't have any personal items to put on top of her locker as some of the others did. It would be nice to have had a photo of her family, but her precious book would look just fine there.

The beds ran down the centre of the room, leaving a space at the foot end just big enough for a personal locker, four pegs and a narrow passage to walk up and down. There was only a couple of feet between each bed, but Minnie had slept top to tail with two of the little ones when she'd been at home, so having a bed to herself was a real luxury.

Mabel and Barbara had made friends with a different group, leaving the four of them to themselves, which Minnie preferred.

'I'm done. I've never had so many clothes in me life and none of them second-hand neither,' she said with a happy smile as she closed her locker door.

'I'm ready,' Clara said from beside her. 'Eileen's helping Grace. I honestly think she's had a maid do everything for her before now. I really think she shouldn't be here.'

'Well, she can't leave even if she wants to. And I ain't going nowhere – I promised me mum I'd send her me wages, not that we get much.'

The other two sidled between the beds to join them. 'We get the princely sum of eleven shillings and sixpence a week,' Eileen said. 'It isn't much, but re-member we have everything paid for including med-ical bills and so on.'

'Thank goodness I have my savings book with me,' Grace said. 'I've also got more than twenty pounds in my purse.' Her crystal-clear voice carried and several heads turned. Minnie saw a speculative look on the face of one of the girls.

'You shouldn't have said that – you won't have it for long now everybody knows. Don't leave it here, for gawd's sake.'

Grace rushed back to her locker, removed her purse and with her back to those who'd been watching she hastily pulled out the four white five-pound notes and pushed them into an inside pocket in her uniform jacket.

'I really didn't think this through. Do you think there might be a safe somewhere I can put it?'

'Might be – you can ask Endean, she's waiting by the door,' Eileen said.

Grace was delighted to find that she could store her valuables safely at the admin office and went off to find it whilst the rest of them followed the others to the rec room.

They had to pass the ablution block, so Minnie decided to use the facilities and also see where they had to wash. 'Are you two coming with me?'

'No, we'll see you there. It's the building next to the mess so you can't miss it,' Eileen said and with a cheery wave she and Clara wandered off.

In the ablutions block, there were twenty lavs on one side and twenty wash basins with hot and cold water opposite. Each one of these had a small shelf and a mirror above it. There were no baths in this block, so Minnie supposed they had to wash at the basins in full view of each other.

As she didn't have a towel, she dried her hands on her skirt. She stared at her reflection. Her hair and eyes were her best features, nut-brown curls and hazel eyes, but her nose was too pointed and her mouth too small, in her opinion.

She was smiling as she strolled out into the April sunshine. The building she wanted was a brisk ten minutes' walk away and she set off, head up, eyes forward and arms swinging the way Eileen had shown them.

She marched past the young officer she'd literally bumped into earlier. Without pausing, she turned her head and saluted smartly and then marched on. She could hear him laughing and she knew it was a good laugh, that he wasn't taking the mickey.

The rec room was heaving as it seemed all the new intakes were in there. Finding her friends was going to be hard for two reasons. One, she was shorter than most of them, and two, they all looked the same.

Minnie moved away from the door and started to walk around the perimeter of the large noisy room. There were three long tables down the centre where girls were sitting knitting, sewing or playing board games and cards.

There must have been over a hundred girls packed in there, and the racket was deafening. After a fruitless few minutes peering through the shoulders of the crowd, she gave up looking for Eileen and decided to have a gander around the barracks. As long as she was back for supper, no one would miss her.

'Hey, Minnie, wait for me,' someone called.

She turned and saw her friend pushing her way towards her. As Eileen was tall and a redhead, she was easy to spot. 'Blimey, I was just giving up. I ain't fond of crowds like this. Fancy a wander around to see what's what?'

'Yes, it's unpleasantly stuffy in here,' Eileen said as they squeezed their way outside into the fresh late April afternoon.

'To put it bluntly, a lot of those girls should have had a bath before putting on their lovely new uniform. I would have thought, being the army, someone in authority would have thought of body odour,' Minnie added.

'I can assure you we think of nothing else,' an amused male voice replied from right behind them.

Minnie turned and, seeing the familiar face, couldn't help herself. 'Not you again. Haven't you got something better to do than creep up on ATS girls?' A shocked gasp from Eileen made her regret her words.

She jumped to attention and saluted; Eileen did the same. This forced the officer to respond in kind and gave her a few moments to gather her wits, which had buggered off or she wouldn't have said something so stupid to an officer.

He was no longer smiling, and she guessed she was about to be put on charge for insubordination. He stared icily at them for a second, then his eyes flashed, and he laughed.

'At ease, ladies. I can see the pair of you are going to shake things up here. Such a shame we aren't allowed to fraternise. Toodle pip.' He nodded and, still chuckling, strolled off.

The two of them watched open mouthed until, as before, he vanished down one of the narrow paths that ran between the buildings.

'Golly, Minnie, you were lucky to get away with that. Whatever possessed you to speak to that officer so rudely?'

Minnie shrugged. 'He's not a proper officer, is he? Wasn't he saying that if he wasn't an officer, he would ask one of us on date?'

'It certainly sounded like that. What an eventful day it's been. Grace fainted on the train, Rigby might have had a breakdown, and you told an officer where to get off.'

'I'd like to know where the NAAFI is and where we can have a bath. There ain't none in the ablutions block.'

'Grace's coming our way. She's not seen us. Should we nip down this alley?'

Minnie shook her head. 'No, she might know where them things we want are to be found.'

'Cooee, Grace, do you want to find the NAAFI with us or go into the rec room with everybody else?' Eileen called.

The girl smiled and for the first time since they'd met on the train it was genuine. 'Oh, yes, the NAAFI, please. I'd love a decent cup of tea and a bun of some sort.'

'Blimey, I'm still stuffed from lunch. How can you be so blooming slim and lovely if you eat buns?'

'I'm just lucky. I eat like the proverbial and don't put on an ounce. I used to ride every day, play tennis and croquet so got plenty of exercise.'

'Did you put your money somewhere safe?' Eileen asked as the three of them started to walk towards the end of the road.

'I did, thanks. It's the same place we have to go to get a pass to leave the base, near the guard room at the exit.' She pointed ahead. 'Look, is that a field up there?'

The buildings ended ahead and there was an empty space but no sign of trees or grass. It was the parade ground where they would have to do their drill every day.

'Good grief – l don't like the look of that,' Grace said. 'It's far too big.'

'You can only just see the far end,' Minnie said, 'and we'd never hear the person drilling us unless he or she marched with us.' Grace was right. Drill was going to be exhausting on this huge concrete area.

'Imagine how horrible it would be in the winter,' Eileen said. 'The weather's all right now and will get warmer. It'll be May next week. Good thing it says we have PT in the gym, wherever that is.'

'I've never been one for exercise,' Minnie told them. 'Waste of time and energy if you ask me.'

'A healthy mind in a healthy body is the motto for the ATS,' Eileen said. 'What I'm not looking forward to is being seen in public in those flimsy shorts and top. Have you noticed there seem to be a lot of soldiers on this base doing very little?'

Grace frowned. 'I've a nasty feeling this is where useless officers and other ranks are sent to keep them out of the way of the serious action.'

'That daft lieutenant is recovering from a broken leg. He don't seem to have much to do, that's for sure,' Minnie said. 'I wonder if he's walking about to strengthen his damaged leg.'

'Makes sense. You'll never guess what Minnie said to him, Grace.'

The three of them were smiling and sharing anecdotes when they turned yet another corner and finally found the NAAFI. Over a proper cup of char and a rock cake, cheerfully paid for by Grace, Minnie revised her opinion of this girl. She might be a bit sniffy but underneath the prickly exterior she was nice. Mum would be chuffed that on her first day as a soldier her daughter had already made three good friends and impressed a couple of officers. Not bad for a girl from the East End.

* * *

Eileen had learned something that Minnie didn't know, and she'd forgotten to tell her. 'Oh, by the way, we've got to hand in our suitcases with our civilian clothes and then the army will send them home. I didn't realise we wouldn't have our civvies. This means even if we go to a dance we've got to be in this ugly uniform.'

'It ain't too bad, there must be a lot of short-arses in the ATS as mine fits better than I'd thought it would.'

'I was expecting the same and for my skirt to be

well below my knees. Mind you, I think you're as tall as Clara, aren't you, Eileen?' Grace said.

'I am, but I'm not lovely and slim like either of you. I've always been well-covered.'

Grace glanced at her expensive gold wristwatch. 'Golly, we need to hurry. I've got to collect my irons – I know they said we've got to keep them with us but there's nowhere to put a tin mug even if we put the cutlery in a pocket.'

'I ain't got mine either. What about you, Eileen?'

'I don't think they meant that we have to carry it around the base, only that if we're posted, or off base doing something, we need to have them with us.'

They dashed back and quite a few of the other girls were doing the same. Everybody seemed in better spirits and there were more smiles than sour faces. The next thing they'd have to face were inoculations, visits to the dentist, optician and so on. Minnie wasn't too bad with needles but was sure there'd be plenty of girls who were.

* * *

It was strange being in a room full of other people, listening to them snoring, muttering, and turning over. There was also the irritating ticking of a dozen alarm clocks that had been placed lovingly on the top of the owners' lockers. The beds creaked when you moved, which made it worse. Eileen slept fitfully, waking with a start several times, disorientated and wondering where she was.

Then she remembered she was no longer under the control of her husband but more or less a free woman. She had, like all the ATS, to answer to the army but that was a lot better than answering to Danny.

Both Clara and Grace were sleeping soundly, as was Minnie. She sighed, wriggled a bit to try make herself as comfortable as she could on the nasty hard biscuits which pretended to be a mattress, and eventually dozed off.

Eileen woke before reveille, which would be someone with a bugle walking up and down past the various barracks. The windows in this room were at shoulder height, but at least there were a dozen on each side and this let in sufficient light for her to see one of the clocks. It was just after five.

If she wanted to have a wash and use the loo without having to queue, now was the time to do it. With a hundred girls and only twenty WCs and sinks, things were going to be horribly busy once everybody was awake.

Eileen slipped quietly out of bed, put her feet in her slippers, crept over to the locker and removed her greatcoat from its peg. This was long enough to act as an all-concealing dressing gown.

There was a slight sound behind her; she smiled and raised a hand at Minnie, who had obviously had the same thought as her. Together they tiptoed past the sleepers and quietly opened the double doors that led onto the landing. Once they were safely closed, they were free to talk.

'I wonder how many others will do the same. It's all very well nipping across to the ablutions and latrines now when it's warm and dry – but I don't fancy it in the winter.'

'I'm going to the bogs and then round the back where we found the baths. I've only had a proper bath a couple of times in me life, when I went to the public ones. We have a tin one in front of the kitchen fire once a week and it ain't pleasant being the last in the queue, I can tell you.'

'Actually, I think we have to bathe on specified days and aren't supposed to have one at any other time.'

'I'll plead ignorance. What would a girl like me know about indoor plumbing?' Minnie said.

'I'll do the same. I know it's only five o'clock, but

you'd think some of the others might have had the same idea.'

The trip to the latrines was brief and Eileen was grateful there were doors on the cubicles. She was careful not to put more water in the tub than the allowed five inches. As there was a black line painted around the bath, nobody had any excuse for breaking this rule.

Minnie had been right to suggest they had an illegal dip as she felt so much better afterwards. They were safely back in the other block, cleaning their teeth and combing their hair, when a few others arrived with the same idea – although they'd not come nearly as early.

'Shall I wake Clara and Grace? It's still twenty minutes to six so they've got time to wash before the general rush,' Eileen said.

'I'll wake Clara as she's in the next bed to me, you do Grace.'

The other two were up and out in minutes and there were now four other empty beds. The trumpeter stopped directly outside their windows and the liquid sound filled the room. There were moans and complaints, but everyone got up.

Eileen and Minnie had re-stacked their bedding and were ready to leave when Endean poked her head through the doors. 'I thought you two might be the first. The next two days will be medical days but after that you don't get into uniform at reveille but into your PT kit. It's exercise before breakfast.'

'When do we start doing drill? I'm looking forward to that,' Eileen said.

'After breakfast. You were given a label yesterday. Write your home address on it and tie it to your suitcase and then take it to the postal depot after breakfast. It's on the way to the parade ground.'

Surely they'd not have to have their irons when they did their first round of drill? 'Excuse me, Corp, if we have to bring our irons back after breakfast then wouldn't it be better to take our suitcases then?'

The woman scowled, unhappy about being shown up. 'Leave the cases here and collect them when you bring your irons back. The extra half a mile added to your morning exercise will do you good.'

Eileen exchanged a glance with Minnie, who shook her head slightly. 'Do we make our own way to the mess or march together?'

'You march everywhere together in alphabetical order and three abreast,' Endean snapped, no longer friendly.

Sitting on the beds was forbidden – they were just for sleeping – and as there was only one chair, it was either sit on the floor or stand. Eileen nodded towards the corner where they couldn't be overheard.

'Blimey, you certainly pulled her chain. She seems nice enough, but I reckon she's going to be a right tartar. I think we should have taken our suitcases yesterday and she forgot to tell us,' Minnie said, once Endean had left the room.

'We thought Rigby wasn't much good but I'm not sure her replacement's much better. She should have thought about the suitcases and the irons herself.'

When all the girls had returned from ablutions, it was time to leave for breakfast. The squad was definitely in lines of three but that was where the resemblance to marching ended. Endean was in front and she either didn't see or didn't care about the shambles behind her.

They arrived at the mess hall and regrouped so they were sitting at the tables in the same order as yesterday lunchtime.

'Crikey, I hope we don't get her teaching us to drill. It'll be blooming chaos,' Minnie said with a grin as she tucked into her porridge.

5

Minnie wasn't sure if being in the last row of three was an advantage or disadvantage when learning to drill – time would tell. At least she got the best view, and nobody was going to step on her heels or cannon into her.

An angry-looking male sergeant strode up and down, giving them the once-over. He didn't look too pleased by what he saw. He came to a halt in the centre two yards from the front row.

'You lot, listen. If I yell "Attention", you bring in your left foot and put it next to your right.' He scowled at them and then called out. 'Atten-shun!'

Minnie kept her back straight and brought her left foot in smartly. All but one of those in front of her did the same. Thanks to Eileen, it was one thing they could all do.

'As you were,' the sergeant roared. 'Now, r-i-i-ght turn!'

Minnie swivelled a quarter turn to her right and snapped her feet back together. She couldn't keep back her snigger. Several girls were facing in the wrong direction.

'Don't you know your right from your left? I knew you were a useless lot but gawd help me, you're even worse than I feared.'

The girls who'd got it wrong giggled and shuffled around so they were facing to the front. Minnie was enjoying this and even those who'd turned left instead of right didn't look too upset.

Next the sergeant wanted them to march. Eileen had told them you step off on your left foot with your right arm up. They should be able to do this and keep the grumpy soldier happy.

'By the le-e-ft, qui-ick *march*!'

They set off briskly whilst the sergeant bellowed after them, 'Left, right, left, right, left, right, left, right.'

Everything might have continued smoothly if he hadn't bellowed at the girls, 'Stop slouching and keep your legs open. What are you, a bunch of pregnant virgins?'

Two girls in the middle stopped dead in shock. The row behind them kept marching and suddenly there was a pile of girls on the concrete.

Those who weren't involved with the collision were doubled up with laughter. 'Good thing we're wearing our knee-length passion killers,' Minnie said as she mopped her eyes. 'Otherwise, them lot would be giving the soldiers over there a treat.'

The poor sergeant was purple in the face and screaming at them to get in line. Once they were organised, he began again. They had to keep looking forward and never look at him. After a few more attempts, the squad was able to march, about turn and halt without anyone bumping into each other or falling over.

The sergeant stalked from the front to stop a few feet from Minnie. 'You, Curly Locks, get your hair cut before I see you again. Two inches off the collar.'

Minnie was fuming. She wasn't going to cut her hair unless she absolutely had to. Maybe she could put it up if she borrowed some pins. She'd ask the girls later.

After half an hour of further marching, they were dismissed.

Endean was waiting for them. 'Quick march, eyes front. Follow me.'

They were marched to another building and this time it was for a lecture. The hall was already full so obviously all four squads were present. Minnie supposed it made sense to do things together when possible.

The lecturer was the lieutenant Minnie had met the day before. He had a nice voice, spoke clearly but she reckoned that even if he'd mumbled and had been boring, every eye would have been fixed on him. He was a real dish; not her type, but she could see that other girls might fancy him.

He was telling them about rates of pay, which trades got more money, how to parade fortnightly for their wages and other things that she didn't listen to. She was more concerned by the way Eileen was staring at him. Her friend had a husband, Danny; why would she be gawping at another man, even if he was ever so handsome?

Eventually, much to her relief, the lecture ended. They had to stand up and were then dismissed by a sergeant. Each squad was collected by their own corporal and peeled off to do whatever came next. Her lot were taken back to the place where they'd had their FFI and this time it was to look for nits.

'Blimey, what next?' Minnie asked as she joined up

with the other three. 'I hope no one has nits in our squad. Wonder what would happen if they had?'

'They used to shave off your hair a few years ago,' Clara said with a smile. 'Think they've got something you can put on it nowadays to kill the lice.'

Minnie shuddered at the thought.

They had a break to use the bogs and then collected their irons and headed for the mess. 'What did Endean say we were doing this afternoon?' Eileen said.

'We've got more drill on the parade ground. I do hope we have the same sergeant, he made me laugh. I loved the way he pretended to tear out his hair when we went wrong,' Clara said.

'He was rather vulgar, don't you think?' Grace said with a disapproving sniff.

'I reckon all of them are. Ain't there a saying, "swear like a trooper"? Stands to reason a soldier would swear and that.'

Dinner was another stew but just as tasty and the afters was jam roly-poly with custard. Just the ticket. Tea last night had been bread and jam and a slab of cake, and they'd got cocoa and cake for supper at nine. Minnie wasn't going to go hungry, that was for sure.

After dinner, they endured a further hour of drill,

which wasn't half as much fun as before, as Endean took it. There was another boring lecture, this time by an old grey-haired doctor who talked about VD. There were lots of red faces in the hall when he'd finished.

'Into order. Right, quick march.' Endean set off briskly and they trooped along behind.

They were headed for the far side of the base towards what Minnie guessed was the medical block. There were a couple of ambulances with a red cross on the side which she reckoned was a dead giveaway. It was blooming miles and after all the drill her legs were hurting something rotten, and the new shoes were heavy and giving her blisters.

Next, they were ordered to line up and wait for some inoculations. Minnie had never been inoculated for anything and wasn't looking froward to being jabbed in the arm.

The two girls with her at the end of the line were Yates and Watson. She turned to Yates. 'Do we get these jabs in our arms or in our bums?'

'Arms, I think. At least that's where I had it the last time I had one.'

'What are we being injected against, do you know?'

'Typhoid.' Yates frowned. 'God knows why as I've never heard of anyone getting that.'

'It's what you get if the water's polluted. If thousands of people had been killed in air-raids the water could be polluted and we'd all have got typhoid,' Watson said.

For a moment, Minnie didn't follow the logic but then the penny dropped. 'You reckon they thought it'd be so bad that no one would remove any bodies for burial? Blimey!' She shuddered. 'I thought being gassed was bad enough.'

Being at the end of the queue wasn't nice when you were waiting for something nasty to happen. The girls filed in but so far none had come out again. Where were they? By the time it was her turn to remove her jacket and roll up her shirt sleeve, she was feeling sick.

A nurse held her arm and Minnie thought this was in case she snatched it away, and it was the same doctor with the needle who'd peered down her knickers yesterday.

'Relax, dear, it won't hurt,' the nurse said, but she was lying.

Minnie barely held back her yelp as what felt like a thick nail was stabbed into her upper arm. When the doctor removed the needle, a trickle of blood followed.

Her arm was on fire and the cotton wool she'd

been given was red in seconds. The orderly handed her a larger piece.

'Go through that other door over there. You get to sit down for a bit. The needle was blunt after being used for all your squad. Not fun being end of the alphabet.'

* * *

Eileen had a high temperature by the following morning and her arm was red-hot and too stiff to move. From the moans and groans echoing around the dormitory, she wasn't the only one to be suffering from the side effects of yesterday's jab. None of her particular friends were as unwell as she, but everybody was complaining about having a sore arm.

'No PT or drill today, ladies,' Endean announced as those able to were attempting to get dressed with only one good arm. 'Those with a temperature come with me. The medic will check you're well enough to remain with your squad and don't have to be in hospital.'

Minnie was dressed and slid between the beds. 'Crikey, you don't look too clever.' She put her hand on Eileen's forehead. 'You're burning up. You stop where you are, you're not well enough to even get dressed. How does Endean think you and them others can march almost a mile to the hospital?'

Before Eileen could summon the energy to intervene, her friend was striding down the room to speak to their leader. Eileen couldn't see or hear what was said, but she'd never felt so ill in her life and if she didn't know it was just a reaction to the injection, she'd think she had some sort of fatal illness.

She closed her eyes and tried to imagine she was back in her own bed at home. Her mind wandered and she was drifting into a fevered sleep when she was abruptly woken up by someone shouting into her ear. 'Private Ruffel. Can you hear me?'

Eileen wasn't deaf and the loud voice had made her head hurt even more. She forced her eyelids to open and stared blearily up at a face she didn't recognise. 'Go away. I'm not well.'

If she kept her eyes closed, hopefully she'd be left in peace. The voices faded and she floated off to a lovely hot place where a fair-haired man was smiling down at her.

'Eileen, Endean's sent for the doctor. You might have to go to hospital.'

'No, thanks,' was all she could manage.

Someone held up her head and slipped some pills into her mouth. This was followed by a lovely cold drink of water. She swallowed this gratefully and let the fever take her away again.

* * *

When Eileen next opened her eyes, the room was quiet but not empty. She couldn't move her left arm as it was too painful, but she did feel a bit better. Minnie appeared at her side.

'Crikey, you gave us all a scare. You've been ever so poorly but I never let them cart you off to the hospital. I volunteered to look after you and the others what are feeling bad so the doc allowed you all to stop here.'

'Could I have a drink of water?'

Her friend held the tin mug whilst Eileen sipped from it. 'Thanks, that's much better. I have to get up. I need the loo.'

'There's a bucket with a lid behind the screen in the corner we made with a couple of blankets. Use that. You won't be the first.' Minnie laughed at her expression. 'Blimey, don't look so horrified. I've blooming well emptied it every time.'

Eileen's legs worked but, not only her left arm, but her entire left side was agony and red-hot to the touch. The jabs had been administered into everyone's left arm on the assumption they were all right-handed. She wasn't, which made things even more tricky for her.

She stood up, glad she was still in her pyjamas but undoing the cord around her waist was going to be difficult one handed, and the wrong one too.

'I'll help you, then leave you to it and come back after,' Minnie said kindly.

With her help she managed not to pee on her feet and to emerge from behind the makeshift screen still decent. She looked around the room. There were five other beds occupied – she was glad she wasn't the only one.

Her head was a bit clearer, her temperature a bit lower and she didn't want to sleep, which was surely a good sign. She sat on her bed and drained the mug of water Minnie handed her. 'What are the others doing? What time is it? I've lost track of the day.'

'Just after four. Everything's cancelled for today 'cos so many girls had a rotten reaction to the jab. Them what are fine are over in the rec room. Some were moaning they couldn't go off base but seems we've to pass some sort of marching test before we're allowed out.'

'I can't see many of us being able to march for a few days. I can't even lift my arm, let alone swing it.'

One of the lumps under a blanket slowly sat up. 'I'm starving. Do we get anything to eat today?'

'You won't get no dinner but you'll get some tea and that soon. Endean has arranged for two orderlies to fetch it over. I'm going to empty the po', won't be long.'

Minnie was a brick to do this for them. Eileen wasn't sure she'd have stepped up like this to take care of her squad mates. She thought the other girl awake was called Jones. 'Are we expected to be back on full duty tomorrow, do you know?'

'Minnie said the medic has us on two days' sick leave but we've got to get up tomorrow. Seems staying in bed during the day in a billet isn't allowed. They made an exception today as you refused to go to hospital.'

'Golly, did I? I don't remember doing that. I suppose we can spend the day in the rec room. I wonder if the other squads have used their dorms as a temporary medical centre.'

'No, the poor things were forced to get up and stagger to the rec room. Minnie persuaded our corp to let us stay up here.'

'That means she'll have a black mark against her name, the officers won't appreciate a very junior private forcing a rule change.' Minnie really was proving to be a good friend and Eileen was glad she had met her.

Minnie returned, closely followed by their tea. They got Spam and pickle sandwiches, hot tea and two slices of cake. It was delicious, and after eating, Eileen felt almost better. Her forehead was still hot, but she was over the worst. Her arm was horribly painful but at least she could move about the room now. The screen had gone as well as the bucket – thank goodness. All the invalids made it to the latrines and ablutions before lights out.

A nurse came to check on them and take their temperature. Everyone else was passed fit enough to be up but not on duty for another day, except Eileen. 'I'm afraid you still have a high fever, Ruffel. You'll have to come back with me where we can keep an eye on you.'

This time Eileen didn't argue. 'I'll get dressed...'

'No, put your greatcoat on over the top of your night things. I came across in an ambulance, so you don't have to walk.'

Clutching her washbag, she made her way carefully down the stairs and, with some effort, managed to get into the rear of the vehicle.

Eileen had never had a day's illness in her life until now and she just hated being so feeble.

6

The next day, her friend was back with them and Minnie got all the poorly people up and dressed in time for breakfast, but it was a close thing. Eileen, who'd been the worst, had needed help to get buttons and that done up, but she was ready before the others.

'Come on, you lazy layabouts, if Ruffel can get up in time then so can you,' she yelled down the room.

The remaining three from yesterday unwillingly sat up. None of them looked too good, but they were in the army and had to get on with it. If a bomb dropped, they'd move sharp enough.

'You're not our leader, Wolton, so what's it to do with you?' The speaker was a tubby girl with ratty pigtails that she pinned around her head. Minnie thought her name was Jackson or Johnson.

'Better I yell at you than you get put on a charge when Endean arrives in a few minutes.'

With a lot of grumbling, the remaining girls grabbed their wash bags but none of them bothered to put on their greatcoats. Minnie wasn't sure if running about the place in their pyjamas was a chargeable offence or just plain stupid.

Eileen was attempting to stack her bedding with one hand. 'Here, give over, I'll do it for you.' She turned to the girls who'd done their own beds and were ready to head for breakfast. 'You lot, why don't you stack them beds? It ain't possible to do it one handed.'

'Righto, Minnie, good idea,' one of them cheerfully replied.

This meant that when Endean arrived ten minutes later the room was perfect and all twenty-four of them were dressed and waiting for her. They now automatically arranged themselves in the correct order so getting into threes once they were outside was easy.

The six with arms too stiff to get into their shirts and jackets waited anxiously to be put on a charge. Minnie and Clara had gone round tucking in the loose sleeves so they looked smart enough and their damaged arms were folded across their front, held in place by the empty shirt sleeve.

Endean nodded and spoke to Andrews, second in line. 'Who suggested that arrangement?'

'Wolton, Corporal Endean. She knows what to do.'

Endean stared thoughtfully at Minnie and her heart sank. Now she was for it. She pretended she'd not noticed the stare and was dreading being sent for by the officer in charge of the trainees.

They regrouped for breakfast, but her anxiety didn't stop her devouring her scrambled egg, toast and tea.

'I don't care if I get put on latrine duty,' she said as she wiped up the remains of her scrambled egg with her last morsel of toast. 'I reckon that dried egg ain't too bad when it's done like this.'

'The cakes and buns are made with dried egg too and they're splendid,' Clara said.

'Why do you think you'll be doing fatigues?' Eileen asked.

'Stands to reason; I messed with the rules and that, didn't I?' Minnie shrugged. 'Don't bother me none. I was just looking after me friends.' She nodded towards the girls in the other squads who'd somehow stuffed their swollen arms into their uniforms. 'They don't look as smart as our girls with their blooming arms hanging down all useless like.'

Eileen shook her head. 'They should be giving you a promotion, not a punishment.'

Minnie shrugged. 'Any road, there's nothing I can do about it now but wait and see. You malingerers can spend the day in the rec room but the rest of us have got lectures. From tomorrow it's PT before breakfast in them flimsy tops and shorts and then drill after.'

'I can't see my arm being okay for drill and PT, but they must know better. After all, they've been giving these horrible injections to ATS girls for months now,' Eileen said.

Minnie had been keeping an eye on the door and her fingers clenched when she saw Endean heading in her direction. It was hard to tell from her expression if she was on the war path.

'Private Wolton, Junior Commander Davies wants to speak to you.'

Minnie was already on her feet. 'Yes, Corp.'

'No, finish your breakfast first. Someone will escort you when you're ready.'

With a sigh of relief, Minnie flopped back into her seat, not sure what to make of it. 'I expected to be quick marched by two military policemen. What do you reckon, Eileen? Am I in trouble or not?'

Grace was staring at her. 'Hardly, I'd say that you're going to be promoted. One of the girls in a different squad told me that someone had already been given a stripe.'

'I'll believe it when I hear it. If anyone's going to be a lance corporal it'll be someone like you, not a common girl from the East End.'

Eileen smiled. 'Of course it's for promotion – look what you've managed to organise for us and we've only been here two days. You might be small, but you've got something about you that makes you a natural leader.'

Grace laughed but it sounded forced. 'Good heavens, next you'll be suggesting that Minnie will get a commission before Clara or I do.'

'I wasn't suggesting that,' Eileen said, 'but now you've mentioned it, I think that's exactly what will happen. It's not...'

Minnie interrupted. 'I ain't going to be no officer. I'd never fit in with them toffee-nosed lot what talk with a plum in their mouth. I don't want to be saluted and called ma'am.'

'Neither do I – officers spend all their time at a desk and I want to be active. Actually, I was thinking I might train to be a PT instructor,' Eileen said.

'Rather you than me,' Minnie replied. 'It'll be a

laugh if we both stay here training the new volunteers – you doing the PT and me doing the drill.'

Minnie finished every last scrap on her plate and drained her second mug of tea. Eileen offered to wash her irons and mug and return them to the billet.

'Ta ever so, that'll be helpful. I'll find you in the rec room if I'm allowed to. I might have to go straight to the lecture.'

* * *

When Minnie emerged from the mess hall, she'd expected to find an orderly waiting to direct her to the building where the company commander was waiting to speak to her.

'Good morning, Wolton, are you finally ready for me to escort you?' Lieutenant Sawyer said with a charming smile.

She was so shocked she forgot to salute, and he laughed at her confusion. She found her voice, snapped smartly to attention and belatedly did what she should have done immediately. 'Good morning, sir.'

He didn't return the salute. 'Come along, I've got better things to do with my time than ferry the lowest of the low about the place.'

'Then just tell me where to go and I'll find it me-self... sir.'

He raised an eyebrow and that made her want to stamp on his shiny boots. Somehow she managed to keep silent and not make matters worse.

'Perish the thought, I follow orders to the letter, unlike others that I could mention.'

Minnie hid her smile. Maybe he wasn't so bad after all. He was quite funny.

He didn't march, just strolled in a military sort of way. She'd always walked straight, making every one of her sixty-one inches count. If you were small, you couldn't afford to slouch.

She wasn't exactly sure what the protocol was – should she just walk alongside him without saying a word or was a bit of chat allowed? She decided to risk it.

'Do the injections always cause so many problems?'

'Afraid so. Just as many men keel over but I must admit that this time the reaction from quite a lot of you was more severe than usual.'

'That doctor used the same needle on all of us. I've got a St John's first-aid certificate and I reckon using the same needle introduces infection.'

He looked down at her, his expression unreadable.

'Are you quite sure? How could you possibly know that?'

'The orderly told me she felt sorry for the girls at the end of the alphabet because of the blunt needle. My arm didn't stop bleeding for an hour and it's still sore.'

'I'm sorry to hear that. To be frank, I'm not exactly sure why it's necessary to give you girls the same inoculations that we get. ATS won't be posted to India, Africa and so on and are unlikely to get typhoid in Blighty.'

'My friend suggested the government thought there'd be so many rotting bodies under the buildings when the bombing started the water would be polluted.'

'What a very depressing thought. Here we are. Don't look so apprehensive, I can assure you it's good news.' He nodded and strolled off in an aimless sort of way. She didn't know him well, but she was sure he was fed up with being on the barracks with nothing important to do.

But Minnie couldn't think about that now. She had to find out what was in store for her. Squaring her shoulders, she marched into the admin block a private and emerged as a lance corporal.

* * *

Lieutenant Ben Sawyer was terminally bored with his current posting. The medics had assured him that the leg he'd smashed up when crashing his motorbike last Christmas was almost healed and he would be fit for duty soon. Why the hell was he still mouldering in this backwater somewhere outside Chelmsford?

He'd expected to be back with his regiment in Africa by now. His father had died suddenly, and he'd shipped home on compassionate leave and then skidded on black ice on his way back to London after the funeral. Six weeks in bloody hospital, then crutches and now here, where he was doing sod all instead of doing what he was trained for. Giving lectures to the ATS, for God's sake, was something a chap too old to fight could do, not someone his age.

Teasing the new intake, flirting with them a bit, was mildly amusing but he wanted to ship out and soon. He was scheduled to give more lectures about the options they could take after their four weeks' basic training. Some weren't especially interesting but having girls working in the stores, driving, doing office work and so on would release men to take on actual fighting.

The recruits now had the choice, if they were

bright enough, to be trained in radiolocation. They could also be trained to work in an operational anti-aircraft gun site. Not firing the guns, obviously, but operating range-finders, height-finders and so on and using the searchlights. He was sure some of them would end up doing these more technical jobs.

With each encounter he had with the diminutive Minnie Wolton, he was becoming less bored by this posting. What was it about the girl that interested him? She definitely had lovely eyes, wonderful curly nut-brown hair and was rounded in all the right places. No one would call her beautiful, though it wasn't her looks but her personality and intelligence that intrigued him. She was the most interesting person he'd spoken to since he got here.

He grinned ruefully. Who was he kidding? He'd grown up expecting all females, young, old, married or single to be dazzled by his good looks and charm. However, she'd not only shown zero interest in him, but she appeared to actively dislike him. Maybe not dislike, but certainly disdain. He was an adult, an officer, and it was time he stopped this flirting nonsense and behaved like one.

Persuading this girl that he was actually a decent chap was exactly what he needed to keep him occupied until he returned to active duty in Africa. The fact that officers and other ranks were not allowed to fraternise was something he intended to ignore.

Showing any interest apart from purely professional was strictly forbidden, and that just made the whole thing more interesting. He'd been told that Minnie would be given the option to stay at the barracks and train new intakes, but she might well opt to go elsewhere for further training in some other trade.

He'd drawn the short straw again and had three lectures to give today. Major Bentley, his CO, had said he was half the age of the other available officers and senior NCOs and far better looking so the girls listened to him, which they didn't to the others.

'Excuse me, sir, Junior Commander Davies would like to speak to you,' a lance corporal said as he saluted.

'Thank you, I'm on my way.'

He walked briskly, not exactly marching, but it covered the ground just as well. All this saluting and marching nonsense was for trainees – it knocked them into shape, so they followed orders automatically when under fire – but he found it increasingly irritating. On active duty, only the most senior officers were saluted.

'Junior Commander Davies is expecting you, sir, if you'd care to follow me,' a nervous ATS girl said when he stepped into the ATS admin block. This was occupied solely by the hierarchy of the ATS stationed at this barracks.

Davies was the equivalent of a captain so outranked him, but he ignored that, knocked on the half-open door and walked in without waiting for an invitation. She glared at him, and he pinned on his most charming smile.

'How can I be of help?'

'I've received a complaint from one of my girls. She says that you made an improper suggestion to her.'

He laughed, which wasn't appreciated. 'Good God, and you believed her? Do you honestly think that I'd abuse my position in that way?'

Whilst he'd been talking, he was racking his brains to think of who it might have been, but the only volunteer who actually had reason to complain he was sure hadn't done so.

'Am I to know exactly who has made the complaint and what it is I'm supposed to have said? I can assure you it's total b... total nonsense.' Probably best not to swear in the circumstances.

Davies was a middle-aged woman with steel-grey hair scraped back and not a smidgen of lipstick to improve her pale complexion. There was no ring on her finger, so she was obviously a spinster too, which no doubt explained her overreaction.

'I've absolutely no intention of revealing the complainant's name. I don't intend to pass the complaint to your commanding officer this time but if there are any further complaints than I'll not hesitate to do so.'

Ben was no longer smiling. 'I insist that you do pass on the accusation. I wish to have this falsehood fully investigated and the person who made it severely reprimanded. I am an officer and a gentleman.'

She looked less disapproving and slightly nervous. 'I suppose it's possible the girl misunderstood an innocent remark...'

'I'm not aware that I've made any remarks, innocent or otherwise, to any of the new girls. I've given three lectures and answered questions afterwards but any other interaction between myself and any ATS girl has been official and professional.'

Davies didn't answer and was obviously regretting having sent for him. He'd also overreacted and there'd been no need for him to be so heavy-handed and upset the poor woman.

'I think this was no more than a misunderstanding. Shall we forget about the incident?'

'Thank you, Lieutenant Sawyer. I'll speak to the girl again, and make it abundantly clear that specious complaints are not appreciated. I'm sorry to have accused you.'

He nodded and wandered off, lost in thought. These girls had only been in the barracks for a couple of days and his interaction with any of them, apart from Minnie, had been negligible. Good God! It had to have been her as she'd just left this office after being promoted.

It seemed a petty thing to do and he couldn't believe he'd got her so wrong. The only way to find out was to speak to her. The problem with this was that if it had been her there'd be a second complaint winging its way to Davies and this time, he wouldn't be able to wriggle out of it so easily.

He glanced at his watch – he was due to give his lecture on a career in cookery or becoming a medical, mess or office orderly. Riveting stuff and there was very little he could do to make it sound more interesting. With any luck, Minnie would be attending and he might be able to snatch a few words with her without drawing too much attention.

It occurred to him that if it wasn't her then there was someone, not necessarily in her squad, with an axe to grind and they might well be watching him closely, ready to report him a second time.

The lectures were supposed to last around three

quarters of an hour and then there was a quarter of an hour for any relevant questions. He could have delivered it in half the time as there wasn't a great deal to say on either trade. He filled the extra time with what he hoped were amusing and pertinent anecdotes and they seemed to go down well enough.

A hand went up to ask a question and he nodded for the girl to stand up. 'Why do we have to have inoculations when we aren't being posted abroad? Lots of us have still got arms too stiff to move and what's the point of that?'

Good question – and one he didn't have a sensible answer for. 'The army's trying to see that you young ladies are treated as equally as possible to the men. Therefore, if the men have inoculations, then so do you. I'm afraid that there will be at least two more.'

There was a discontented muttering which rapidly spread around the hall. The tall red-headed girl, the one who seemed to be a particular friend of Minnie's, put her hand up and he nodded.

'I understand the logic behind your answer, sir, what I don't understand is why the same needle was used for all members of my squad. Is there a shortage of needles?'

He ran his finger around his collar, which had become unaccountably tight. He'd got himself into this mess and had to come up with a valid answer that wouldn't criticise his superiors or the War Office.

'I'm afraid I can't answer either question, but I can assure you I intend to find the answers. I believe we have two further lectures this afternoon and I'll endeavour to obtain the information you want by then. Thank you, ladies, dismissed.'

He hadn't spotted Minnie, the ATS girl he particularly wanted to speak to, and wondered where she was. Perhaps this promotion meant extra training of some sort if she was to fulfil her role as lance corporal effectively. Why the blazes the bigwigs hadn't decided to change the officer ranks to coincide with the men last year he'd no idea. In fact, it rather blew his answer, that the War Office was trying to keep the male and female sides of the army in step, right out of the water.

7

Eileen expected Minnie to come into the rec room after her visit to the admin office, but she didn't. Whilst those in her squad who were fit enough were drilling or marching somewhere on the base, she decided to write her duty letter to Danny. She'd brought with her one of the letter cards she used for her correspondence with him. All she had to do was put his name and number and the British Forces Postal Service did the rest.

> *Dear Danny,*
> *I haven't heard from you, but I expect things are busy wherever you are. Don't worry about*

writing to me but I'll continue to write to you if I have the time.

I left my job at the Co-op and am now in the ATS. I didn't think doing the books for Co-op coal yard was good enough. It's now my third day and I had a horrible reaction to the typhoid inoculation so am sitting in the rec room with twenty other girls who are also unable to do drill.

It's not exactly how I expected it to be but what I've learned from watching you train has really helped me settle in. I've made some good friends and decided to train to be a PT instructor. You know I like to keep fit and can play a decent game of netball and tennis.

I have to stop now as I have to attend another lecture.

Eileen scrawled her name underneath and then moistened her finger and ran it around the gummy edges of the card and pressed them firmly together. Using one of these cards meant that it was basically only one sheet of paper per letter. She wrote occasionally as she felt it was the least she could do as he was risking his life every day for his country. She knew Danny wouldn't reply as she'd only received two letters in all the time he'd been away. She guessed she wasn't uppermost in his thoughts. In fact, he'd never been an affectionate husband and, like her, might be relieved to be away from a marriage that wasn't happy.

She hadn't seen a bright red post box anywhere and wasn't quite sure where she should post this letter. She glanced at the gold wristwatch she'd bought for herself when they'd got married and saw there was half an hour before the first of the three lectures everybody had to attend today.

A helpful private gave her the directions to the postal department and she arrived at the lecture hall with ten minutes to spare. Her arm, after all the rushing about, was throbbing painfully and the thought of having to do PT and drill in the morning wasn't a happy one.

'There you are, I've been looking for you everywhere,' Minnie said as she rushed up to her. 'You were right – it was a promotion. I'm a lance corporal now, can you believe it? I'm not attending these lectures as the four of us what have been given stripes have got a meeting with a sergeant major to learn how to give orders and that.'

'Lucky you, even with that handsome officer giving them, these lectures are dull. They could give us a printed copy and we could read the information in the evening.'

Her friend grinned. 'You're not the only one who thinks he's a bit of all right. I reckon there's a fair number what don't read too well so telling them what's what is better. I'll see you at dinner. How's your arm?'

'Ghastly, but I'll soldier on,' Eileen smiled, and Minnie dashed away, laughing.

The lecture was about becoming a driver and Eileen noticed several girls were taking notes. Both Grace and Clara were listening avidly. She couldn't see either of them as drivers, but they were obviously interested. As Eileen already knew what she wanted to do, she paid little attention and was relieved when they were dismissed. Her tummy had growled several times and she was ready for lunch – or dinner, as Minnie called it.

'Private Ruffel, could you spare me a moment of your time?'

What did the handsome young officer want with her? 'Of course, sir.'

'I need to speak to Lance Corporal Wolton. She didn't come to the lecture. Could you tell her I'm looking for her?'

'She'll be at the mess hall for lunch in five minutes, sir. I'll tell her then. Where do you want her to meet you?' Clearly, he couldn't stroll into the ATS canteen.

'Presumably she'll be attending this afternoon's riveting events. I'll be there ten minutes early. Ask her to come then.' He nodded and walked away. He was a very attractive young man and she couldn't help watching him as closely as most of the single girls were.

He was tall, probably around six foot, broad shouldered, with narrow hips and lovely fair hair – not that there was much of it as even the officers had a short back and sides. His eyes were a piercing grey and his best feature. Eileen frowned. What was she thinking? She shouldn't even be noticing another man.

Danny wasn't tall, had plain brown eyes and mousey hair, but she was married to him. She was nothing to write home about either and they'd started courting when she was only sixteen, had got engaged two years later and had been married four years now. If only she'd been able to have a baby, then she might feel differently. She wouldn't be in the army but at home looking after a little one. As she watched Lieutenant Sawyer leave, she realised she was glad she hadn't had a baby so she could be here dreaming what it would be like to have a husband like him and not be tied to a bad-tempered, controlling man like Danny.

'What did he want?' Grace asked, gazing longingly after the departing officer.

Eileen had forgotten the brief conversation would have been observed by Grace and Clara. 'He was looking for Minnie. Something about her promotion, I expect.' She smiled and started walking briskly after the others who'd been in the hall. 'I'm starving and I've done very little today either.'

Grace caught up with her and continued her interrogation. 'Why would he ask you? He's an officer and could just send an orderly to fetch Minnie. Is there something going on between them?'

Clara overheard this and shook her head. 'Don't be silly, Grace. Are you hoping to interest him in yourself by any chance?'

Grace smiled. 'If I wasn't in this uniform and therefore not allowed to fraternise with an officer, I would be. He's an absolute dish.'

This seemed at odds with her previous remark. 'So, you're accusing Minnie of breaking the rules? I think that you're jealous that she got the promotion and you didn't. Grace, I don't want to hear you being unsupportive of our new lance corporal.'

Instead of being offended by the criticism, Grace laughed. 'Good heavens, he wouldn't look twice at someone like Minnie. No, I was wondering if she's going to be moved somewhere else, given some sort of special duties.'

They'd been seated for a few minutes before Minnie and the other three newly promoted girls rushed in. Eileen noticed that they'd already sewn on their stripes. There were mostly smiles and nods of congratulation, but she spotted a few sour faces – strangely Grace's wasn't one of them.

'Sorry, meeting went on a bit. Did I miss anything interesting at the lecture?'

Eileen gave her the message and her friend nodded but made no comment. Today they were allowed an hour for lunch, but Minnie told them that from tomorrow it would only be half an hour.

'PT before breakfast, then drill for an hour, then kit inspection and in the afternoon another three lectures. The day after – it'll be Saturday and 1 May – we parade first thing and if we pass muster, we get permission to leave the base. Imagine – a whole day to explore Chelmsford.'

'Do we go to church on Sunday?' Clara asked.

'We have church parade along with the men – nothing was said about going to an actual church. I don't reckon Him upstairs will care where we are, do you?'

After eating, Minnie dashed off to her meeting,

but Eileen and the others had time for a stroll to the NAAFI before the first lecture. Word had gone round that they had chocolate for sale. It didn't seem necessary to take their irons and mug back as they wouldn't be doing anything more energetic than sitting and listening to more tedious information.

* * *

Ben decided it might be more sensible to wait inside the lecture hall rather than talk to Minnie on the public thoroughfare and possibly cause further speculation. He didn't go to the Officers' Mess for lunch but grabbed a sandwich at the NAAFI. He passed Minnie's friends but carefully avoided eye contact so none of them had to salute.

He stopped and pretended to look down the nearby alley but actually stared at the tall redhead, Minnie's friend. For some reason he was drawn to her, and she was wearing a wedding ring. This made her doubly out of bounds.

Minnie was standing in the foyer reading the noticeboard when he walked in. She glanced over her shoulder and smiled. 'There's a dance at the NAAFI on Saturday night. Is that just for other ranks?'

'Unfortunately, it is, officers can't attend as that

would mean none of you could relax and enjoy yourself. We have our own shindigs.'

'There ain't many ATS officers so you blokes will all be dancing together, I reckon.'

'We can invite girls from the town, our wives, fiancées and girlfriends, so there's usually sufficient females to go round.'

She looked different somehow, the addition of the smart stripes on her left arm had given her presence. He liked the way she talked to him, not treating him as anything special – which he wasn't, of course.

Now he was about to ask her if she'd made a complaint about him, he rather wished he hadn't made that decision. He cleared his throat, unaccountably nervous. 'Forgive me, but I was hauled over the coals by your CO for making unwanted comments to one of your girls. I've not spoken to anybody apart from you.'

To his immense relief, she didn't take offence at his implied suggestion. 'Crikey, whoever it was is a silly moo. It wasn't me in case you're wondering. I like a bit of banter and I think you're a decent sort of officer. You wouldn't take no advantage of no one.'

'Thank you, if you hear who it was would you...'

'If you're asking me to sneak on one of me own then you can forget it.' Minnie glared at him, jumped to attention, saluted and marched off without giving him an opportunity to explain what he'd been going to say. He wasn't usually so ham-fisted and was determined to explain when he got the opportunity.

He was half amused, half irritated by her reaction, but then Minnie Wolton was an original. However, it was definitely her tall red-headed friend who stirred his senses.

8

Minnie had only travelled a hundred yards when she realised she was going in the wrong direction, as everybody else was trekking towards the lecture hall. She was a sensible sort of girl, but that man seemed to rile her in a way no one else could.

She bent down and pretended to retie one of her shoelaces and then turned and was about to stroll back when she saw Eileen, Grace and Clara approaching. She wasn't going to tell anyone but Eileen what happened, so she'd keep quiet about it for the moment.

'Look what we got,' Eileen said and waved a couple of bars of chocolate. Sweets, like most things, were rationed to 3oz a week and were hard to come by.

'I got you a bar of Cadbury's Fruit and Nut before they all went.'

'Ta ever so – I love a bit of Cadbury's chocolate. How much do I owe you?'

'Nothing, call it a celebration gift for being promoted,' Eileen said with a smile. 'Or you could say I was trying to butter you up.'

'You go ahead, slather as much marge as you like in my direction. Don't reckon there's any butter going spare.' Minnie laughed.

They found their seats in the hall. The first lecture was about working in the stores and it didn't sound as boring as she thought. Mind you, it was more for the girls who'd already worked in shops as there was a bit of bookkeeping and such involved.

The second was emphasising how much stuff each girl was given free which would have to be paid for if they were still civilians – not just clothes, board and lodgings, but also medical things.

There were questions about leave and about what might happen when they were posted, and all those answers were worth listening to. As they were sitting at the back, they were able to escape before Lieutenant Sawyer. He'd instructed them to return to their billets for a briefing from their new lance corporal.

This was for their benefit as Endean could have done this task instead.

Minnie was proud of herself and knew her family would be surprised and over the moon by her being promoted so fast. She reckoned she would be the first girl from the East End to have this happen to her.

Strangely Minnie wasn't nervous about talking to her squad. Endean had been the one to recommend her promotion and was being ever so supportive. Once everybody was perched on the springs at the end of their beds, she told them about the dance at the NAAFI first.

'No officers and no civilians allowed. No alcohol neither.' This news was well received, even the lack of booze. 'Saturday first thing, no PT but we have to parade and there's going to be a full kit inspection immediately after. If we do all right then we get the day off base and then the dance in the evening.'

'Golly, a whole day to ourselves, how absolutely spiffing,' someone said, and she sounded just like Grace and Clara. Minnie hadn't realised there was another posh bird in the squad.

'Only if we do the drill as it should be done, and we pass the inspection.'

'Do we all miss out if just one person gets it wrong?' Eileen asked.

'That's up to Endean, but it means you've all got to be on top form. I ain't missing a day out, not for no one.' She stared pointedly at two of the girls who'd been the worst at drill and at keeping their space tidy.

'I wish we were volunteers, then we could pack it in,' the taller of the two said.

'Well, you can't. You're only allowed to leave on compassionate grounds.' The two girls exchanged glances. 'So, too late to be having second thoughts about being in the army as you're here for the duration.'

'Does compassionate mean like being up the duff?' a girl said and most of the girls laughed.

'Right, you lot, it's time for tea. I reckon we should have a practice tonight to make sure we can get our kit out proper in the fifteen minutes we'll have after the parade.'

This was agreed and Minnie stood aside to allow those desperate to use the latrines before tea to rush off.

'You did really well, Minnie, I just couldn't stand up and talk like you did,' Clara said.

'Ta, I enjoyed it. I might be a short-arse but no one will mess with me, that's for sure.'

She nodded at Eileen and her friend hung back. 'Something I went to tell you, in private like.'

'We can go to the NAAFI for tea. My treat.'

'You've already brought me chocolate. Are you made of money?'

'Sort of. My grandmother left me an annuity and I made sure my husband couldn't touch it. It bought our lovely house, which is rented out now, in St Albans.'

'I'm shocked. You didn't look like Clara nor Grace when you turned up. Your things were nice but not expensive.'

'Gosh, I'm not as rich as either of them. It's £100 a year. I inherited four years ago, which was why we decided to get married even though he was finishing his apprenticeship as a cabinetmaker.'

'A babe in arms at the altar.'

Eileen nodded. 'I was nineteen and he was a few months older. We'd been going out since we left school so always knew we'd get married eventually. The money made it possible.'

They were talking as they walked slowly down the cut that led between two blocks and came out not far from the NAAFI. This was open to all, men, women and civilians, so was a lively and noisy place.

'Shall we grab a sandwich and tea and bring it outside? The grass is dry enough to sit on over there.'

Eileen pointed to a field, probably used for football, and Minnie nodded. There were already a few soldiers and ATS scattered about. The men were smoking their smelly Woodbines so she didn't want to be near them.

'I'll come in with you. It's ever so kind of you to treat me twice. I've got to watch me pennies as I've to send me pay home to help out.'

Inside it was hot and the air thick with fag smoke and steam. There was a short queue at the counter which they joined. They emerged with a mug of decent rosie lee, a corned beef buttie each and a rock cake to share. After finding a quiet spot away from the others, they continued their conversation. She'd not yet told Eileen about what Lieutenant Sawyer had said.

'What's your husband think about you signing up?' Minnie asked.

'He doesn't know. I've just written and told him. He won't be happy, but as we all have to do something useful for the war effort, he'll just have to lump it.'

'I've not told you what happened.' Minnie explained and Eileen was shocked but not for the reason she'd expected.

'How awful to think a girl would run and tell tales like that. I hope it's not anyone in our squad.'

'I was miffed that he thought I might have done it and that I'd tell on me mates.'

'To be honest, you do seem to get on rather well with him. Grace thinks he couldn't possibly have any interest in you other than professional.'

'For once she's got the right end of the stick. We've hit it off as friends like, it'd never be nothing else. I've decided that now I'm going to make the army me career, I ain't got no time to spare for men or any of that malarky. I reckon as I've been given this promotion so quick, I'm going to do well.'

'Who do you think made the complaint?'

'I'm certain it ain't anyone from our platoon. I'll ask the other lance corps to find out and give whoever it was a talking to.'

Eileen carefully divided the rock cake between them. 'I always thought I'd have a big family, but in all the time me and Danny have been married, it's never happened. There's probably something wrong with me and I'm not sure how I'll feel if I can't ever have babies.'

Minnie munched her cake before answering. 'It might be him what's not able to have kiddies, not you. It ain't always the woman's fault. My Auntie Nell was widowed and married again and had a baby the next year when she was forty. Just goes to show.'

'I'm not thinking of abandoning my marriage. For better or worse – but I'm not so sure I meant it.' Eileen smiled sadly. 'Between ourselves, I'd not be upset if Danny didn't come back.'

Minnie's eyes widened.

'Goodness, I don't mean I want him to die, but if he just decided he didn't want to be with me.'

They rinsed their mugs in the ablutions on the way past and were the first back to the billet. Minnie made up her bed and spread out her kit in the required way. She wondered if she would ever get married and have babies. Her mum had six and that was too many. But a couple of little ones would be nice. Anyway, she'd meant what she'd told Eileen, until the war was over there'd be no men in her life and she wasn't too bothered if she remained a spinster neither.

As lights out approached, she was satisfied the girls would pass the kit inspection easy enough. The problem was going to be the drill as half a dozen girls hadn't marched to order for a couple of days because of their arms.

She clapped her hands and stood on the only chair in the room. 'Right, we get up at five and have a practice, that's decided. I'll take the parade like what Endean will do. It's worth losing an hour's kip to gain a day off, ain't it, girls?'

There were a few groans but the girls agreed. They all longed for a day off!

* * *

Ben decided an evening in the mess was called for. After a few pints of beer, he'd relax and forget about the way he and Minnie had parted. He liked her name and thought it suited her. He wondered if she knew his? Would she even bother to find out?

The mess was quiet, no one he particularly wished to spend time with, so he took his pint to an empty table by the window and sat down. Most of the officers here were old hands, too ancient to be active or with the boys in Africa and other foreign places. Tomorrow he'd speak to the major and demand that he be allowed to rejoin his regiment. He was wasting his skills here and Britain needed every trained officer it had.

He scowled into his warm beer. First, he'd better get a clean bill of health from the camp doctor as without that he'd be wasting his time. He was gazing out of the window as he sipped his drink when he suddenly straightened. Something was up – that was the third pair of squaddies that had run past him. The only thing that attracted so much attention was some sort of scrap. There was nothing a private liked better than watching two men kicking seven bells out of each other.

He wasn't officially on duty and an NCO should be sorting things out but something about the way the men had been running had him on his feet and heading for the door without conscious thought.

Even the most aggressive squaddie wouldn't hit an officer, so he might well be the best person to defuse the situation. Not only that, but he was also a big man and had boxed for his regiment in the past.

He could hear the noise, the shouting, coming from behind the building that housed the latest intake. It wasn't just ATS girls who were trained here but also conscripts. Some of these were sent by the courts – told to join up or face a long term in prison. These reluctant soldiers were usually the ones that caused the most trouble until they had their belligerence knocked out of them by the NCOs.

'Out of the bloody way, you morons, an officer coming through,' he snarled at a group who hadn't seen him approaching. They took one look at his expression and slunk away before he could identify them.

He shouldered his way through the tightly packed circle surrounding the two men fighting. Where the hell were the NCOs? There was going to be hell to pay when he found out who should have been on duty this evening.

Without hesitation, he stepped into the brawl and grabbed the man on top by the scruff of his neck. 'On your feet, soldier.'

His barked command registered and the man dropped his fists, stood more or less to attention, blood dripping from his nose and his right eye almost closed.

The bloke he'd been pounding surged to his feet and, not recognising Ben as an officer, took a swing at him. Ben swayed to one side and landed a satisfactory uppercut. His attacker went down like a log and the remaining few men watching cheered before sloping off.

Finally, three NCOs pounded up and skidded to a halt. 'We'll put these men on a charge, sir,' one of them said as he jumped to attention and saluted.

'No, they can go.'

The one on his feet was helping his opponent up. They looked at him, not sure they'd heard correctly.

'I take it there'll be no more nonsense like this in future?'

They both straightened. 'No, sir. Thank you, sir.'

'Dismissed.'

God knows what the fight had been about as the cretins were obviously the best of pals. The two of them staggered off and he turned to deal with the NCOs. They should have been here before him. It was gross dereliction of duty in his opinion.

The three were watching him warily, but it really wasn't worth the effort involved. 'You three are a disgrace. You'd better make sure there won't be a next time.' He stared at them through narrowed eyes, and they got the message.

They snapped to attention and saluted. Ben reciprocated and watched them march off, pretty sure it wouldn't be long before they'd be on a charge for something else. With any luck he'd be long gone by then and back with his own men, doing the job he was trained for.

Raised voices, one of them female, attracted his attention as he was making his way back to the mess. He increased his pace.

The woman was angry. He increased his stride and rounded the corner that led to the postal block to see Minnie's friend squaring up to two of the new intakes of privates. They were blocking her way and making ribald comments.

'Come on then, duckie, give us a kiss,' one of them said.

'I'll do no such thing. I'm a married woman. Now get out of my way or I'll have you put on a charge.'

'Hoity-toity, ain't you? No decent bird walks around on her own at night in a base full of soldiers, now do they?' The second bloke reached out to grab the girl's arm.

Ben was astonished to see the girl handle the matter herself. One minute the man was touching her arm, the next he was writhing on the floor clutching his balls. The first one saw him approaching and vanished, abandoning his friend.

'Are you okay?' He ignored the man groaning and puking on the ground.

'Yes, sir, I'm tickety-boo. I know how to deal with men like that.'

'I'll sort this out. No need for you to be involved unless you want to press charges.'

She shook her head. 'Thank you, sir, I'll get back to my billet.' She stepped around the man she'd felled and then looked at him. 'Was I wrong to walk on my own? Our corp didn't tell us not to be out in the dark. I was just posting a letter to my cousin, Ronnie.'

'Where's he stationed?'

'I don't know, somewhere abroad. Anyway, goodnight, sir, and thank you again.'

'You're Private Ruffel, aren't you?' She nodded. 'Are you certain you're okay?'

'I am, sir, but I appreciate you coming to my rescue.'

Ben blew his whistle and two of the NCOs he'd reprimanded a few minutes ago were beside him, eager to ingratiate themselves. 'Escort this man to the glasshouse. Put him on a charge for assaulting an ATS. I'll deal with him in the morning. He had another with him – get him to give up his companion.' He nodded. 'Better get the quack to give him a once-over.'

They grabbed the man from the ground and half-dragged, half-walked him away. Ben was smiling as he headed for his rooms. He'd had more fun tonight than he'd had in his entire time at Great Baddow barracks. This didn't change his mind about speaking to the quack and his CO but that would have to wait until after he'd dealt with the two bastards who'd tried to molest Minnie's friend.

Private Ruffel was tall, only a few inches shorter than him, had copper-coloured hair and a lovely smile. This fiery-tempered redhead made his pulse race.

But Ben wasn't looking for romance and even if he was it wouldn't, couldn't, be with an ATS. Other ranks and officers didn't mingle. Lack of action was making him behave out of character. He had the weekend off so would go up to Town and catch up with some friends and maybe meet with Lydia.

Lydia Hampton was married but her husband was decrepit and as long as she was discreet, he turned a blind eye to her many affairs. A roll in the hay with her would be just the ticket.

Ben scowled. If things were different, he would get to know Private Ruffel and wouldn't bother with the casual relationship he had with Lydia. Then he swore under his breath. Even if she wasn't an ATS, she was married and therefore out of reach.

9

Eileen walked briskly away from the scene of what could have been something far worse, with her head up, attempting to keep her emotions in check. She was proud of herself, although inflicting so much pain on another human being, even that one, had made her stomach clench.

How did ordinary men cope with the horror of war? Most weren't violent, and now they were expected to kill indiscriminately. Imagine what it must be like for those who had to push a bayonet through the stomach of a German.

She had her wash bag tucked under her uniform jacket and detoured to the ablutions and latrines before returning to the billet. There was a steady stream of girls – not all of them from her squad – doing the same.

Minnie was waiting for her. 'Blimey, you're as white as a sheet. Is it your arm giving you grief?'

'No, something horrible almost happened to me.'

Quickly she explained and her friend listened without comment. 'If that'd been me, I'd have kicked his head in too. Serves him bloody well right.' She guided Eileen back to her bed and didn't release her hold until they were there.

'You sit tight, I'll fetch you a drink of water.'

'There's no need. It was just a bit of a shock. I was thinking that perhaps you'd better warn the rest of the girls about wandering around the base on their own so late.'

'I'll speak to Endean tomorrow – done more than enough yapping tonight.'

Eileen was just sliding under the blankets when the billet went black. It was a further twenty minutes before everybody stopped talking.

Tonight's adventure wasn't something she was going to mention in her next letter to Danny. The last thing any soldier would want to hear was that his wife could have been raped by a fellow soldier.

* * *

Surprisingly, nobody moaned too much when Minnie got them up an hour early. The weather was clement and although not exactly light, it wasn't too dark to practise their drill on the parade ground.

From Monday they would be doing the PT that had been postponed because so many of the girls had had an adverse reaction to the first round of jabs. They would also be seeing the dentist, but further inoculations had been postponed to allow everybody to fully recover.

'Right, sort yourselves out and we'll go down the stairs in our threes and then march to the parade ground,' Minnie told them. As she was now the lance corporal, they had to do what she said whether they liked it or not.

Minnie took her place in the last row and then eyes front, arms and feet in unison, the girls marched and it was a shame there were no senior NCOs wandering about to see how splendid they looked.

They right turned, about turned, and saluted when asked and after twenty minutes, Minnie ordered them to halt. 'At-ten-tion.'

As one, they brought their heels together and when Minnie saluted as if she was the officer, they responded perfectly.

'Fall out,' Minnie yelled and the girls relaxed.

'That was perfect, ladies. I reckon we'll be the best of the bunch on parade today.'

Clara and Grace rushed up to join Eileen. Minnie was talking to a group of girls who were asking her questions. They'd only been at the base a week, but how things had changed. She scarcely recognised this group as the ones who'd arrived in civilian clothes last Saturday.

'I wish Minnie could take the drill,' Grace said. 'She makes it so much easier than the drill sergeant or Endean. I wasn't sure about her being promoted but they made the right choice.'

'They certainly did,' Eileen replied. 'We've just got time for a lick and a promise and to clean our teeth before breakfast.'

The ablutions were busy with most of the girls in their pyjamas with their greatcoats over the top as a dressing gown. The fact that they were in uniform raised some eyebrows, but nobody asked why.

Immediately after breakfast, they raced back to lay out their kit for inspection. Endean and an officer would be coming round at eight thirty. After that, they had to put everything away and then march to the parade ground to demonstrate how good they were at drill.

The kit inspection was over in less than a minute

as there was nothing on any bed out of place or missing. Endean congratulated them and told them to be ready to leave for the parade ground in a quarter of an hour.

For the first time, everyone was bubbling with excitement as they got into their threes. As long as they weren't asked to do anything new this morning, they would pass with flying colours, which meant they had the rest of today free and apart from church parade tomorrow they had Sunday as well.

* * *

Eileen was right and all but one squad was given permission to leave the base. Clara and Grace talked about going up west, but this didn't appeal to either her or Minnie. The last time she'd been in the West End, she'd been propositioned every few yards by overeager American GIs. They'd flashed their money and their non-rationed goodies about, and silly girls had flocked to their sides. She was certain there'd be a lot of unwanted illegitimate babies with American fathers next year.

'There's the dance at the NAAFI tonight so why go to London when we've got what we want here?' Eileen said.

'If it's the expense then I'm happy to treat you all,' Grace replied. 'We can have a smashing lunch at the Ritz and then go to the cinema in the afternoon and to a club in the evening.' She smiled. 'Why attend a dance here when we can go somewhere much more exciting and dance with officers and gentlemen?'

'That's ever so kind, Grace, but I ain't one for clubs and posh places. Eileen, you go if you fancy it. I'll be just fine here.'

Eileen hesitated but then changed her mind and nodded. The expense had been her real concern, not the risk of GIs accosting her. 'If you're sure you don't mind then I think I'll go with Grace and Clara.' She'd never been to a grand hotel or a night club. It would be something to remember but better not to mention it in her next letter to Danny.

'Don't forget you've to be back here by ten. That don't leave you much time for going to a night club. Them trains ain't too clever after dark neither.'

'Golly, I didn't realise the curfew was so early,' Clara said. 'I've changed my mind, Grace, I'll stay here. I really don't want to be AWOL and get into trouble.'

'You're right, Clara, better to explore Chelmsford this time and leave the bright lights until we have a weekend pass,' Eileen said.

This change of plans didn't please Grace and she turned her anger towards Minnie and not the those who were letting her down.

'This is your fault, Minnie Wolton. Trust you to ruin things for us. I'm going on my own and I won't be back by ten. You can put me on a charge if you want.' Grace flounced off. Eileen shook her head and sighed.

'It was generous of her to offer to pay for us. I'm going after her to see if she'll stay and we could go to the flicks together later. I'm sure there are plenty of places to get a decent lunch in Chelmsford as well.' Eileen dashed after Grace and found her in the ablutions, putting on her lipstick. The row of sinks and mirrors was crowded with other girls doing the same.

'Grace, don't go off in a huff. If Minnie hadn't reminded us about the fact we can't be off base after ten, then we'd have all been in trouble. She wasn't doing it to ruin anything but to protect her friends.'

'I know, but I was so looking forward to a day out.'

'We can still have a good time. There's bound to be lots to do in Chelmsford and we've got the dance tonight.'

Grace frowned. 'It's other ranks only, no officers. I don't want to dance with ordinary soldiers. It's not what I'm used to.'

Eileen lost patience. 'You joined the ATS, what did

you expect? Even if you were an officer, you'd still not be allowed to mingle with the male officers. Don't be daft. You'll not fit in if you don't make the effort.'

Grace blinked back tears. 'I've made the most colossal error, haven't I? I'd have been better off marrying the silly man my mother picked out for me. He's incredibly wealthy and I'd have everything I could possibly want.'

'But you don't love him. In fact, you don't even like him. Spending the rest of your life with someone you don't like would be awful. Far worse than being in the ATS.' Grace was listening. 'Also, why isn't he in the services? Is he something important in the government?'

'Nothing interesting like that. He's deaf in one ear and has flat feet. He runs his vast estate near Guilford and does something boring in the city too.'

Minnie and Clara joined them. 'Come on, you two, there's a bus due in five minutes and we'll have to run to catch it,' Clara said.

There was a mass exodus from the washroom and thirty eager ATS girls raced through the camp and arrived outside just as the bus was pulling away.

* * *

Minnie watched the bus go and laughed. 'We'd never have got on anyway, it's bursting at the seams already.'

'When's the next one?' Eileen asked.

'I ain't no idea. It's only a couple of miles to town. We can walk easy enough.'

To Minnie's surprise, a girl she didn't know from another squad made a suggestion. 'You lead us, and we'll march. Give the locals something to see.'

Eileen, Clara and even Grace agreed and five minutes after missing the bus they were in threes, with her in front calling the time and marching, smart as you like, towards Chelmsford.

People stopped to watch and cars, the few that there were on the roads, hooted. When a lorry approached from the rear and needed to pass, they stepped onto the pavement and marched on the spot, in perfect time, until the vehicle lumbered past.

In no time they were approaching the centre of the town and she brought her squad to a halt. 'We're there. Ta ever so, ladies, you did us proud. I reckon word will get back to the camp, though.'

'I never imagined that I'd actually enjoy marching but today I did,' Grace said.

'Not all the girls were our lot, so it just goes to show how well we've been drilled that we managed to keep in step,' Eileen added.

'I need a coffee, real coffee, not the horrible Camp stuff which tastes disgusting,' Grace said. 'There must be good hotel here where we can get some.'

'I ain't fond of coffee, I prefer me tea. Endean's from somewhere around here and told me there's a smart hotel called Saracens Head, ever so old, that does posh food and that.'

'Lead the way, Minnie,' Clara said.

'It's in Tindal Square, what's at the end of the High Street,' Minnie told them.

'That's all very well, but as we don't have the foggiest where we are or where that is, it's not going to help us,' Grace said as she gazed around as if looking for inspiration.

'This is called New Writtle Road, if that's any help,' Eileen said as she pointed to the road sign high up on the side of a nearby house.

'I know where we go. This leads to New London Road and then we turn left and keep going. Eventually we'll be in the High Street and Bob's your uncle.'

'How in heaven's name do you know all this? Surely Endean didn't tell you all the street names?' Eileen said.

Minnie grinned. 'She showed us a map and I'm good with pictures and that. I can remember it all clear as day.' She nodded, happy she'd been able to impress her friends. 'Also, The Empire Theatre and The Regent Theatre ain't far from where we're going.'

This news was greeted with enthusiasm. Today was going to be a good day, and Minnie reckoned the future, despite there being a war on, looked good for her.

It was no more than half a mile to the hotel and she was impressed with the shops, banks and businesses they passed. The shop windows were crisscrossed with sticky tape like those in London and there were sandbags piled up around doors. What blooming good either of those did when a bomb dropped she'd no idea. The good thing about this town was that there were no blooming Yanks cluttering up the place.

'Have there been air-raids on Chelmsford?' Eileen asked.

'Endean said there have been some, they've got important factories and that but they're the other side of the town. Don't see no sign of bomb damage here, do you?'

'No, and everybody seems relaxed and going about their business. Apart from all the queues at the shops, it all seems like before this lot started,' Eileen said.

'We're lucky we get three meals a day regular as you like, I reckon a lot of folks don't.'

Those they passed looked prosperous enough, all carrying gas masks, and mostly smiling when they saw them. Not many kiddies around, they must be in school or evacuated.

They found the Saracens Head, but it looked a bit grand for Minnie. She hesitated, about to suggest she went to the caf they'd just walked past, but Grace grabbed her arm.

'No, I won't let you slope off. I'm determined to buy you a lovely lunch and this is just the place to do that.'

'I'll keep me trap shut and not show you up, don't worry.'

'Minnie Wolton, I might be a snob, but I consider you a friend now and you can say whatever you want, wherever you want. Believe me, no one will turn their noses up when I order us the most expensive things on the menu.'

Grace and Clara took the lead and soon they were being ushered to a table in the window with a white cloth, sparkling glasses and silver cutlery.

'Blimey, what's all this lot for? We only need a knife and fork to eat our dinner.'

The waiter smirked and shook his head at her

comment and that really got her goat. Minnie was about to give him a piece of her mind when Grace stepped in.

'I am Miss Grace Sinclair, my father's Sir George Sinclair, he is a member of the government. Lance Corporal Wolton is a personal friend of mine and I won't tolerate your insolence. Do I need to speak to the hotel manager?'

The poor bloke opened and shut his mouth like a stranded fish. Then he recovered and, to give him his due, he apologised handsomely.

'I meant no offence, Miss Sinclair, to you or your friends. I apologise if inadvertently I did so.' Whilst he was speaking, he moved around the table, pulling out the chairs so they could sit down. A waste of time in Minnie's opinion, but she knew nothing about the way the posh folk lived. Perhaps they were too feeble or stupid to move the chair for themselves.

'We would like a jug of coffee and a pot of tea served immediately. We shall peruse the menus whilst you bring our drinks.' Grace nodded regally and the man sort of bowed.

He returned immediately with the menus – these were presented in a leather cover with gold writing. When Minnie flipped it open, she was disappointed to see how little choice there was.

Her friends were reading and exclaiming as if there were dozens of things to choose from. 'What's this when it's at home?' She pointed at the words that she thought were French but she wasn't going to risk trying to say them.

'Boeuf bourguignon,' Clara said. 'It's a French beef stew. I'm going to have that. I'll have the vegetable soup to start. I should have the same, Minnie, unless you like fish.'

'Fish and chips, but I ain't sure about what's on here. I'll have the beef stew and the soup – can't go wrong with that.'

The waiter returned with a silver tray with the coffee, tea and a plate of biscuits – they didn't look like something you got at the shop.

'Thank you, we'll serve ourselves. We will all have the soup and boeuf bourguignon. The wine list won't be necessary.'

After the cups and saucers, cream, milk and sugar had been put in the centre of the table, the waiter removed most of the cutlery, leaving them with a butter knife, soup spoon and knife and fork.

Eileen preferred tea as well and they shared the pot. Grace and Clara drank the coffee. They all tucked into the biscuits.

'Well, if everything else is as good as that, we're in

for a treat,' Eileen said as she brushed a few stray crumbs from her uniform.

Minnie had been looking around the large dining room, already busy even though it was only just midday. 'Here, I reckon that's the local rag on that table over there. That old gent's reading a newspaper so I'm going to get one too. It might well tell us what films are on at the flicks this afternoon.'

Their soup arrived whilst she was reading but the waiter wisely made no comment. She pushed her chair back a bit so the paper didn't trail in the soup.

'There's *21 Days* with Vivien Leigh and Laurence Olivier at the Regent and *Band Wagon* with Arthur Askey and Richard Murdoch at the Empire.'

Minnie carefully folded the *Chelmsford Chronicle* and replaced it with the others in the wooden rack. No one had started eating. They were gazing over her shoulder for some reason.

'Ta for waiting. Looks a bit of all right and smells good too,' she said. Still the others didn't pick up their spoons. 'What's up? What have I missed?'

Eileen leaned closer. 'Lieutenant Sawyer has just walked in with a very elegant woman.'

Before they could prevent her, Minnie swivelled in her chair just as the lieutenant's companion looked in her direction. The posh bird nodded and smiled, and Minnie did the same.

She turned back and picked up her spoon. 'Don't like cold soup. Not sure why you're bothered by having them in here.'

The table was far enough away for them to talk without being overheard.

Grace answered. 'He couldn't have anticipated being seen by anyone from the camp and now we've spoilt it for him.'

'Why would he come here and not meet his friend in Town?' Clara said.

'Let's change the subject. Shall we decide which film to see after lunch?' Eileen was right, officers and their lady friends were none of their business.

10

Ben had been surprised and annoyed when Lydia insisted they meet in Chelmsford and stay at the Saracens. He'd agreed, reluctantly, and now bitterly regretted having done so. The group of ATS being in the same dining room was a disaster.

'Don't look so stricken, darling, those little ATS girls are not going to cause us any trouble.' Lydia smiled and for the first time since he'd begun this affair, her casual attitude to things grated.

'I know two of them and you can be sure us being seen together will be circulating all over the camp by tomorrow.'

Lydia was carefully removing her gloves and her broad gold wedding band and expensive diamond engagement ring was clearly visible. Why in God's name had he agreed to register as her husband? The fact that he was unmarried was common knowledge and it would be hard for those girls to miss the flashing diamond and the wedding band.

Lydia's tinkling laugh echoed around the dining room and two tables nearest to them looked round and smiled, obviously thinking them to be a happily married couple. If they left now, that would just draw more attention to themselves, so he'd have to endure the meal and try to look as if he was enjoying himself.

'I'm going to have the egg mayonnaise and the Dover sole to follow, darling. What are you going to have? I think I'd like some bubbly – this is a special occasion, after all.'

'That sounds splendid, I'll have the same.'

The attentive waiter returned to take their order. The noise from the champagne cork attracted further unwanted attention and it was obvious that the four ATS girls were deliberately ignoring them. He wasn't sure if this was good or bad but did know he'd no intention of spending the night with Lydia.

As soon as the meal was over, he'd bundle her back into his most prized possession, his bright red MG, and return her to the station. In fact, he was prepared to drive her back to Town if that was what it took to get rid of her.

God knows why he now found her so annoying. Might it be because it was the first time he'd been seen with his mistress – if that's what she was – by people who knew him, even if they were just ATS girls?

The food was remarkably good and, despite his reservations about his situation, he enjoyed the meal but only drank one glass of champagne. It seemed only fair to buy her whatever dessert she wanted and she settled for sherry trifle.

Minnie and her friends had left some time ago, all studiously looking in the opposite direction as they passed his table. Thank God he hadn't brought in the overnight bags, although the room was reserved.

'Excuse me, Lydia, I won't be a moment. Shall we have coffee?'

'Yes, that would be lovely. I'll order it, shall I?'

He nodded and hurried to the desk, where the day manager was patrolling back and forth, keeping an eye on things. Must be difficult to run a good hotel like this with so many shortages – not just food, but also labour, as all able-bodied men were now conscripted.

'I'm Lieutenant Sawyer, we have a room reserved

but have decided not to stay. I'll pay for lunch now if I may.'

The man didn't raise any objection or suggest that he had to pay for the unwanted room. 'I'll collect your bill for you, sir, if you'd care to wait here.'

'Actually, we're going to have coffee before we leave. It was a splendid meal and we both enjoyed it.' He knew roughly how much the meal had cost and handed over more than enough. 'I'm sure this will cover it. Thank you.'

'I'm sure it will, sir, and the surplus will be divided as it should be amongst the staff.'

Ben returned to the table, knowing it was highly unlikely any of the money would find its way into the pockets of the waiters. He wanted to be able to walk out to the car with Lydia thinking they were going to collect their bags. If she then objected to the change of plans, at least in the car park at the rear of the hotel they would probably be unobserved.

She disappeared to the ladies' room to powder her nose and he hovered in the foyer. Thankfully she didn't keep him waiting long.

'That was remarkably delicious, darling. Who would have thought that a dull place like Chelmsford would have such a good hotel and restaurant?'

There was a rear exit to the hotel that led directly

to the car parking area and she made no objection to going out there – she could have asked him to bring up her bag and that would have been a problem.

'I'm sorry, Lydia, but we can't stay. Being seen with you where I'm not recognised was one thing but you insisting on coming here has put me in an awkward situation. Those girls know that I'm not married and if they report me, I could be accused of conduct un-becoming.'

She raised an elegant eyebrow. 'My dear, are you giving me my congé? I suppose I must be glad you fed me first. Are you tired of me?'

He could have lied, flattered her, promised to make it up to her but told the truth. 'I've enjoyed our liaison, Lydia, but having it made public like this has rather changed things, don't you think? Are you happy to catch the train or do you require me to drive you back?'

'Take me to the station. I've absolutely no desire to travel any further than I have to in your ridiculous little car.'

With considerable relief, he watched her stalk across the station forecourt. It had been fun whilst it lasted but he was glad the relationship was over. Un-bidden, an image of the tall redhead came into his head.

Why did he keep thinking about Eileen? There was absolutely no chance of him ever being involved with her. Not because he thought her beneath his notice but because he was an officer and, of course, she was married. The sooner he got the all-clear from the quack the better. One thing he did know was that spending time in her company wouldn't be good for either of them.

* * *

Eileen had never had close girlfriends and the more time she spent with these three, even Grace, the happier she was. Danny hadn't been one for talking about feelings, making plans and so on, and for the first time in her life she had someone to share her dreams with. When she came to think about it, her husband had never talked to her in the way she chatted to her new friends. He told her what to do, complained about something he'd read in the newspaper, but never discussed things.

'Penny for them, Eileen,' Minnie said as they walked together towards the cinema.

'I was just thinking I'm really going to enjoy being in the ATS and having good friends like you. My husband was an excellent cabinetmaker, he made wonderful bespoke furniture, but he spent more time in his workshop than he did with me in the house. He wasn't a good husband.'

'Men ain't built for conversation. All they want when they're with a woman is to get in their knickers. It ain't them that get in the family way. I'm not throwing me life away on no man.'

'Don't you find men attractive? Don't you wonder what it would be like to be intimate with them?'

'Blimey, no,' Minnie said. 'I reckon I'm not like you or the others. If I was pretty like what you are then maybe when I was growing up the boys would have paid attention and things might be different.'

'Goodness, don't you look in the mirror? You might be small but you're quite lovely. You've got the most beautiful hazel eyes and wonderful nut-brown curls. As for your figure, it's absolutely perfect.'

A hundred yards ahead of them was a small queue outside the Empire in Springfield Road. Minnie had explained that there were two larger cinemas, but the Regent and the Empire had the best films on this afternoon. The doors opened and they moved forward. One and six was a lot to pay but would be worth it.

There was no need for the usherette to lead them to their seats using her torch to guide them as the auditorium was lit. The lights didn't go down until the afternoon performance started. From then the films were shown continuously and you could stop there for hours if you wanted.

'Cor, this is a treat. I'm used to watching the second half of the major feature before the first,' Minnie said.

The Pathé news was good, all the servicemen smiling, no pictures of anything nasty or actual war. According to the commentator, who spoke with a plum in his mouth, and was explaining the images they could see on the newsreel, everything was tickety-boo. She hoped this was true but had a nasty suspicion it wasn't.

There was a cartoon, *Mickey Mouse*, then *Band Wagon* came on. Eileen really enjoyed the film and couldn't remember having ever laughed so much. After being in the dark for so long, the bright sunlight outside made her blink.

Grace had insisted on paying for them and there hadn't been time to argue before they went in. Now they were outside and heading for the bus stop, Eileen decided it was time to speak up.

'You paid for lunch, Grace, and I don't think you should have paid for the cinema as well. Please let us pay you back.'

'No, that would be silly. I'm quite sure my quarterly allowance is more than you and your husband have to live on for a year. Minnie comes from the East End and Clara's family have cut her off. Therefore, it makes sense for me to be your banker whilst we're together for our training.'

'If you put it like that, we can hardly refuse. It's strange, isn't it, that we've only been together for a week and already know more about each other than I know about anybody apart from my husband.'

Minnie overheard this and laughed. 'We've certainly seen more of each other than we expected to. My mum would be shocked to think I've shown me drawers and me boobs to all and sundry. And then there's the dentist on Monday and more inoculations, lectures, drills and parades.'

'When do we get to choose what trade we want to go into?' Clara asked.

'Two weeks from now we'll all get a form to fill in. By then we'll know what's available and can make what Endean calls "an informed decision". If you ask me, we won't get much say in it. The clever ones will go to technical posts and possibly become officers.'

'That makes sense,' Eileen replied. 'I want to be a PT instructor and you already know that you'll stay here and train new recruits. What about you two?'

'Grace and I have decided we want to be dispatch

riders. Imagine the fun it will be racing around the place on a motorbike.'

'Can either of you drive a car?' Eileen asked.

'We can and I've actually used my brother's motorbike on occasion,' Grace said.

'In which case I reckon you two will be first pick when it comes to choosing girls to be drivers. Me, I ain't keen on cars, I prefer me own feet.'

'I think you should go for something more taxing than driving. You've both got a good education.'

Grace laughed. 'So far, we've not heard about anything else that appeals. Maybe we'll change our minds if something more interesting comes up.'

Minnie was taking them around Chelmsford as if she'd lived there all her life. She must have a remarkably good visual memory.

'There's a bus stop just ahead,' Eileen said. 'There are a few women waiting so I think there must be a bus coming soon.'

'It might not be going to the camp, but we can ask.' Clara looked at her watch. 'We don't have to go back immediately as the dance doesn't start until six.'

'Why don't we have a cup of tea in that little café over there?'

'That's a good idea. I'll nip over and ask them ladies what bus stops there and when the next one is,'

Minnie said. 'You know what I like, so you can order for me. I won't be a tick.'

She went to speak to the women, leaving the three of them to enter the café alone. There was one free table at the back and Grace headed for it without waiting to be conducted there.

Eileen thought that rather rude as the table could be reserved. She hung back and a waitress who looked no more than fourteen years of age staggered out from behind the bead curtain carrying a heavily laden tray.

'Is it all right if we sit at that empty table?'

'Yeah. I'm rushed off me feet, but I'll be with you when I can.'

'Is there a ladies' room I can use?'

'Yeah. Out the back but it's clean as a whistle.'

Eileen used the facilities, and the girl hadn't been exaggerating, there was even a small vase of garden flowers above the sink and everything was spotless. Minnie was back and said it was the right bus stop and the next bus went in forty-five minutes.

'Plenty of time to drink our tea and eat our cake,' Clara said happily as she tucked into an iced finger.

They left the café with ten minutes to spare. 'I saw a tobacconist and confectioners just across the road. I'm going to pop across and see if I can get a newspa-

per. I'm hoping it might have more up-to-date information than the newsreel,' Eileen said.

'What if the bus comes early and you ain't here?'

'Then that's my own fault and I'll have to walk
back. I'm not that fussed if I miss the dance. You get
on the bus regardless.'

'Well, you be quick. It looks like it's going to rain,'
Minnie said.

Eileen was dismayed to find three people in front
of her and decided it might be wise to give up on the
idea of getting Grace chocolates to say thank you for
her generosity. Then an elderly lady with pebble
glasses and very few teeth came out from the back to
help with the queue.

With a small tin of Rowntree's Dairy Box in her
hand, she emerged from the shop to find she'd missed
the bus. To make matters worse, heavy drops of rain
began to fall. It was going to be unpleasant making
the return journey and she would be soaked right
through to her underwear.

She was trudging along the pavement, not looking
forward to exiting the town and being obliged to walk
on the side of the road where she was more vulner-
able to passing traffic. After only a few minutes, a
bright red sports car glided to a halt beside her. The

window was wound down and Lieutenant Sawyer looked out.

'Would you like a lift back to base?'

'Oh, yes, please. But I do hope we won't get into trouble because we're *fraternising* in your smashing MG.' She'd not spoken to him since her unpleasant encounter with the drunken soldiers a few nights ago but she had thought of him more than she should. He didn't get out but leaned over and opened the door. She hurried up and dropped into the comfortable leather seat. This was the first time she'd been in any sort of sports car – in any car as expensive as this one.

'Giving a lift to a private doesn't count as far as I'm concerned. Why didn't you catch the bus?'

'My friends did but I needed to buy something.' She showed him the tin of chocolates and he nodded.

'I hope whoever the gift's for appreciates the sacrifice you made for them. Did you have a good day out?'

Should she mention that she'd seen him with his friend or pretend they didn't both eat lunch at the Saracens Head? 'We had a delicious lunch and then went to the pictures. It was an Arthur Askey film called *Band Wagon* and was very funny.'

He laughed and banged his gloved hands on the steering wheel. 'What a coincidence! I went to the Ritz and watched *Gone with the Wind*. God – what a complete waste of money that was.'

She'd obviously misunderstood the situation at the hotel and his lovely companion had been just a friend – otherwise he'd be with her now.

A few minutes later, he overtook the bus. She swivelled in her seat, wondering if her friends had seen them pass and what they would have made of it if they had.

'I'm going to be back before them and I'm only slightly damp, which is even better news than being transported in your luxury sports car. Do you make a habit of offering lifts to random ATS girls?'

For some reason, she found talking to him easy, not something she was familiar with as Danny was a man of few words. Just being so close to Lieutenant Sawyer made her pulse race.

'I've given lifts to people many times but you're the first ATS girl. The others have been... umm... let me think. Two soldiers, other ranks, not officers, a vicar, a couple of middle-aged ladies who, like you, had missed the bus and, on one never to be forgotten occasion, a local good-time girl.'

'Golly, I didn't know there was so much petrol available for private jaunts.' This was a silly thing to say but his casual reference to giving a lift to a prostitute had shocked her.

'As an officer I still have access to fuel, but it won't be long before I'm reduced to travelling on public transport or by Shanks's pony.' He turned his head and smiled at her with a quizzical expression. 'I thought you might be going to ask me to explain what happened when I gave a lift to a lady of the night.'

Eileen couldn't help herself. 'I'm a married woman so I'm sure nothing you can tell me will shock me.' This was patently untrue, but she really did want to know about his unfortunate experience.

'It's nothing too alarming. We'd not been travelling more than a hundred yards when she asked me for ten shillings in advance. I thanked her for the offer and hastily pulled into the kerb and she hopped out. Fortunately, nobody saw us or I might have got an unsavoury reputation.'

'Perish the thought, everybody on the base knows you're the perfect gentleman.'

His smile vanished and he looked at her through narrowed eyes. For a moment she was slightly uncomfortable, then he smiled again.

'I'm going to tell you something in confidence. A complaint was made against me by an ATS and although the matter was dropped, it's made me wary.'

Now it was her turn to laugh. 'If this is you being wary, sir, then I'd hate to see you being foolhardy. It might be better if you stopped a distance from the gates and you entered on your own. The rain's eased a bit and I won't get all that wet.'

'Absolutely not. I don't give a damn what anybody thinks. As you just said, I'm a gentleman and was helping a lady in distress.' His charming grin was back. 'I suppose I'm not being inappropriate calling you a lady in distress?'

She giggled – not something she'd done since she was a girl. 'Better than calling me a lady of the night. Perhaps a woman in the wet might be better.'

'I'm Ben, am I allowed to use your name?'

'It's Eileen, but you can't call me that and I certainly won't be calling you anything but sir.'

'You never know. We might meet under different circumstances one day.'

There was no opportunity to reply as they were rapidly approaching the gates. He hardly slowed down and was waved through. This wasn't surprising as his little red sports car must be the only one at the base.

He leaned across her to open the door and his arm brushed her breasts. She held her breath. He turned his head and his eyes blazed. Was he going to kiss her? Then the moment passed and he was back where he should be.

'There you are, out you get.'

She thanked him for the lift and scrambled out. He drove away, leaving her very unsettled. Even when she and Danny had been courting, he'd never made her feel like this. Why had spending so short a time with him had this strange effect on her?

This was so wrong. A married woman shouldn't be having feelings like this for another man. Tonight she'd pray for forgiveness and in future keep her distance from him. She daren't use his name even in her head as that would be admitting that he was beginning to mean a lot to her, even though it was impossible and she scarcely knew him.

11

Minnie hadn't told Clara or Grace that she'd seen Eileen in the front seat of the little red sports car. She jumped off the bus before them, hoping to know all about it before the others.

'Nature calls, see you in a minute.' Eileen was hovering between two of the buildings, presumably waiting for her. Minnie waved. 'Blimey, talk about riding in style.'

Eileen grinned. 'He offered me a lift and it would have been silly to refuse. I found him an amusing companion and can see now why you like him.'

'Like him? I ain't sure about that. But he's all right, I suppose, for an officer.'

'I missed the bus to buy these for Grace. I'm going

to give them to her now. She's a bit prickly but I'm beginning to think that she's quite nice underneath all that.'

Minnie agreed. 'We're the best of the bunch, I reckon. Here they come. Are you going to tell them how you managed to be here first?'

'Of course I am – why shouldn't I?'

Grace and Clara were envious that they hadn't been the one to travel in the MG with the handsome officer. The chocolates were well received and the four of them hurried back to their billet in order to get ready for the dance.

Upstairs it was deserted. 'Goodness, where is everybody?' Clara asked, viewing the empty dormitory. 'I think we must be horribly late if there's nobody here.'

'They could all be in the rec room,' Eileen suggested. 'Maybe we're early.'

Grace checked her wristwatch. 'Don't panic, ladies, it's teatime. They will all be in the mess gobbling down bread, margarine, jam and an indifferent slice of cake.'

'I ain't sure why I came back here, I'm not changing nor nothing,' Minnie said.

'Aren't you going to put on a bit of lipstick at least?' Grace said.

'No, I don't have any so couldn't even if I wanted to.'

'You can borrow mine,' Eileen said but Minnie shook her head. Her mum had called girls with make-up 'painted ladies' and that had put her off using it ever since.

'Should we go to the NAAFI and see what's what? It'll be unusual for me being first in the line for a change,' Eileen said.

Minnie had hoped that Grace would open the chocolates and hand them around, but she'd hidden them in the back of her locker, which seemed a bit mean. She found herself walking next to her and decided to mention it.

'I was hoping for one of them chocolates. I can't remember the last time I had one.'

Grace didn't answer immediately then looked at her. Minnie was shocked to see tears in her eyes. 'And I can't remember the last time anyone gave me an unsolicited gift of any sort. I'm going to share them, of course I am, but I just wanted to enjoy the moment and see them in my locker for a day or two. I do hope the others don't think I'm mean or greedy.'

'Me and my big mouth – both feet right in as usual. You hang onto them as long as you want. It ain't none of my business anyway.'

'I promise you'll be the first to choose. Do you have a favourite?'

'Any chocolate's all right with me. Blooming heck, there's a right old to-do coming from behind the NAAFI. I'm not going anywhere near it.'

Eileen agreed. 'There's still time to get a cup of tea even if we don't want anything to eat or we could wait in the rec room. What do you think?'

They were just considering would be best when half a dozen redcaps ran past. The military police would soon sort out the ruckus, which sounded like some sort of fight.

'Not tea, I'm awash with it,' Clara said firmly. 'We could play Monopoly whilst we wait.'

This was a board game Minnie loved but it took a blooming long time to complete. 'We won't finish it, but we can work out who wins by who's got the most houses, money and owns the most property.'

'I've not played since I left boarding school – my parents didn't approve of something as frivolous as board games. Reading – books that they'd selected for us – and piano practice was their idea of suitable en-tertainment for children.'

'Sounds like you had a miserable childhood,' Eileen said sympathetically. 'Being wealthy doesn't always make you happy.'

Minnie laughed as they walked into the empty rec room. 'It helps, though, don't it?'

* * *

The four of them became so engrossed in the game that they were reluctant to leave it. Eventually, it was Grace who said if they were going to the dance they'd better leave or it would be over.

'I reckon Eileen's the richest and I'm second,' Minnie said. 'That was ever so much fun, ta for suggesting it, Clara.'

This time when they approached the NAAFI they could hear the music, laughter and people having fun, but it was all rather subdued. 'Blimey, no wonder it's quiet, they've left three redcaps at the door.'

'It's a live band, not records. How absolutely spiffing,' Grace said and without waiting for them she rushed through the door.

Minnie wasn't a good dancer but that never stopped her getting onto the floor and enjoying herself. What she really liked to dance to was the music of the American bandleader, Glenn Miller.

Even with the windows and doors open, the NAAFI was stuffy and hot. A blue haze hung over the room, and she halted at the door. There were so many khaki-coloured uniforms, both male and female, squashed into the space that Minnie realised dancing would be more like shuffling about on the spot.

'I ain't going in. It's too crowded. You go ahead, I'm going to find a book and read until it's time for cocoa.'

Eileen and Clara didn't try to persuade her to join them and she liked that they respected her views. They too disappeared into the crush. After watching for a few moments, Minnie couldn't even distinguish them from the rest of the ATS who were milling about.

It was a warm evening, still light, and she decided to have a stroll before going in to read. There were still parts of the camp she'd not explored but tonight she was just going to walk round the parade ground.

She was on her way back when she heard desperate crying from somewhere behind the latrines. Slumped behind the block was a young girl, a civilian, sitting in a tangled heap on the ground. Her hair was mussed, her legs scratched and she was missing a shoe. Even more telling was the fact that the bodice of her pretty spotted frock was ripped. This poor girl had been assaulted.

'I'm Lance Corporal Wolton. Can you stand or shall I fetch the ambulance?'

The girl was too distraught to answer and continued to sob. Her face was snot covered, her eyes swollen, and red lipstick was smeared over her face. The bastard who'd hurt this girl was going to pay for this.

There were heavy footsteps approaching. Minnie jumped up and stood in front of the girl, fists clenched, in fighting stance, ready to protect her with her life if necessary.

* * *

Ben hadn't known what to expect when he went to investigate but it certainly wasn't Minnie ready to take a swing at him. He took one look at the crumpled heap behind her and guessed what had happened.

'Is it what I think it is?'

Minnie nodded. 'Yes, sir. This young girl has been assaulted and is too distressed to tell me what happened or even give me her name.'

Ben crouched down next to the quivering girl – hardly more than a child, really. He had a good idea who the bastard might be, the same one who'd attempted to molest Eileen, and this time the man wouldn't get away with a week's fatigues. He'd go to the glasshouse for years if he had any say in the matter.

'Sweetheart, I'm Ben, I'm going to pick you up. Is that all right?'

The girl still cried but didn't struggle when he slipped one arm under her knees and the other under her arms and gently hoisted her up.

'Medical block?' Minnie said.

'Yes, can you double there and have them meet us with a trolley?'

'Yes, sir. She's lost a shoe and has no handbag either. I don't think the attack took place here.'

'I agree. We'll look for her things once she's safe and being taken care of.'

Minnie took off, leaving him to carefully edge his way down the narrow passageway between the latrines and the ablutions block and exit onto the main route through the camp. The girl was light, he'd have no problem carrying her the half a mile even if the trolley party didn't materialise.

He talked to the inert girl, telling her it would be all right, that they would take care of her, but it wasn't true. If, as he suspected, she'd been raped, the repercussions for her could be horrendous. She could be pregnant. Bad enough being an unmarried mother but to carry the child of your rapist didn't bear thinking of.

If it was rape, then the perpetrator deserved to

swing for it. Jail wasn't sufficient punishment. He was halfway to the hospital when two medical orderlies appeared with a trolley. Minnie was beside them as they trundled it at the double towards him.

'She's either unconscious or fallen asleep,' he told them.

'We'll take her now, sir. The doc has been sent for and the MPs.'

Carefully he put the limp girl down and stepped aside as they tucked a blanket around her, leaving only her head showing. Her dignity was now restored, and he prayed his suspicions weren't true, that she'd just been robbed and beaten up. That was bad enough, but if rape was to be added, that would be intolerable for her to deal with.

Minnie wasn't even flushed or breathing heavily from her exertions. He was impressed by her fitness. 'You'd better wait for the redcaps, they'll want to know what you saw, how you found her and so on.'

'I've told you, so I don't need to repeat myself to them. You stay, sir, I'm going to look for her shoe and her handbag. She can't have come very far as she was.'

Ben stared at her without answering and instead of looking uncomfortable, she grinned. 'I beg your pardon, sir, I should have asked you if you'd be kind enough to remain here whilst I search for her things.'

'Yes, Wolton, you should. However, you're right, you go ahead and I'll come and find you. I can see Sergeant Finbarr and two of his men approaching.'

She nodded, smiled, and dashed off. She might be small but she was a veritable powerhouse. It didn't take long to tell Finbarr, the senior NCO in charge of the MPs tonight, what he knew as it wasn't very much.

'I think it might be the man who attempted to assault another ATS a few days ago. Find him and see if he's got an alibi.'

He left them to it and jogged after Minnie. He'd been here for almost six weeks, had seen two cohorts of ATS come and go, but this was the first time he'd been on first-name terms with any of them. Both young women were attractive, funny, intelligent and must be absolutely out of bounds to him, especially Eileen, as she was married. He might be many reprehensible things, but he wasn't a home wrecker or a seducer of innocents.

There was a hum of noise coming from the NAAFI but nothing too alarming. At least the majority of the other ranks and ATS girls would be safely contained at the dance. The girl who'd been attacked must have come onto the camp in order to attend, so it made sense to start looking for both the attack site and Minnie in that direction.

He eventually found her not by the NAAFI but on the parade ground. She saw him and beckoned. For a moment he thought she was going to yell across the empty space, but she waited until he got there.

'She was attacked here. Look – the grass is flattened, and her shoe and her bag are over there.' Minnie pointed to a pile of stones painted white to make them more visible at night. 'I didn't move them in case there's evidence of some sort. I ain't sure what anyone could find out, but I thought it better to wait.'

He crouched and studied the flattened grass more carefully. 'You're right. This is clearly the attack site. Show me where the bag and shoe are – did you look inside to see if her purse is still in there and her identity card?'

'I ain't touched nothing. I just told you that.' Her tone was sharp and he was beginning to find her distinct lack of respect for his position irritating.

She followed him and pointed to where the bag and shoe had been hidden. 'I don't understand why the bastard who did this bothered to hide one shoe and her bag.'

'I thought that, but I reckon when he'd finished she surprised him and took off, leaving them behind. Makes sense that he'd hide the evidence, don't it?'

'Good point.'

Minnie might be abrasive, but she was very bright. He leaned down and retrieved the two items. 'Here, it seems better if you look inside. Less intrusive for a woman to do it.'

She didn't comment but half-smiled as if approving his suggestion. 'There's a bus ticket from Chelmsford, three and sixpence and her ID card.' She handed this to him.

'Sally Smith, aged sixteen, and she lives at 60 New London Road. For Christ's sake – what was someone so young doing here?'

'I reckon she came with friends, maybe an older sister. They probably don't even know she's missing.'

He digested this information and came to a decision. 'If I go into the dance, you can imagine the reaction I'd get. Officers stay away from these events. The MPs settle any problems and we only see the culprits the following day.'

'I'll go in – it should be easy enough to spot any civilian girls. I won't be a tick. Are you going to wait outside or go back to the hospital with Sally's things?'

He sighed. This couldn't be allowed to go on. 'Wolton, you appear to be ignoring the chain of command. I am an officer, you are not. It is for me to make suggestions, issue orders, not you. Do I make myself quite clear?'

'Lieutenant Sawyer, sir, I ain't got time to discuss that now. I know me place, and I reckon I'm just doing me job, nothing else. Put me on a charge if you want but I've got to find Sally's friends.'

Before he had time to respond, she was gone, leaving him feeling rather foolish. Minnie was right. She was putting her duty to Sally Smith first and was prepared to take the consequences of being insubordinate.

His brief acquaintance with this dynamic girl had turned his belief in his innate charm and natural authority upside down. She seemed impervious to both. If he was honest, she hadn't actually been disrespectful, just not as subservient as he was used to from someone in her lowly position.

He was smiling, despite the dreadful situation, as he sauntered after her. He would hang about – it wasn't urgent for the doctor to be told the girl's name. There were a few couples wandering about outside the NAAFI and with the two redcaps standing outside the door they were unlikely to do anything untoward.

It was doubtful that the perpetrator would return to the dance – if he'd been there in the first place. Ben put things in the order that they might have occurred.

Sally had turned up at the dance with a couple of older friends. They'd split up and Sally had maybe been asked to dance by the man who later attacked her. She was young and innocent and had been easily persuaded to go outside. How she ended up on the parade ground, which was quite a distance from the NAAFI, he'd no idea.

Scarcely ten minutes later, Minnie and Eileen came out accompanied by two civilian girls. You could see even from that distance that they were upset. God knows how she'd found them so quickly and Ben, not for the first time, was struck by Minnie's efficiency. That girl would be promoted again in no time.

Eileen was walking with one of the girls and Minnie was comforting the other. They didn't need him to intervene as they had the situation well under control. He dodged out of sight and jogged to the hospital. It might make things a bit easier if the medics were made aware of who was coming.

* * *

Eileen had been horrified when Minnie had pulled her to one side and explained what had happened. Together they pushed their way through the crush of dancers, looking for any girls in frocks rather than uniforms. They'd spoken to three who'd said they hadn't come with anyone called Sally Smith when she spotted two more standing on the edge of the dance floor looking anxious.

'Over there, it has to be them,' she told her friend.

'I reckon you're right. Quick, we need to speak to them before they start making a fuss,' Minnie said. 'The dark-haired one looks just like Sally – must be her older sister.'

They reached them and Minnie naturally took the lead. 'Excuse me, are you looking for Sally?'

'We are, we were dancing and didn't notice she'd gone until just now. Is she all right? Mum wasn't keen on her coming, but we promised to keep her safe.'

Eileen knew when they discovered how poor a job they'd done they would be devastated. Minnie ignored the question.

'It's too noisy to talk in here. Let's go outside and I'll explain why I'm here.'

As soon as they were outside the door, Minnie told them that Sally had been attacked and was in the hospital.

'Oh my God, poor Sally. It's all my fault. She was sitting at one of the tables talking to another girl and promised not to move.'

'She obviously did and must have been missing for an hour at least. Blooming heck, how did you not see she was gone from the table?' Minnie didn't mince her words.

Eileen stepped in. 'There's no point in recriminations now. Let's get you over to the hospital where your sister's being looked after.'

The sister was the most distraught, but her companion seemed a lot calmer considering the circumstances. Eileen was escorting the friend and thought she'd take the opportunity to talk to her and find out a bit more about what had actually happened.

'Did you look over at the table at any time before you missed her just now?'

'When I looked across a while ago, Sally and the girl she was with were dancing together. I thought that was harmless so didn't tell Elsie.'

'What was the girl wearing?'

'A blue frock with flowers, she had reddish hair and I don't think she was any older than Sally.'

'Thank you, I'm going to see if I can find her. You catch up with your friend. Would you tell Lance Corporal Wolton what you told me and that I'm going to look for this girl?'

Eileen ran back and entered the fray again. She was almost certain there was no red-headed girl in a blue floral dress anywhere in the NAAFI. It was just possible she was in the ladies' room and she was going to just check there first. If her suspicions were right, then this other girl could well be in danger.

It took her ten minutes to be certain the girl she was looking for was missing. The two military policemen were on high alert as they'd seen her rush in.

She quickly explained what was going on. 'I think you need to look for this girl. The other attack took place on the parade ground. I pray I'm wrong, but I've a horrible suspicion that I'm not.'

It didn't seem possible that two young girls could be enticed from the safety of the NAAFI without anybody noticing. Surely the second girl must also have come with others. A dance on an army base wasn't something you attended alone.

Her hands clenched and her stomach tightened. Had those horrible men from the other night attacked these poor girls?

12

Minnie delivered the sister – she now knew her name was Elsie – to the hospital and was surprised when the friend turned up without Eileen.

'The other ATS has gone to look for another girl who was sitting with Sally. She told me to come on here by myself,' Elsie's friend said.

'You go on in then. Hope everything turns out all right for Sally.'

On the way back to the NAAFI, Minnie was stopped by a redcap. 'There's another girl missing. A redhead with a blue flowery frock – she was sitting with the girl who was attacked and now she's vanished.'

'Bleeding hell – that's not good. Do you mind if I

come with you, Corporal? If we find her in the same state as Sally, then she ain't going to want to talk to you.'

'That's what your mate said so she's gone with the bloke on duty with me tonight. He's searching the left-hand side of the parade ground and I'm doing the right.'

It was starting to get dark and if they didn't find the missing girl soon, it would be much harder to locate her. Torches could only show a pinprick of light – not enough for what they were doing.

She jogged alongside the corporal, keeping up despite the difference in their sizes. In fact, she was breathing easily and he was already beginning to puff. They'd seen nothing to indicate that a girl or her possible abductor had come this far.

Then the shrill sound of a whistle echoed across the ground. 'That's an officer's whistle – it means I need to get there pronto. You follow as best you can. I can't wait for you.'

Minnie didn't bother to answer. She took off at full speed and she was soon several yards ahead of him. The whistle sounded again, coming from behind a building a short distance from the NAAFI.

Her stomach turned over. Lieutenant Sawyer was kneeling beside the body of a girl. She increased her pace and skidded to a halt and dropped down next to him.

'She's unconscious, has definitely been raped, but her pulse is strong.'

He'd taken off his jacket and covered the girl from the waist down. The corporal and two other MPs arrived.

'The three of you go into the NAAFI. Have the ATS leave immediately. Ask any civilian females to wait outside. I need to speak to them. All the squaddies are to remain inside. Wolton, go with them and telephone for an ambulance. Come back with a couple of blankets.'

Eileen joined her as she hurried into the NAAFI and then went straight to the office. There was a telephone there which connected directly to all the buildings in the barracks. The telephone operator answered promptly and connected her. She explained what was needed and put down the receiver.

'Do you think it's the same two bleeders what had a go at you the other night, Eileen?'

'It could be – in fact, in a way I hope it is because to have several dangerous men loose on the base is a horrible thought.'

'It has to be the two of them. One bloke couldn't attack both girls at the same time.'

Whilst she was talking, Minnie had been searching the office for a rug, a blanket, even a couple of tablecloths would be better than nothing.

Eileen opened what looked like a stock cupboard and found what they wanted. 'Here you are, a couple of picnic rugs. They'll do very well.'

They joined the flood of unhappy girls being escorted from the premises. From what she could overhear, they didn't know the reason – which was probably a good thing – and were just moaning that the dance had been curtailed.

Once outside, it was easier to move as the ejected girls were heading either for their billets or if they were civilians they were standing about looking fed up. It made sense to send them away as they obviously couldn't have been involved in the two attacks, but she thought it might have helped to have interviewed some of them. One of the ATS girls was far more likely to offer up information as they wouldn't be snitching on a possible mate.

There was still no sign of the ambulance but if the operator was to be believed, the message would have been delivered instantly. It shouldn't be much longer before it arrived. She hoped a medic would come as the girl didn't look too clever.

Minnie knelt down beside the injured girl and

then carefully tucked her under one of the rugs and folded the other and placed it beneath her head.

'There, you'll be more comfortable now.'

She regained her feet smoothly and turned to the officer – now she knew his name was Ben, it was becoming more difficult to think of him as her superior. 'Do I have your permission to speak to the girls waiting?'

He nodded. 'Yes, but I'll come too. Ruffel, stay with the girl. Tell Major Clark that I'll be with him shortly.'

Presumably this Clark bloke was the doctor in charge of the hospital. She'd only met two doctors, one the useless young one who'd caused so much pain to her girls, and the other a grey-haired bloke who'd given a couple of lectures and he didn't seem up to much either.

'Shouldn't both girls be transferred to the hospital in Chelmsford? It's not a proper hospital here, is it?'

She'd spoken out of turn and he'd already warned her about doing that. She braced herself for a reprimand but instead he nodded and smiled sadly.

'There's a decent one, the Essex and Chelmsford Infirmary, at the town end of New London Road. Both girls will be transferred there. However, the officer in charge of the investigation needs to speak to them and hopefully get a description of the bastards.'

'Do you think they might talk to me or Eileen rather than another man in uniform?'

'Possibly. It wouldn't hurt for you both to be there. Someone has been sent to collect Sally's parents, but we don't know the identity of the other one. Time to speak to the remaining civilian girls. You might as well accompany me.'

A less than enthusiastic suggestion, but Minnie was happy to do as he asked. Back at the NAAFI, there were five girls waiting. None of them looked worried, more annoyed at being denied an evening's entertainment.

She touched his arm to attract his attention and he looked down. 'What's wrong?'

'Look at them, sir, they ain't bothered about a missing friend. I don't reckon you'll learn anything useful from them.'

This proved to be correct. The girl in the blue frock wasn't known to any of them, which was strange. They were sent on their way after a few questions. Suddenly a staff car screeched to halt and a very angry grey-haired major jumped out.

'What the devil's going on, Sawyer? Absolute bloody chaos. Why are you involved? Aren't you off duty tonight?'

Minnie slipped away. This was nothing to do with

her really, and the best thing for her to do was to return to her billet and talk to the girls there. It was almost lights out, ten o'clock, so everyone, apart from Eileen, would be getting ready for bed.

She frowned. Actually – they were all off duty so could go to bed when they liked. The rule was that they had to be in by midnight, so most likely the girls turfed out from the dance would all be in the rec room.

It was possible one of them had seen something and if they had she'd take the information to the MPs. She'd risk being torn off a strip by the major – which she didn't mind – or by the lieutenant, which she did.

The racket from the rec room meant she'd been right in thinking most of the girls were in there. At least a few of them must have guessed why the dance had been abandoned by now, so she wouldn't be breaking any rules telling them what had happened.

Clara and Grace saw her come in and rushed over. 'Everyone's saying there's been a murder,' Clara said.

Minnie was about to explain when Grace chimed in. 'It's something to do with the fight before the dance. It doesn't surprise me. I was told that a lot of the conscripts are sent to the army instead of being sent to prison. Therefore, it's hardly surprising such dreadful things happen.' She shuddered dramatically. 'I really should have listened to my brother and not joined the ATS. I'm sure this doesn't happen in the WAAF or the WRNS.'

'I'm sure it does,' Clara said firmly. 'Anywhere you have a lot of uneducated men; they are bound to drink too much and end up fighting.'

Minnie had heard enough of this nonsense. 'You've got it wrong. Two girls have been attacked and raped. Nothing to do with fighting or drinking.'

* * *

Ben stood loosely to attention and let his CO rant until he'd run out of invectives to sling at him. 'Two civilians have been assaulted by two of our men, sir. That's catastrophically bad for the base's reputation, don't you think? The redcaps are interviewing the men who were there. If they can ascertain who was in attendance at the start and is now missing, then we'll know who we're looking for.'

'Assaulted? Do you mean raped?'

'Yes, sir, I do.'

'Jesus Christ. I'll nail the bastards who did this to the wall. Get all the men on the parade ground and have a roll call taken.'

'That's being done, sir. I sent half a dozen senior NCOs ten minutes ago.'

'Good man. Sorry for the bollocking. Didn't know the facts. Should have waited for you to explain.'

'Shall I get on with it, sir?'

'Who's supposed to be on duty tonight, do you know?'

Ben did but had no intention of dropping his fellow officer in the mire. 'Haven't the foggiest, sir. I'm going to see how things are progressing inside.'

The sergeant had got the men sorted into platoons and was barking orders at them. He stood by the doors and waited to be noticed. When the sergeant glanced in his direction, Ben nodded.

'Have you got anything useful from this shower?'

'Yes, sir. Three men have been mentioned more than once as being here earlier but are now absent. I was about to send my men to find them.'

As they were speaking, the loud note of the bugle indicated all men were to fall out and assemble on the parade ground.

'Get this lot over there, Sergeant, the CO's waiting to address them.'

'Yes, sir.'

'Continue the search for those three men.'

Ben had the names and wasn't surprised that two

of them were the ones he'd put on a charge earlier in the week. It seemed likely that the third one had left the NAAFI for legitimate reasons. As he'd already flagged the two names to the MPs, it shouldn't be long before they were arrested.

The courts were sending the scum of the country into the army thinking they'd instantly be knocked into shape. Maybe if they were on the front line this would be the case, but loafing around here being trained wasn't enough to deter the hardened villains.

Bill Hempstead, a fellow lieutenant, also recovering from a serious injury sustained in Africa, should have been all over this. He'd received a bullet in the guts and although repaired, the poor sod spent half the time unable to function and had to retreat to his bed. That was where he'd be now. Bill knew he should be invalided out but vainly hoped he'd make a full recovery and be able to fight again.

He headed for the room they shared and, as expected, Bill wasn't in good shape. He was in bed with the lights out. Ben switched them on and his hands clenched.

'Sorry, old bean, but I'm not able to function this evening. Another of my funny turns. Sorry you had to step in.'

'Not to worry, I've handled it. You look bloody awful. White as a sheet, in fact.'

'Been worse than usual, I'll be fine tomorrow.'

'I'm calling an ambulance. You need to be in hospital. This is more than a funny turn, as you call it.'

He rushed off and snatched up the telephone in the office next door. The fact that Bill didn't argue about the ambulance was a very bad sign. If he hadn't been faffing about dealing with those two bastards, he'd have come over to see how his friend was hours ago. He prayed he wasn't too late.

The doctor listened. 'He needs to be transferred to Chelmsford immediately. The two ambulances are taking the girls. Bloody hell!' There was a pause. 'I'll find something to transport him in. He needs to be flat so not in a car. I'll be there in five minutes.'

Ben tore back to his room, relieved that Bill was still conscious and coherent. 'The quack's on his way. I'll pack what you need. God knows what you'll be travelling in, but it will get you there, don't worry.'

The doc arrived with a stretcher and two medics to carry it. 'I'll just get this drip up, old boy, then we can get you to the hospital.'

The bag of clear fluid was attached and the doctor held it as Bill was gently moved onto the canvas stretcher. Ben followed them out and if the situation hadn't been so desperately worrying, he'd have smiled. Bill was going to Chelmsford in the back of an open truck. A comfortable bed had been made for him from a paillasse and blankets.

He tossed the overnight bag alongside his friend and the doctor. 'I'll come and see you tomorrow, Bill,' he called and hoped this wasn't wishful thinking.

He'd only met Bill when he'd arrived at Great Baddow barracks six weeks ago but in the services friendships were made fast and dissolved just as quickly. That said, he'd come to like his roommate. But he was pretty sure that Bill was on the way out. In fact, now he came to think of it, the poor sod had been going steadily downhill for the past couple of weeks.

Ben flopped out on his bed, boots still on, too dispirited to return to duty. He remained where he was for a bit and then decided he'd already upset the major tonight, so it was better not to exacerbate the situation. He wanted to rejoin his regiment and it was the major who had the last say on the matter. Bentley was usually a docile sort of chap but tonight he'd been unusually vehement.

His injured leg was painful after so much activity and somehow, he doubted he would be considered fit for active duty for another few weeks. Considering he'd almost lost the leg, and his life, he was lucky to still be in the army at all.

Thinking about his near demise made him think of Bill. No point dwelling on things, better to get up and get on with it.

There were squaddies wandering about so the major had finished with them. Therefore, no necessity for him to go to the parade ground. He didn't enjoy the stultifying atmosphere of the Officers' Mess, neither was he a heavy drinker, so instead, he headed for the NAAFI. He glanced at his watch – still plenty of time for a brew.

The main room had been returned to its usual layout, tables and chairs scattered about and the counter open for business. There were no soldiers there, just a sprinkling of ATS. Eileen was standing in the queue. He looked around and saw Minnie sitting at a table with the two other girls he usually saw with her.

'Good evening, Ruffel, do you know if the girls identified their attackers?' He spoke quietly, making sure no one could overhear.

Eileen nodded. 'It was the two who accosted me, sir. They've been apprehended already. The second girl actually works here, in the post office, and had come over after her shift finished. She's young, but not as young as Sally.'

'That explains why she was on her own. What a dreadful thing to have happened to such young girls.'

'A dreadful thing to happen to any woman, whatever her age, sir.'

She turned back to the counter and gave her order. He hoped to God this incident didn't lower morale.

He collected his tea and a sausage roll, probably more breadcrumbs than meat, and retired to a far corner. He was the only officer in here tonight, although this was the one place all ranks could socialise. From his tucked away position, he could watch Eileen without being observed.

He was drawn in purely a platonic way to the diminutive Londoner, Minnie, but he found the tall, statuesque, married Eileen dangerously attractive. He half-smiled into his mug. The sooner he was gone from here the better.

Then he shook his head at his stupidity. The intakes only spent four weeks being trained before being posted to whatever trade they'd been selected for. In three weeks, those two would leave even if he didn't.

13

Eileen was glad to have company on the way back to their dormitory as it was now completely dark and only two of them had remembered to bring their torches. It didn't matter that the vicious men who'd attacked the girls were now locked up – everyone was nervous, suspecting there could be others just as bad lurking around the next corner.

'Tomorrow we've just got church parade and then the rest of the day free,' she said to her friends as they approached the block where they were living.

Minnie replied, 'If it wasn't compulsory, I wouldn't go, I'm not a God botherer, none of me family are.'

'As long as we attend church, does it have to be the

service they put on here?' Clara asked. 'I really don't feel comfortable standing alongside a lot of soldiers after what just happened.'

'I ain't sure where the nearest church is but you're right, we can go off base.'

'How would they know if we actually went to a service? They just have our word for it,' Grace said. 'My brother and I were obliged to attend the local church twice every Sunday. Do you know that sometimes the vicar droned on for two hours? It's put me off religion for life.'

Eileen smiled in the darkness. If Grace had a true faith, then a boring vicar wouldn't have made her give up on God, whereas she went to church because she wanted to, not because she had to. 'There's a map of Great Baddow pinned on the notice board at the end of the dorm. The church is bound to be marked on that.'

'We might as well call in at the bogs on the way past,' Minnie said. 'I don't think me teeth will fall out if I don't clean them just this once.'

At the top of the stairs, Eileen shone her torch at the map and saw that the Church of St Mary was less than a mile away. 'If we add the walk to the gate, we'll need to leave half an hour to get there,' she told the others.

There were still a few stragglers heading for their billets but the four of them were the only ones from their squad. Upstairs the girls were in their pyjamas, some reading, some chatting, and a few were writing letters.

They had twenty minutes before mandatory lights out, which was more than enough. Minnie moved the only chair in the room to the far end and hopped onto it. She didn't have to clap her hands or call out, within seconds the room fell silent and every girl was looking in her direction.

How was it that some people were just born with the ability to command, Eileen thought, while others like her struggled to be seen even though they were half a head taller?

'It's been a horrible night. Two girls from the village were raped but the men who did it are now locked up. There's nothing for us to worry about. The redcaps will be keeping an eye on things from now on.' Minnie waited for the chatter to stop before continuing.

'There's a church in the village and we're going there. I thought the rest of you might like to come too. We can march like what we did before and give the locals something to smile about.'

One girl put a hand up as if still in the classroom. 'Will the church be big enough to take all of us?'

'I ain't got a clue. But we can stand at the back if we have to.'

There was a chorus of agreement as nobody was keen to attend a service that meant being surrounded by squaddies, even if the two villains were in custody.

* * *

The next morning, immaculately turned out, they were ready to march to Great Baddow. This time Minnie took her place in the penultimate row of three. Even after just a few days the squad were able to march in step and didn't need her at the front calling the time.

They certainly turned a few heads as they left the base and headed for the village. It didn't seem possible that this group of girls who'd turned up from all walks of life, all parts of London, had somehow been turned into smart members of the ATS so quickly.

As they marched in perfect step to the village, Eileen let her thoughts drift. So much had happened in just a week but the most astonishing and worrying thing was that she couldn't stop thinking about Ben. Just referring to him by his Christian name in her head made her flush. She must pray harder for the strength to keep her distance, as adultery was a sin.

As they were three abreast, they marched on the road and fortunately there was no traffic on this Sunday morning. Minnie had explained to the girls they were to march on the spot – something they'd just mastered – whilst she spoke to the vicar.

It turned out this was unnecessary as the elderly gentleman approached the head of the column, beaming. 'What a magnificent sight to see you young ladies marching so splendidly. Welcome, welcome, as you can see this is a very large church and there's ample room for all of you.'

They split into their friendship groups and walked into the dimly lit interior. Candles were in short supply – like everything else – so there were none lit. There were a few pretty arrangements of garden flowers scattered about. The church was huge, far too big for such a small village, so it was no wonder the vicar had been so pleased to see them. It would need a congregation of several hundred to fill all the pews.

The arrival of a handful of officers from the base had caused a few comments from the girls but the men wouldn't have heard and took their seats towards the front of the church.

'Glad Sawyer didn't come,' Minnie whispered. 'I think I get on his nerves.'

'He's quite nice really, I like him,' Eileen said.

The organ began to play and the congregation stood. The procession of choristers, vicar and verger processed down the aisle.

'Did you see that?' Minnie hissed. 'One of the choir boys has got a mouse. I saw it run up his sleeve just now.'

'Little devil. Let's hope it doesn't escape.'

'It'll certainly make being here more interesting,' Minnie said, grinning.

* * *

The service was excellent and the familiar words came easily to Eileen without her needing to follow in the book. The organ accompanied the hymns with gusto but not much musicality and the sermon lasted only twenty minutes. The vicar mentioned the two girls attacked last night in his prayers and until then Eileen hadn't considered the possibility khaki uniforms might not be popular here.

Luckily the mouse remained with the small boy and kept both him, Minnie, and several of the girls amused during the service.

They trooped out and avoided having to shake hands with the vicar as he was chatting to his regular parishioners. They'd agreed to return in the same way as they'd come. Marching was fun and even the most reluctant were now enjoying the drill.

They'd been on the move for a few minutes when Minnie called out, 'Car coming,' from her position at the rear of the column.

This meant they smoothly moved into single file whilst continuing to keep in step. Impressive – and this was the first time they'd had to do it in public. Minnie had taught them a couple of days ago after the regulation drill had been completed.

The staff car with the five officers sailed past and as soon as it had, Minnie called instructions again and they were back to three abreast. Eileen reckoned even the blokes couldn't have done it any better.

They swept into the barracks and this time there was quite a crowd watching, some of them were the officers that had been in church earlier.

As soon as they were back to their billet, they fell out and dashed upstairs to collect their irons and mug.

'Do you think we'll get a roast today as it's Sunday?' Clara asked.

Minnie nodded. 'Yes, it was something I was told

at my meeting. Sunday and Christmas we get a roast, other days it's a stew of some sort.'

The mess was full of eager ATS wanting a proper Sunday meal. 'I hope there's still some roasties left for us,' Minnie said. 'All that exercise has given me an appetite. I could eat a horse.'

'You might very well have to,' Grace said with a smile. 'The French love horsemeat. It's a bit chewy but rather like steak.'

'Blimey, I'd have thought you'd ride a horse, not eat it,' Minnie said.

'I much prefer to ride one,' Grace replied.

They always sat in the same places and their squad was last to come in. If this meant they got meagre rations then they'd attend the service on the parade ground in future.

'Cor, that looks a bit of all right, don't it?' Minnie said as an orderly plonked heaped plates in front of them. 'Plenty of everything, although they've boiled the guts out of the cabbage and carrots. I reckon they've had them on since last Sunday.'

After eating, some of the girls were going to play tennis, others opted for a stroll around the field that bordered the parade ground. However, most, like Minnie, Grace and Clara, decided to spend the afternoon in the rec room playing board games and chatting.

'We've got more jabs and the dentist on Monday, but first it's PT. I ain't looking forward to wearing those outfits in public.'

'I thought we could turn up one pair of knickers and wear them underneath. That should keep us decently covered,' Clara said.

The girls giggled and several of them agreed with Clara.

'After what happened at the FFI and then with the kit demonstration outside, what with brassieres being waved about by Rigby, I don't think anything will ever embarrass me again,' Eileen said. 'And I'm going to do what you suggested, Clara, and double up on my knickers.'

* * *

Minnie and the rest of the squad headed for the gym where they were to do their PT before breakfast and she wondered where the other two squads were going for their morning exercise. With any luck she could stand in the middle of a row and not be so exposed.

'Crikey, don't we look a sight? I heard some of the girls say they were going to breakfast in their PT kit but I'm going to change even if it means being late.'

'I'm looking forward to it. I want to train to be a PT

instructor so I'm going to stand at the front,' Eileen said.

'I'll stand behind you, then nobody will be able to see me.'

There was a different corporal waiting for them in the big gym. She was almost as tall as Eileen but instead of being nicely rounded, she was thin as a stick. Minnie hadn't seen her before. The woman didn't introduce herself and watched them milling about getting into lines without yelling, which was a good sign. Once they were in place, she stepped forward.

'Good morning, girls. I'm Corporal Smith and you'll be seeing me most mornings for your daily PT routine. Follow what I do. I'll face forwards and call out the names of the exercises.'

There followed warm-ups, bungee jumps, star jumps, sit-ups and press-ups. They then did a series of stretches to cool down. It hadn't been half-bad, Minnie decided, as she wiped the sweat from her forehead.

Not everybody agreed with her and half the girls were panting and red-faced. Eileen was fresh as a daisy and even Grace and Clara were smiling.

'I need a wash before I get dressed – I think if we run we should just about have time,' Eileen said.

'At least we ain't limited to a few minutes like we were when we came last week,' Minnie said. It appeared that their group had finished before the other two, so the ablutions weren't too busy.

It was more a lick and a promise than a proper wash, but it would have to do. As she was about to go up the stairs to her dormitory, Endean waylaid her.

'Lance Corporal Wolton, I'm afraid you're going to have to miss breakfast. I'm sure you'll get time for something in the NAAFI later on.'

'What's up? I ain't going nowhere in this, I don't care what you say.'

'I wasn't asking you to, Wolton. You've got five minutes to change. I'll be here. Don't keep me waiting.'

Minnie flew up the stairs and was into her uniform – which, like everyone else, she'd laid out ready on her bed – and hurtled back with a minute to spare. There'd been no time to tell her friends where she was going but she was pretty sure Eileen had seen her speaking to Endean so would guess something was up.

'Am I for the high jump? I ain't done nothing wrong as far as I know.'

'The exact opposite, Wolton. It seems you were seen yesterday marching to church with your squad.'

'Blimey, that's good.'

No point in asking anything else as she would be told when she got there. Endean seemed cock-a-hoop so it had to be something special. Minnie glanced down to check her uniform was neat, her heavy shoes polished and her stockings on straight.

She was surprised they were walking away from the ATS admin block and towards the army one. Why would anyone in the real army want to see her? Endean seemed happy enough so it must be something good, but she couldn't imagine what it might be.

The main admin block for the army was a lot posher and twice the size of the one the ATS had. She noticed there were several ATS girls working in the offices – not something that appealed to her. They were expected and ushered into what looked like the commanding officer's room by a smiling corporal.

She snapped to attention and saluted the major, who returned the gesture with a smile. 'There you are, Wolton, take a pew.'

Minnie sat in one of the chairs waiting opposite his desk and Endean took the other. She kept her knees together, the heels of her shoes touching, and sat up straight. She hoped they didn't notice she had to be on tiptoe or her feet would have dangled in mid-air.

'Right, I've been hearing excellent things about you and your platoon, young lady. I don't suppose that you are aware that there is a drill competition for the ATS. I want to enter you and your girls. This is the first time we've had ATS trainees that have proved good enough to warrant entering them in the competition.'

Minnie swallowed a lump in her throat. It was all very well marching about the place but to maybe to do it in a competition wouldn't be so good. 'We haven't learned to do anything really fancy yet, but I reckon we could.'

He beamed. 'You were seen leading your girls on the way to church yesterday. I've already had several phone calls from local dignitaries saying how impressed they were. Not only because of your marching expertise but also because you attended the local church. The first time anyone from here, apart from a few officers, has done so.'

Minnie hesitated, wondering if she should or shouldn't explain why they'd gone, then decided he looked a nice enough bloke, a bit like someone's grandad, so she'd risk it.

'We enjoyed it, sir, but we only went because we didn't want to be with the men after what happened the day before. I'm not sure if it will be a regular thing, especially if it's tipping down.'

He shook his head. 'A dreadful thing, I'm not surprised you felt insecure. Obviously, you can attend or not as you see fit, but I'd like you to at least go next week as I believe there are going to be quite a few local people coming out to watch.'

'In that case, sir, we'll definitely go.'

'Good show. Splendid, splendid. Now, shall we get down to details about this competition? Endean won't be taking you for the necessary extra drill to make sure that you're up to scratch. My sergeant major will do so, as under his instruction our boys have won for Great Baddow barracks for the past two years. It will be a feather in our cap if we can take the ATS cup as well. No other barracks has done so yet.'

Being yelled at by a sergeant major didn't sound much fun. She glanced across at Endean, who smiled reassuringly.

'Permission to speak, sir,' requested Endean.

'Yes, go ahead, Endean.'

'I'll be there learning alongside you, Wolton, and once we've mastered the routine then I'll take over. I'll be supporting you at the competition. It's in two weeks' time.'

Minnie just nodded and smiled. She was finding

being in the same room as the major rather unnerving. Better that she kept her gob shut and didn't risk offending him.

'Excellent. Off you go. Do us proud. Your training starts this afternoon. You and your platoon will have to miss the lectures.'

Endean was on her feet and Minnie followed suit. They both saluted a second time and marched in perfect step from the room and out of the building. As soon as they were away from it, they relaxed.

'Blimey O'Reilly, that's a turn-up for the books. I hope the girls are as enthusiastic about doing extra drill as I am. I ain't sure some of them will want to do it.'

'I believe that you marched a mixed group of girls into Chelmsford on Saturday. I've arranged for those girls to join us and for the reluctant members of your squad to temporarily transfer.'

'I'll give you their names. Make it official like. It's only for the extra drill, they won't have to change billets?'

'No, of course not.'

'Whereabouts is this competition when it's at home?'

'Oh, didn't I say, it's being held here this year. Less chance of us being bombed than in London,' Endean said. 'Not that there have been many bombs anywhere since last year, but they still get the occasional dive bomber coming across the Channel, don't they?'

'That's even better. I ain't one for travelling far. Chelmsford's the furthest I've been from home in me life.' Minnie grinned. 'Excuse me, but if I run like, I'll maybe get me breakfast after all.'

14

Ben had started jogging around the playing field every morning to strengthen his injured leg. He often stopped and watched the men and the women practising their show-drill routines.

He thought the girls had the edge and would be disappointed if they didn't take the cup. The entire barracks was invested in these two teams – there was a feeling of expectancy, of excitement as if waiting for the football cup final. Everywhere was being spruced up, hedges clipped, white stones re-whitened and every bit of grass had been mowed.

The unpleasant atmosphere that had hung over the place for a few days after the two girls had been assaulted had thankfully dissipated and mainly because, for the first time, the two drill events were being held at Great Baddow barracks. A bind for those having to travel but excellent for them.

There were several betting pools, illegal and frowned upon but inevitable, and they were being ignored as long as they didn't get out of hand. He'd had a flutter on the girls himself.

The lectures were finished – thank God – and next week the girls would be filling in the forms indicating which trade they wanted to go in. Then they would be posted away to start work or for further training. They still had drill, PT, and various medical inspections as well as smaller talks telling those interested to hear more about the trade they intended to choose.

Ben was determined to join the exodus himself and this was why he was taking the extra exercise. Five months away from his regiment was more than enough.

He finished his run, returned to his billet and changed back into his uniform. He was strolling to the mess for breakfast when suddenly, and painfully, he was flat on his face on the concrete.

'Bloody hell, sir, you went a purler. Here, let me help you up.' The speaker was his sergeant and a good friend.

'I don't know what happened. I do know my

bloody leg hurts. I think it gave way.' With some difficulty, he rolled over and sat up. The pain in his injured ankle was excruciating.

'You stop where you are, sir, I'll fetch a couple of blokes to carry you.'

'You will do no such thing. Grab my arm and help me up. That's an order. If I lean my weight on you, I think I'll be able to make it to my billet.'

This was wishful thinking as he couldn't put his foot down at all. The slightest movement sent shafts of pain up his leg. 'Give the medic a buzz. I need transport to the hospital. In fact, I've a nasty feeling I'm going to be on my way to London to see my specialist.'

'Righty ho, stop where you are, and I'll fetch you a chair. Some bugger in here is bound to have a spare one.' His sergeant left Ben propped against the wall and elbowed his way into the nearest building, returning moments later with a much-needed seat.

'Thank you. I'll perch here, you make that telephone call.'

What the hell had happened to his leg? He'd done nothing untoward to it as far as he knew and exercise had been positively encouraged. He recalled being told just after the accident that some sort of metal had been put in to support the shattered tibia. Had this given way? The pain was definitely in his shin. A bloody awful thing to happen just as he was getting ready to be shipped out to join his regiment somewhere near Egypt.

One of the ambulances arrived speedily and he was carefully lifted into the back and willingly stretched out on the padded bench that ran down one side. Every minuscule bump sent bolts of agony up his leg and he was gritting his teeth by the time the vehicle glided smoothly to a halt outside the small hospital.

The senior quack jumped in. 'Stay where you are, young man. I'm going to have a quick dekko but I've a nasty suspicion something catastrophic has happened. Judging from your extreme pallor and expression of foreboding, you must suspect that too.'

'My leg collapsed under me, sir, I was just walking. I've had no pain, have been having a gentle jog around the playing field every morning and now...' He couldn't continue as agony engulfed him as the doctor slid up his trouser leg.

'I'm going to give you something for the pain. Then I'm afraid it's straight back to London. Your shin is a very strange shape and I can only surmise that the pin put in to support the broken bone has itself broken.'

An orderly helped Ben remove his uniform jacket and then the doc jabbed him in the arm. Whatever it was, it worked and he drifted off into a drug-induced sleep. He was vaguely aware of the journey, of being transferred to a trolley and taken into the hospital. It was almost certainly St Thomas's in Westminster, where he'd had the original surgery.

They kept him doped up, which was good for the pain but bad for knowing what was going on. He was wheeled into X-ray and then straight to theatre. He tried to ask if they intended to amputate his leg but his mind was woolly and he couldn't find the words.

He came round in a side ward with various bottles of liquid attached to his arm – one clear and one obviously blood. There was a protective cradle over his lower leg and as he could feel it, he thought it was probably still attached to his right knee.

'Good, you're very lucky, Lieutenant Sawyer,' Mr Forsythe, the senior consultant, said to him.

'I don't feel very lucky. Do I still have both limbs intact?'

'You do, I can only apologise that the pin I put in failed. Faulty workmanship by the manufacturers. I have replaced it and in a few weeks you'll be as good as new.'

Unwelcome tears trickled down his cheeks. He

still had both legs. He could serve his king and country again and that was all that mattered.

* * *

Eileen was sitting in the rec room with the other girls, filling in the form they'd been given so the powers that be could decide which trades they'd go into.

'I'll be glad to finish with these lectures. I didn't enjoy the sessions of gas training – if the Germans had been going to drop gas on us then they'd have done it already,' Eileen said to Minnie, who was sitting next to her.

'Blooming heck, I reckon that was the worst. Having to take off our respirators in that tin hut and then nearly choke to death is something I ain't keen to repeat.'

'The pamphlet we've been given on all the sections of the ATS is extremely useful but does go on rather,' Grace said as she flicked through the dozens of pages. 'I'd no idea there were thirty-six trades and occupations available to us and I'm definitely going to put down work on the anti-aircraft gun sites as my preference. What about you, Clara?'

'I think AA operational duties are definitely for me too. Although I must admit I still rather see myself astride a motorbike, racing about the place taking messages,' Clara replied.

'I definitely want to do PT training,' Eileen told them.

'We've got the intelligence tests tomorrow, and we've also got to write an essay about our lives before we joined up,' Clara said. 'Then on Saturday the drill event. I'm actually rather looking forward to that.'

'At least we won't be doing any more practice,' Eileen said. 'We can't miss these aptitude tests, can we?'

'We don't need any more training. I reckon we're better than the men. It don't seem possible next week we'll be going our separate ways. Do you know where you'll be going to learn to be a PT instructor, Eileen?'

'I haven't a clue – I'm hoping when I'm trained that I can come back here but I don't suppose I can.'

'Look, our corporal's heading our way,' Grace said. 'She doesn't look very happy.'

Endean spoke directly to Eileen. 'Private Ruffel, would you come with me, please?'

Eileen frowned. She didn't know why she was being summoned but didn't ask and didn't argue. 'I hope I won't be long, if I don't get back before we have to go for tea, can you take my papers back for me, Minnie?'

'Course I will. See you later.'

They marched everywhere – very little strolling if they were moving from one assignment to another. Eileen looked around at what had been her home for the past three weeks and was astonished at how much she and the other girls had changed. They'd metamorphosed into soldiers and were scarcely recognisable as the civilian girls they'd been when they'd arrived a short time ago.

They weren't going to the admin building for the ATS but to the main block. Her heart began to thump, her stomach turned over. She could only think of one reason she'd be going here. Something had happened to Danny. She sent up a fervent prayer to the Almighty that he wasn't dead or badly injured – even being taken prisoner would be preferable to that.

Eileen was ushered into an office where a major was waiting. He was on his feet, his expression serious; this definitely wasn't good news.

'Private Ruffel, I have to inform you that your husband Corporal Ruffel has been seriously injured. His condition is critical, and he's already been flown home. You have compassionate leave to visit him. A car is waiting to transport you to Chelmsford and Essex Hospital where he is presently being treated.'

Eileen stared at him, unable to speak. Endean

took her arm and guided her out. 'He's not dead, Ruffel, that's something to hang onto. You have permission to remain at his side as long as you wish.'

'I have to take my tests tomorrow, there's the drill competition in three days. I can't miss that.' It was easier to talk about things she could understand and not about the fact that Danny could die.

'Family first, Ruffel. I'll let Lance Corporal Wolton know what's happened.'

Eileen was bundled into the waiting car and was on her way to Chelmsford with her head still spinning. She'd not seen Danny for over two years, hadn't expected to see him until the end of the war, and she couldn't take in this dreadful news.

As if in a dream, she made her way into the hospital and was directed to the wards – used for servicemen and women only – where Danny was being looked after. It wasn't visiting time but the sister in charge of the ward was expecting her.

'Mrs Ruffel, your husband is very poorly. I don't know if you were told that the lower part of his left leg has been amputated. He'll be discharged from the army with a disability pension if he recovers.'

'Lost his leg? No, I didn't know that. Is he conscious?'

'In and out, but he's been asking for you. Corporal Ruffel is in a side ward. I'll conduct you there.'

Danny was burnt brown from the sun. There was blood from a glass bottle hanging above his bed dripping into his arm, a cage over his legs, and she didn't recognise him as the man who'd left her in September 1939.

As she approached the bed, his eyes opened. He managed to smile, his teeth startlingly white against his brown skin.

'Eileen, love, sit with me. I don't want to die alone.'

* * *

Minnie gave the bad news to the others and they were all as upset and shocked as she was. Eileen wasn't the only married woman in their squad and the other two, naturally, were the most concerned.

'I don't think she'll be back unless her hubby pegs it,' one of the girls said, which was something Minnie had already considered.

'The important thing is that Danny gets better. I'm going to pack her haversack with what she needs and go and see her tomorrow afternoon after the tests. She doesn't even have her gas mask, let alone her toothbrush.'

'Will you need permission to leave?' Clara asked as she wiped her eyes.

'I do, of course, but I'll get it. They ain't inhuman,' Minnie replied.

* * *

The next morning, immediately after breakfast, they were shepherded into a large hall – from the smell of sweat and fags it was used by the men – where there were desks set out. Their squad went in first, which was good as it meant she'd have the rest of the day to get to Chelmsford and back.

After three hours of scribbling, Minnie was relieved to put down her pen and escape into the warm May sunshine. 'Blimey, I'm glad I don't have to do that every day. I'm going to the admin block to ask Junior Commander Davies for permission to find Eileen. I'll miss me dinner today.'

'Give Eileen our best wishes,' Clara said, as did everybody else.

Davies saw Minnie immediately and didn't leave her hanging about for an hour, which she could have done. Minnie explained the reason for her visit.

'An excellent idea, Lance Corporal, I applaud you for thinking of it. I'll write you a slip right now. I see that you have what Private Ruffel requires. If you hurry, you'll catch the bus as it leaves in ten minutes from outside the barracks.'

Clutching the vital piece of paper, Minnie ran to the gate and waved the permission slip at the guard, who waved back and didn't ask to see it. The two gas masks bounced around her neck along with Eileen's haversack filled with clean underwear, stockings, toilet bag, clean shirt collars and a few other personal items her friend would need.

The bus pulled up as she arrived at the stop, and she jumped aboard. It was half empty and she had no difficulty finding a seat. She paid the elderly conductor the necessary fare and gazed out of the window, mulling over what she was going to say to Eileen.

If Danny died then her friend could stay in the ATS, and train to be a PT instructor as she wanted, but if he didn't then she'd have to leave on compassionate grounds in order to look after him. Minnie was glad she wasn't in that position and it confirmed her decision that if she met someone she fancied, she wouldn't get married until after the war was over.

Eileen didn't love her hubby and having to spend the rest of her life as his carer would be a nightmare.

The bus stopped not far from the hospital, and it didn't take her more than ten minutes to walk there.

There were half a dozen wards put aside for service-men, so she headed that way, ignoring the large sign that indicated no visitors were allowed out of visiting hours.

After asking a helpful student nurse, Minnie eventually arrived at the right place. An officious nurse in a dark blue uniform intercepted her.

'No visitors until three o'clock. I'm afraid you must return then.'

'I ain't visiting no patient, I've come to bring necessities to Private Ruffel as she's been here all night and not even a toothbrush to her name.'

The nurse looked a bit less disapproving. 'Yes, Corporal Ruffel is still critically ill but stable now. His consultant is more hopeful that he'll recover.'

'That's good. Where's me friend? I've got to be back on base in a couple of hours so can't hang about chatting.'

'If you would care to wait here, Lance Corporal, I'll fetch her for you. There's an excellent restaurant no more than five minutes from here – why don't you take Mrs Ruffel for some lunch? She's not eaten more than a couple of biscuits since she arrived yesterday.'

'Okay, ta ever so, I'll do that.'

The nurse rustled off, her white starched apron crackling as she walked. Minnie thought this woman was probably a sister or perhaps even a matron – she wasn't too sure about how things worked in a hospital.

A few minutes later, Eileen emerged looking pale, dark circles under her eyes, but she didn't look particularly tearful, which was a good thing. They fondly embraced.

'I'm sorry about your Danny. Everybody sends their love and best wishes.' Minnie handed over the gas mask and haversack full of essentials.

'I can't tell you how glad I am to see you. You angel – I can see you've bought me what I need. Sister Robertson said that you're in a hurry – can you wait a few minutes whilst I have a quick wash, clean my teeth and change the collar on my shirt? I assume you've put one of those in.'

'I ain't in a hurry really, I've got until lights out. You take your time. Do you mind if I wait outside – the smell of hospitals turns me stomach.'

'Yes, you do that. I'll be out in a jiffy.'

Eileen was true to her word and fifteen minutes later, arm in arm, they hurried to the restaurant that had been recommended to them. In these British Restaurants you got a main course and afters, plus tea. Last time Minnie had eaten in one, she'd had roast beef and two veg plus treacle pudding, bread and butter and tea and it had cost only 11d.

It was a little after midday and there were already a dozen or more people waiting. The jolly waitress, on seeing that they were in uniform, beckoned them to the front of the queue.

'You come next, ladies, I don't reckon you've got time to waste standing about like them lot.'

'Thank you so much,' Eileen said. 'My husband has just been shipped back from abroad and is critically ill. I can't be away from him for too long.'

'Come along then, it's a lovely lamb hot pot today and spotted dick and custard for afters. Do you want tea or coffee?'

'We'll have tea, ta, we ain't fond of coffee,' Minnie said as they followed the woman into the steamy interior.

They walked up to the counter – no waitress service in these sort of places – and, with a laden tray each, they took one of the few vacant tables.

There was no talking until both the dinner and afters were eaten and they were pouring out the tea.

'What happened to Danny?'

'A shell hit his left lower leg and he had to have it amputated in the field hospital,' Eileen said. 'He then got an infection in the wound and it's that that's been making him so ill. It's still touch and go, but he's not as bad as he was.'

'Blimey, lost a leg, that's blooming awful. He'll be in hospital for weeks, then on crutches. I reckon after that you'll have to look after him.'

'I know, but I spoke to his doctor this morning and he said Danny would have either a wooden or tin leg fitted before he comes home, so at least he'll be mobile. He said it was unlikely that he'd be discharged until July or August.'

'Does that mean that you'll still train to do that PT malarkey?' Minnie asked.

'I certainly will. I've thought of nothing else whilst I've been sitting next to his bed holding his hand. His father died when he was young, but he's got a devoted mother and an older sister – I'm hoping that they'd look after him so I can stay in the ATS.'

15

Ben made excellent progress and was transferred to Chelmsford on the third day after the operation to repair his leg. This time he was in a ward with three other junior officers. One another soldier who was too ill to communicate, the second a jovial chap who had, he told him, pranged his kite and almost gone for a Burton. The RAF bods had a language all their own. The third officer wasn't in his bed.

'Bally bad luck breaking your leg on your motorbike, old bean,' Flying Officer Freddie Jennings said.

'Worse luck to have the pin fail and have to be mucked about with a second time. I was about to rejoin my regiment so I'm bloody fed up, I can tell you.'

'I get a week's crash leave after I'm discharged from here. Do you brown jobbies get the same?'

Ben grinned. 'We don't crash, just get blown up, so no, we don't. What's wrong with you, you didn't say?'

'Lacerations mostly, blood loss and broken ribs. Will be tickety-boo in no time,' Freddie said. 'Should be out of here in a week at the most. What about you?'

'I'm bedbound until the stitches are removed and then onto crutches. I'm hoping I can go back to my barracks and do desk duties until I'm fully fit.'

'Jonny, the chap missing from that bed, is in theatre. He's another brown jobbie like you. Not sure why he's here but think it might be his appendix.'

'Don't know him so he's not one of mine,' Ben said. 'What about the chap in the last bed?'

'Haven't the foggiest – I came in yesterday and he's not made a peep nor moved since I've been here.'

'So, we're the two able to communicate – glad of the company even if you are a Brylcreem boy,' Ben said with a smile. There was always a friendly rivalry between the two services.

'There's a poor sod in the side ward. Lost his leg, at death's door. His wife has been at his side since he arrived. Lovely girl, tall, spectacular red hair. In the ATS. Have seen her wandering about during the last couple of nights.'

'I think I know who it is. She's from my barracks. Private Eileen Ruffel. Lost his leg – that's awful. I almost lost mine.' Ben leaned over and rang the bell next to his bed.

A young student nurse arrived. 'Can I help you, sir? Do you need a bottle?'

'No, thanks. Could you please give Private Ruffel my sympathies and best wishes? She's at Great Baddow where I'm stationed.'

'Yes, of course I will. Corporal Ruffel is doing really well now. He's serious but no longer critical.'

'That's good news. I don't suppose there's a cup of tea going spare. I've not had anything to eat or drink since seven when I was shoved into the ambulance and brought here. Now it's almost two o'clock and I'm parched.' His stomach rumbled loudly and the girl giggled.

'I'll get you some toast as well. You poor old thing. I won't be a tick.'

Ben wolfed down the very welcome toast and Marmite and drank three cups of tea. He felt considerably better after that. The long journey in the uncomfortable ambulance had tired him out and his lower right leg was unbearably painful. He wasn't going to ask for more drugs and would suffer in silence until somebody came round to dose him up again.

Half an hour later, the orthopaedic bod came in to check he'd travelled safely and the starchy sister accompanying him handed over two very welcome pain-relieving tablets.

He woke some hours later. The small ward was in darkness apart from the light that filtered in from the corridor, the three beds were now occupied and all the occupants were sleeping or unconscious.

Bugger it! He'd missed the evening meal. The three slices of toast he'd consumed several hours ago were going to have to suffice until breakfast. Although his watch had been removed for surgery, it was now back where it should be. He tilted his wrist so he could see the glowing luminous figures. Just after midnight – no chance of a friendly young nurse being on duty who'd make him more toast and tea.

Ben was silently bemoaning his fate when he saw Eileen stop at the door. 'I'm awake. How's your husband? Bloody bad luck about his leg.' He kept his voice quiet, but she still heard him and hurried in to perch on the side of his bed.

'Danny's off the danger list, thank goodness. He's eating and looks a lot better. What happened to you?'

Ben explained. 'I could have lost my leg too, I'm bloody glad I didn't. I don't suppose you could trespass in the nurses' cubbyhole and make me a tea and possibly some toast? I was asleep when they brought the food around and missed it.'

'They've now taken to feeding me at the same time as they bring Danny's meals. I was going to make myself a cup of tea and I'll see if I can find some biscuits to go with it. I shouldn't think there's any bread left at this time of night.'

'Anything will do – thank you.'

She slipped away and he pushed himself up the bed so he could look around at the other humped shapes in the beds. Not even the chatty Freddie had woken up to demand a cup of tea for himself.

His leg ached but he didn't need further medication. It was a bit of luck for him that Eileen was at the bedside of her husband and could come in and visit him too. Spending a few precious stolen moments with her was better than nothing. Rotten luck for her husband – but there was nothing Ben could do about that. Possibly being able to talk about her problems would make things a bit easier for her – it would certainly do so for him.

She crept back in, carrying a tray, and carefully placed it on the small locker beside the bed. 'There wasn't a teapot so I've poured us two cups each. I've made you two jam sandwiches. I'm sorry I've been so long but I needed to check on Danny. He's fast asleep.'

Conducting a conversation in whispers was strangely exciting. Ben grinned in the semi-darkness at his totally inappropriate and reprehensible thoughts. He was glad this setback hadn't altered his carefree attitude to life.

'This is manna from heaven. I can't thank you enough. Excuse me whilst I slurp and munch – very quietly.'

A jam sandwich with slightly stale bread had never tasted so good. The tea was delicious and by the time he'd finished, he was a new man. Eileen tucked into the biscuits with equal enthusiasm.

'I'm going to remove the evidence and wash it up. I'd better return to my vigil – I don't want Danny to wake up and discover that I'm missing.'

'How's he adjusted to the news? It must be a terrible blow. Will he be able to go back to his original employment?'

'He was a cabinetmaker and even with a false leg I can't see him being able to do what he did before. I was able to get in touch with his mother and ask her if he could go there to recuperate – well, for the duration of the war, really – unfortunately, she's moved in with her daughter and said that there's no room for him.' She sighed loudly. 'That means I'm going to have to leave the ATS and look after him myself.'

'That's a shame. But he'll get a decent disability pension and you'll probably be able to do part-time work of some sort.' It was none of his business and he didn't know why they were discussing her personal life like this, but she obviously needed to talk to somebody and he was the one available.

'We have our own house, but we have tenants in and can't get it back. I suppose legally we could evict them but I'm not going to do that – they moved in on the understanding they would have it for at least three years.'

'Then you need to find somewhere else to live. Chelmsford's a nice enough town, a bit dull, but there are lots of employment opportunities. There's Marconi's, Hoffman's and Compton's – they're all major players in the war.'

'I've not heard of any of them but if they're crucial to the war then that will make them a target for bombs, surely?'

'I'm sure they were but since Hitler's turned his attention to Russia, the regular bombing has stopped and I think Chelmsford's as safe as anywhere else.'

She smiled, her teeth a flash of white in the gloom. 'Food for thought, Ben, and I've got plenty of time to sort things out as Danny won't be discharged until he has been fitted with his prosthetic leg and that could be months away.'

Eileen picked up the tray and with another smile, left him to his thoughts.

* * *

Eileen left the little side room that the nurses used as a kitchen as spotless as it had been when she'd trespassed in there. After using the WC, which was only in the next corridor, she returned to the side ward where Danny was sleeping peacefully.

The sister who Minnie had thought was a bit bad-tempered had proved the opposite. She had arranged for Eileen to have a comfortable camp bed, a pillow and blankets so she could sleep beside Danny and not remain upright on the hard visitors' chair.

She smoothed the blankets over Danny and clambered into her own bed. Strange that Ben had ended up in the same ward with more or less the same problem. She smiled – he had more and Danny had less where legs were concerned, but they were both lucky to be alive. She was finding it hard to accept that for the rest of her life she was going to be little more than an unpaid nurse for someone she didn't love and wasn't sure she even liked. Danny felt like a stranger to her now, she scarcely recognised him, but even before he'd left, they'd not been that close.

When no baby had arrived in the first year of their marriage, intimacy had all but stopped. Occasionally when he'd had a few too many beers he demanded his marital rights but, thankfully, that hadn't happened often.

Until she'd talked to Ben about how her future was going to be, it hadn't seemed real. She'd still clung onto the faint possibility that she could continue in the ATS but that was obviously no longer an option.

There was no point in her leaving to train as a PT instructor, but she hoped they'd let her stay and help with the new recruits as they went through their training. It would be some solace to spend time with Minnie as she'd turned out to be the best friend Eileen had ever had.

The doctor had said Danny would probably stay at Chelmsford for a few weeks, until he could walk about with crutches, then he'd be transferred somewhere for rehabilitation and the fitting of his new leg.

There was no necessity for her to stay overnight any more and tomorrow she'd explain this and return to Great Baddow. She supposed that she'd be expected to visit him twice a week but wished she didn't have to. Danny had no one else, so it was her Christian duty to follow the rules and do what a good wife would do.

Of course, she was thankful to God for sparing her husband but was going to have to draw on her deep faith and belief that marriage vows were sacred to get through the rest of her life with a man she didn't know.

To be honest, it had been a relief when he'd shipped overseas with the British Expeditionary Force. She'd enjoyed being independent, living in her own house, doing a job she enjoyed at the Co-op.

How was she going to be able to spend possibly decades living with him? What made things more difficult was that he had begged her not to leave him now he was a cripple, and she'd given her promise that she wouldn't.

* * *

The next morning, Eileen was up, washed and her bag packed, ready to leave after the morning round of the doctor and his entourage. There was no visiting until two o'clock, but she thought she'd risk a peek into the ward where Ben was. There were no lurking nurses and he saw her, had been watching the door as if he was expecting her to come. She took one of the chairs stacked neatly against the end wall and carried it over so she could sit next to him. The curtains were drawn around two of the beds and the other patient was still either unconscious or deeply asleep. This gave them the illusion of privacy.

'Good morning, Eileen, how's your husband today?'

'He's wide awake and eaten more breakfast than I did. I've told him I'm going back to Great Baddow but will visit him when I can.' She hesitated but then decided to tell Ben how Danny had changed. 'He's refusing to discuss our future, is pretending that he's fine, it's really hard. He was always a taciturn man and now I'm finding it impossible to relate to him.'

'Give him time, it's traumatic losing your leg. I should know as I've almost lost mine twice. Were you close before?'

What a strange conversation to be having with the man she was having very inappropriate thoughts about. She could talk to Ben in a way she'd never been able to with Danny.

'I've asked myself that exact question and the answer is I don't think so. He singled me out when I was still at school, the year before I took my school certificate. I was always a plain girl and he was quite good looking and I was flattered by his attention.'

'Fishing for compliments, Eileen? He was lucky to have you – you're not only lovely but also intelligent and kind,' Ben said.

'Good heavens, I think the anaesthetic must have damaged your eyesight. However, I accept the intelligent and kind compliment gratefully.'

'How long have you been married?'

'As soon I left school at nineteen. I stayed onto take my highers. I'm twenty-three now. Do you know, I've had the most uncharitable thoughts about my marriage. I'm beginning to wonder if Danny only married me because he knew I had an annuity. It's only £100 a year but because I couldn't claim it until either I was twenty-one years of age or got married, it had been building up and was over £1,600 by then.'

Ben's smile was charming. 'A woman of substance as well as beauty. I'm sure if you'd been given the opportunity that you'd have had dozens of offers.' He stared at her in a way that made her heart skip a beat. 'Why do you think that you're not attractive? Did somebody ever tell you that?'

'My mother was slim, several inches shorter than me and with lovely dark brown hair. She told me I was fat and ugly and insisted that I covered my hair with a hideous bonnet when I was a child and an even worse hat as I got older.'

'Your wonderful russet tresses are literally your crowning glory. Is your mother still around?'

Eileen shook her head. 'No, she died three years ago. My father died from injuries he received in the first war several years ago. He was a sergeant major, I believe, and worshipped my mother, but sadly agreed with every word she said.'

'Then the pair of them destroyed your confidence, which was unforgivable. Let me assure you, and I'm an expert on the subject, that you're a very attractive young woman. I can't tell you how sorry I am about the situation with your husband.'

'Thank you, but I'd never leave Danny. I spoke my wedding vows in the sight of God and believe that they're sacred.'

Ben leaned back and his smile was no longer charming but dangerous, wicked even, and for some reason her pulse skipped a beat.

'I wish you weren't married. There's a connection between us, don't you think?' He spoke sincerely, meant every word. This time he wasn't flirting but speaking from his heart.

'I do like you, Ben, but we mustn't even think about that.'

She went to stand up but he reached out and took her hand. The touch was like a fizz of electricity running up her arm. She knew she should pull away, but something held her captive.

His long, strong fingers gently stroked her wrist and she caught her breath. Then he pulled her closer and she couldn't resist. His other arm stroked her face and then their lips were touching. Scarcely a kiss, but it was enough to tell her she had feelings for him and they were forbidden.

Shocked by her actions, she stepped back. 'No, Ben, this is wrong. It doesn't matter what we feel, what we want, I'm a married woman and we can never be together.'

His eyes glittered and his unshed tears were too much. With a gulp, she fled from the ward and, as she was entering Danny's room, a staff nurse came up to her.

'Private Ruffel, your husband will be moved into one of the main wards to continue his recovery. I'm not exactly sure which one it will be, but it will definitely be on this side of the hospital with the other service men.'

'Thank you, that's very good news. He'll do better if he has someone to talk to when I'm not there. I have to go as the bus is due in ten minutes and there's not another one for an hour. Would you be kind enough to tell him that I'll come and see him as soon as I get permission to do so?'

As she clambered onto the bus few minutes later, Eileen knew it wouldn't be Danny she wanted to see, but Ben, and she daren't risk seeing him again.

16

Minnie was still glowing with satisfaction after she and her squad had beaten all the other contenders at the drill contest. She wished that Eileen had been there as she'd have enjoyed it as much as everybody else.

'I say, well done, Lance Corporal, we're very proud of you and your girls. As a thank you, you have the remainder of the day and evening to yourselves to celebrate. I've arranged for special refreshments to be served to you all in the NAAFI.' The major, the barracks CO, patted her on the arm.

'Thank you, sir, we enjoyed the experience.'

He then strode off to congratulate the men who had also done well – but they'd come second this year, not first, so had provided no silverware to go on his shelf.

Endean had stepped back a week ago and left the training to Minnie so wasn't there to be congratulated.

'Well done, ladies. We showed them blokes how to do it,' Minnie said. 'Off to the NAAFI. We've got something special laid on for us and then we can do what we blooming well want after. I'm going to nip into Chelmsford and see how Eileen's getting on.'

'Do we have time to go to the pictures? What time do we have to be back on the base?' Grace asked.

'By lights out, so ten o'clock. Plenty of time to see a flick.'

'Are you going to come with Clara and me?'

'No, ta, I'll stop with Eileen.'

The NAAFI had done them proud. Several tables had been pushed together at one end of the large room and were ready for the triumphant squad. The girls who'd been substituted were obviously included in this rare treat. The food was tasty, sausage rolls, sandwiches with real cheese and pickle, decent ham with mustard as well as a selection of cakes and lashings of tea. Considering civilians only got an ounce of cheese each a week, Minnie was amazed that the NAAFI had used so much of their precious ration for their tea.

'That bread was a bit of all right, weren't it, Clara?' Minnie said as she polished off the last of her sandwiches. 'Better than the usual grey National bread we get most days.'

'It certainly was,' Clara replied. 'I won't need any supper so Grace and I can watch the entire programme. I don't care what films are showing, it will just be a pleasure to be away from here for a few hours.'

'You'll be away from here permanently from the end of next week, don't forget. Everybody's going to find out where they're going in a couple of days and will be posted for further training or their actual trade.'

'That's very true,' Grace said. 'I hope Clara and I stay together at least for our training.'

'Eileen won't be going nowhere now as she's going to have to leave the ATS to look after her husband. Junior Commander Davies said Eileen can stop here and help with the new recruits until he's out of hospital and I don't reckon that'll be for weeks, if not months.'

Grace turned away without comment and spoke to Clara. 'We ought to leave soon if we're going to catch the bus. We've got to collect our gas masks and so on first, so we'd better hurry.'

Minnie was able to catch the same bus as everybody else and thought it a bit off that Clara and Grace hadn't waited for her. They also appeared to make a point of sitting as far away as they could, but maybe she was imagining they were ignoring her.

Grace was sometimes a bit sniffy, but Minnie put it aside as Grace and Clara would both be gone at the end of next week. She and Eileen would be the only ones left from their intake.

* * *

On arrival at the hospital later that day, Minnie made her way to the ward where she expected to find Eileen. Today she'd come at visiting time so there were dozens of people wandering about looking for their loved ones.

She wasn't exactly sure where Corporal Ruffel was but she thought he'd been in a small side room, but when she entered she found this was empty and there was no sign of her friend. She peered into the adjacent ward with four beds and immediately saw Lieutenant Sawyer.

'You look better than I expected, sir, considering you were carted off in an ambulance a few days ago at death's door according to several witnesses.'

Ben had been reading the paper and immediately folded it carefully, put it on his locker and then beamed. 'I'm sure you haven't actually come to visit me, Lance Corporal, but if I can prevail upon you to remain for a few minutes, I'll give you the information you want about your friend Eileen.'

Minnie hesitated but he pointed to a chair sitting to attention next to his bed.

'See, this is ready and waiting, so how can you refuse a poor lonely officer?'

She sat down and raised an eyebrow – not something she did very often but the occasion called for it. He appreciated the gesture and his eyes danced.

'Right, point made and taken. Corporal Ruffel has been moved to another ward and Eileen left a couple of hours ago. You must have missed each other somehow.'

'Bloody hell, what a waste of time.'

Now he laughed. 'Hit a man when he's down, why don't you? I've never been called a waste of time before, which is very humbling for a man like me.'

'Don't be daft, you know what I mean. Any road up, I'm visiting you now, ain't I?'

'Indeed you are and very much appreciated it is too. I'm going to make the most of it as I don't suppose I'll get many visitors whilst I'm here.'

Minnie didn't contradict him but had a sneaking feeling she might find an excuse to come into Chelmsford again in a few days if she got the opportunity. Strange that she didn't fancy him but did enjoy spending time with him. She told him about winning the drill competition and he was suitably impressed.

'I wouldn't be surprised if you get another promotion after this. As far as I can see, you did a damn sight better job than Corporal Endean and without her experience or training.'

'I've been reading up on that and I have to go away for a special course or something before they can make me up to corporal. I've only been here five minutes...'

Lieutenant Sawyer looked very obviously at his expensive wristwatch. 'Actually, you've been here seven minutes.'

It was her turn to laugh. He was really very easy to talk to. 'You know what I meant. Endean told me if I get sent on this cadre thing then I'd be one of the first to be made up so quickly at Great Baddow.'

'It would be unusual but then you're an exceptional young woman. If you made an effort to improve your speech, I honestly think you could be sent to train to be an officer in a few months.'

'I'm proud to be from the East End and have no

intention of improving anything apart from me knowledge of the army.'

He raised a hand as if an apology. 'I'm sorry, crass of me. I don't care how you speak, I just like to listen to what you say, but I'm afraid there are more idiots made up to officers than there are sensible people. It's still who you are rather than what you are that gets you promoted.'

'I forgive you. I reckon that you ain't like any other officer on the base. If you was, I wouldn't be talking to you like this.' Minnie grinned. 'I'm aiming to be a staff sergeant – that'll be six steps up and more than enough for me.'

'And I'm quite certain that you'll get there and far quicker than any other candidate. You're right, you'll have to attend a course to become a corporal. It's only three weeks and then you'll be back to train the new recruits.'

'How long will you be in here, sir?'

'A week at least, possibly longer and then I'm hoping to return to barracks and do desk work. I really don't want to go home – I don't get on with my mother.'

'Fair enough. I better get going as I want to catch the next bus back and find Eileen.'

'If you must. My name's Ben, by the way, and I

know that yours is Minnie. If you use it next time you visit, I won't report you for insubordination.'

'What makes you think I'm going to come again?' She ignored his invitation, as to use his first name would be breaking all the rules.

'I'm sure you'll take pity on a lonely, extremely handsome young officer and visit him on his bed of sickness.'

She waved to him as she left and was still smiling as she joined the queue of housewives with bulging shopping bags at the bus stop. She didn't fancy him but did enjoy his company.

* * *

Ben wasn't surprised when Freddie yanked his curtain back and winked at him. 'Good God, old boy, two pop-sies at the same time. Hats off to you, chum. I thought it was the boys in blue who were successful with the ladies.'

'I'm just amusing myself. The two girls involved are unavailable, so a little harmless flirtation doesn't hurt any of us. I'm sure that in the RAF officers can't fraternise with other ranks, male or female.' He hoped his casual explanation fooled Freddie, it sounded lame to him. He flopped back on the pillows, trying to gather his thoughts. How could he have fallen in love with Eileen after spending so short a time in her company? Love at first sight? He'd not believed that was possible but now he knew it was true. What a bloody, damnable mess this was.

'And quite right too. I was jesting, old bean, and like your style. I have a delightful fiancée in the WAAF but as she's posted on the other side of the country, we rarely see each other now.' Freddie grimaced and settled back more comfortably on his pillow. 'I enjoy the company of young ladies but am absolutely faithful to my Jenny.'

The soldier with a burst appendix appeared to be recovering well from his surgery, but the other chap was still comatose and Ben didn't like to ask any of the medical staff exactly what was wrong with the poor sod.

Not long after Minnie had departed, Major Bentley arrived and spent the first ten minutes extolling the virtues of the ATS team, which had done the barracks proud that morning.

'Rotten luck, my boy, having those screws, or whatever they were, in your leg fail. When do you expect to be fit for duty?'

'As soon as the sutures come out, I'm hoping to return to Baddow and do desk duties until I'm fully fit.'

'Excellent idea, young man. You can take over from me. It will be good practice for you when you get your next promotion.'

'That's splendid news, sir. I'll do whatever's needed. The quack said I'll be able to walk on it in six weeks and all being well this time I can then return to active duty after that.'

'Desperate to get back on the front line? If I was you, I'd stay in Blighty until you're quite sure the inner workings of your leg are going to remain intact. You're likely to lose the leg if anything happens to you overseas. It happens to plenty of men, unfortunately.'

'That's true,' Ben said. 'Corporal Ruffel's one of them. His wife's Private Ruffel, who is based with us. A damn shame that she'll have to leave the army when he's discharged from hospital as from what I've seen and heard, like Lance Corporal Wolton, she's an asset to the ATS.'

'Absolutely, my boy, we need more like those two. Wolton is going to be promoted to corporal and will be leaving to attend that course next week.'

'I'm sure that she'll make an excellent senior NCO in time. Thank you for taking the trouble to visit. I hope to be back with you in a week.'

Ben could hardly salute when in pyjamas so didn't bother. Bentley patted him on the shoulder and with a benign smile around the ward marched out. The major was a relic from the last war, but was a decent sort of chap. Ben knew he was lucky to be under Bentley's command.

* * *

Eileen couldn't believe that she'd missed Minnie and hoped her friend would return on the next bus. They were both off duty until the following morning and she was looking forward to spending the evening together.

Her head was still whirling from her stolen kiss with Ben. This was something she couldn't, wouldn't even, tell her best friend. She believed that everything happened through God's will, but how could falling for Ben be that? No, it was a temptation from God to see if her faith was strong enough to resist her feelings.

She must put aside these thoughts and focus her entire attention on being the best wife she could be to Danny. Maybe a nice hot bath would clear her head and stop her from doing something she knew to be wrong. It would be at least an hour and a half before Minnie could be back, which gave her ample time to have a quick bath. She intended to sneak into the bathhouse despite the fact that this wasn't her allocated time for such a luxury.

Eileen washed her hair whilst she was there and couldn't help thinking about what Ben had said – calling her red hair her crowning glory. Danny had never told her she was beautiful, that her hair was pretty or ever told her that he loved her. She'd asked him and he'd said love wasn't words but deeds and until now she'd been happy with that.

How was it that just spending a short time with Ben had opened her eyes to the woeful inadequacies of her marriage and shown her how wonderful a relationship with a man you loved could be? She'd made her bed and would have to lie in it, as her mother would have told her, regardless of the circumstances. With any luck, when Danny was discharged, he wouldn't insist on his marital rights – he'd never been keen on intimacy even when he had both legs.

That would mean Eileen's dreams of having babies of her own would be dashed too. But there were bound to be lots of unwanted babies, especially in London, where the GIs could take their pick of eager girls. Maybe she could persuade Danny to adopt one or two? She doubted he'd agree, but the thought of being able to have children to love, even if they weren't her own, made her feel a little more optimistic about her future with him.

Fortunately, there were no American bases near Chelmsford at the moment as most of them were near the coast. That made perfect sense as when the Allied forces invaded it would be mainly from Kent, which was only twenty miles or so from France.

Although the Luftwaffe were no longer dropping bombs every night as they used to, there was the constant drone of aircraft in the sky as huge American bombers, called Flying Fortresses, accompanied by their own fighter planes, were rehearsing flying to Germany to bomb their cities.

Dropping bombs on innocent civilians was a horrible thing to do. The invention of aircraft had changed the way wars were being fought.

Eileen emerged from the ablutions with her hair neatly pinned into a French pleat on the back of her head – it would still be damp when she took it down for bed but she couldn't walk around with it wet. ATS were expected to be immaculately turned out at all times, as were the soldiers.

She dropped her wet towels into the laundry basket that sat outside their dormitory and returned her wash bag to her locker.

'Eileen, there you are. What a palaver – but I'm

back now.' Minnie rushed over and they hugged. 'Have you asked Davies if you can stay when everyone else leaves next week?'

'I'm off to speak to Davies now, will you come with me?'

'Give us a minute. Just want to dump me gas mask and haversack. You going to ask about stopping on?'

'I am. Danny's unlikely to be discharged for a couple of months so I'm praying I'll be allowed to remain until then. I've got to find somewhere for us to live as well.'

They marched to the admin building and their CO invited them in immediately. She listened to Eileen's request and smiled.

'I've just been asked to locate someone capable to help out at the main admin block. I think you have relevant experience. Didn't you keep the books for your local Co-op fuel depot?

'I did, ma'am, I took a course at night school in bookkeeping and accounting. I am also a capable typist but don't have shorthand.'

'Perfect. You will report at eight o'clock on Monday. I'm glad your husband's going to make a good recovery.'

'Thank you, ma'am.'

'Lance Corporal Wolton, here's your travel warrant. Your course starts tomorrow. You need to report by three o'clock. You should have ample time to get to London.'

Minnie took the slip and saluted, and they about turned perfectly and marched out. Once outside, they relaxed. Eileen clapped her hands like a child at a party.

'It couldn't be better. I know it's Sunday but if maybe I could go into Chelmsford tomorrow, I can look around and see where I might be able to find a house to rent. I've got £500 in the bank so want something nice.'

'Blimey, you're rich! You'll get a blooming palace for that much.'

'I want somewhere with a garden and a workshop so when Danny's feeling up to it he can use his carpentry skills. He won't be able to make furniture, but ladies love sewing boxes and children are desperate for toys at Christmas, aren't they?'

'None to be had in the shops, that's for sure,' Minnie said. 'He could make little wooden trains, fire engines, tanks, Spitfires, things like that.'

'I'm sure he can but the thing is I don't know if he will. He's a very proud and stubborn man and I have a nasty feeling he'll refuse to do anything if he can't go back to making his wonderful cabinets and so on.'

'You'll win him round. I'll be staying here at least for the next few months, maybe for longer. It'll be grand having you living so close so I can nip in to see you when I get a few hours free.'

Eileen went to bed that night feeling happier than she had since the dreadful news had knocked her sideways. She couldn't leave Danny so had to find a way to live that would suit them both. If he would agree to them adopting, then she was sure eventually she could learn to be reasonably content with her new life.

However much she'd rather stay in the ATS and make a career for herself, that was no longer possible.

17

Minnie had said goodbye to her squad last night and would be sorry to see most of them go. Clara had hugged her, but Grace had just smiled. She was pleased to discover when she arrived at the bus stop on Monday morning that she wasn't, after all, the only lance corporal being sent away to train for promotion. Sandra Thomas was a decent sort and they'd got on all right when they were both promoted two weeks ago.

'It's going to be jolly good fun doing this with you, Minnie,' Sandra said with her usual booming voice. She was a few inches taller than Minnie, had very short brown hair and nice blue eyes.

'Why didn't Davies tell me you was coming too?

We could have walked down here together if I'd known,' Minnie said with a smile.

'I didn't know myself until last night. Bit of a surprise, but a good one nevertheless.'

They were joined by a few soldiers but none of them were NCOs so they didn't cause them any grief. To be sure there'd be no trouble as they left the barracks behind, they sat at the front near the conductor.

'Are you staying at Baddow to train new girls like what I am or going to do something else after?'

'I'm going to do something a bit hush-hush, at least I've put down for that. I think this is why the decision to send me with you was so delayed,' Sandra said.

'I reckon you'll be off for more promotion soon. I'm aiming to be a warrant officer, but I ain't bothered about being an officer.'

She waited for Sandra to confirm that girls like Minnie didn't get to be officers even if they wanted to.

'Golly, why don't you want to be an officer? You'd be perfect.'

'I'd rather be with folk I'm comfortable with. I ain't got a good education. I passed me scholarship, but I couldn't go to the Grammar school as me dad couldn't afford the uniform and that.'

'There you are,' Sandra said. 'You've got the brains,

could be an officer if you wanted. If it's your choice, then that's different. I was going to become an officer because that's what my family would expect me to do. But I'm going to follow my heart and aim for WO2 like you, Minnie.'

'My friends, Clara and Grace, had to do a lot of tests because they wanted to join Anti-Aircraft Defence. Have you had to do all that sort of thing?'

'I'll tell you all about it when we get off the bus. I'd have to shout to make myself heard. I'm surprised this old rattletrap's still running.'

The bus eventually stopped at the station where they were the only two passengers left on. They jumped off with their gas masks dangling around their necks and their kit bags slung over their shoulders. They had had to take all their belongings with them as they'd be sent directly to their new postings after completing the training. Minnie had asked to return to Great Baddow but supposed the officers might send her somewhere else.

They waved their travel warrant at the ticket collector and dashed up the wooden stairs to the platform just as the London-bound train steamed in. There were a few smartly dressed women waiting to get on but only a couple of suited businessmen – the early-morning rush to get to the city was finished by ten.

They found an empty compartment, slid back the door, and flopped into the window seats on opposite sides.

'It don't take long to get to London. I don't reckon there'll be anyone else wanting to come in with us, do you?' Minnie said as she removed her annoying mask and put it with her suitcase on the seat next to hers. She pushed up the armrest to give herself a double space and Sandra did the same.

'Right, to get back to your question about tests. I had to spot aircraft on film, I had to do things to check how steady my hand was and how good my hand-to-eye coordination was. Those tests were for joining the ack-ack. That said, I'm hoping I'll go to the School of Army Experiments, which is where the hush-hush work's done. I've got a physics degree and they want people with science degrees in that department.'

'Crikey, I've never met anyone with a degree of any sort,' Minnie said. 'That means you must be older than me. I'm nineteen and will be twenty in November.'

'I'm twenty – I went up a year early and completed my course last summer. I've been working with my father in the city for the past nine months – he's a stockbroker. I wanted to do something more active for the war and signed up without telling my family.'

'You could have joined the WRNS or the WAAF, so why did you join the ATS?'

'It was the nearest recruitment office to where I was working.' Sandra looked out of the window for a moment before continuing. 'I wanted to work with women – to be honest, I don't find the male of the species at all attractive.'

For a second, Minnie didn't get her drift, then the penny dropped. There'd been a couple of spinsters who'd shared a house at the end of her street and Mum had told her they also shared a bed, but no one talked about that side of things.

'I like blokes as friends but I ain't had a boyfriend, nor never been kissed by one.'

Sandra's eyes sparkled. They were really her best feature. 'What about being kissed by a girl? Have you tried that?'

Minnie was a bit startled by this question, it wasn't something folk talked about so openly. 'No, but I ain't got nothing against it neither. I reckon I don't have them sort of feelings at all. There's a handsome young officer all the girls are mad about, but I can't see it my-self – he's a good mate but nothing more.'

'You're good friends with Lieutenant Sawyer? It

has to be him you're talking about as most of the other officers are either elderly or injured.'

'I'd forgotten you must know him too. Right from the start we hit it off, but he's not made any move on me if that's what you're thinking. I reckon my friend Eileen fancies him, though.'

'I heard that her husband lost his leg. What a shame as it means she'll have to leave the service to look after him. If he was a woman, he'd look after himself.'

The ticket inspector paused at the door, and they held up their pieces of paper. He nodded and smiled and continued on his way. The interruption gave Minnie time to think about this strange conversation. There were men what fancied other men; they got arrested if they were caught but police didn't seem to bother about a couple of ladies doing the same thing.

'Men are bloody useless on the home front if you ask me. They want their womenfolk to stop at home, have their slippers warming by the fire and the supper on the table as soon as they get home.'

Sandra laughed. 'And now women are doing a man's job as well as their own. I'm sure you know that there are women pilots ferrying new and damaged aircraft to and from the factories and the bases. ATS girls are going to be trained to work on the guns, but we won't be allowed to actually fire them.'

'I'm not tall enough to apply for that even if I wanted to. I'm going to train the new recruits for now and see what happens. We only joined up three weeks ago and now we're joining a cadre of lance corporals to train to become corporals. Me mum and dad won't believe me when I tell them.'

'I'm no longer communicating with my family, so they won't hear about my promotion,' Sandra said.

'That's a shame. Me family are one of the reasons I joined up. I can send me wages to them as we don't have to pay for nothing in the ATS.'

'You're lucky to be close to them. I wish things were different for me.'

'I want to be promoted as often as possible as it means I'll get better pay. I'm sending all but a few pennies home to help out me family. We was getting 1s 8d a day when we started and that's already gone up to over two bob. A sergeant gets about 4s 6d a day.'

'I had £14 5s in my post office book so have that to supplement our meagre wages. I'll treat us both to a decent lunch at a Lyon's Corner House. We don't have to report in Fulham until after three.' She smiled. 'Call me Sandy, I prefer that to Sandra.'

Minnie wasn't going to refuse a free scoff and smiled her thanks.

They talked about their families, and it was obvious to Minnie that she was the lucky one; even though her parents often struggled to pay the rent, they were happy. Sandra's parents sounded blooming awful and she wasn't surprised that her new friend had wanted to escape and join the ATS.

The longer she spent with Sandra, the better she liked her, even though they were so different. By the time they arrived at the barracks in Fulham where they would be trained, they were the best of friends.

When Minnie discovered they were to share a billet, she wasn't bothered that her roommate preferred women. There'd been a couple of instances at Baddow where girls had been found in bed together and they'd been dismissed from the service with no further action taken. She reckoned this was the only time women got the better deal.

* * *

Ben was allowed out of bed after three days but only to sit on the uncomfortable upright chair provided for visitors. He was disappointed that neither Minnie nor

Eileen dropped in to see him, but he had plenty of company.

There was now an empty bed as the anonymous chap had died with as little fuss as he'd lived for the past few days. Freddie proved amusing company and they shared anecdotes of their active days.

'I rather wish I'd joined the RAF instead of the army – it seems you have far more fun than we do.'

'True enough, old bean, but we're not called the walking dead by the local populace for nothing. Only one bod I trained with is still alive.'

'Good point – I'll stick with my regiment.' Ben grinned and flexed the toes on his injured leg, delighted that it no longer hurt to do so. 'Not that I had any choice in the matter – I was always destined to be a brown job – as you RAF types call us. I went to Sandhurst, as did my father and grandfather and no doubt countless other ancestors in the past.'

'You'll be in the thick of it as soon as you're back on your feet. Mind you, even with the catastrophic loss of life in our branch of the services, it doesn't come anywhere near the millions who died in the trenches in the last lot.'

A student nurse appeared with a pair of crutches. 'Here you are, Lieutenant Sawyer, Sister says you can start practising as long as you don't put your foot down. Your stitches are coming out the day after to-morrow and then you can be discharged if you're proficient with these.'

She handed them over and he thanked her. 'I'm an expert, nurse, don't forget this is the second time my leg's been rebuilt.'

'Then I'll leave you to it.'

He hadn't lost the knack and within minutes he was swinging up and down the ward. 'I'm going to the ablutions – bedpans and bottles will soon be a dim and distant memory.'

When he returned, he propped the crutches up at the head of the bed and gratefully hopped back onto the covers. This was the most exercise he'd had in a week and he was shocked at how feeble he'd become in so short a space of time.

* * *

A couple of days later, the stitches were duly removed and a staff car was sent from the barracks to collect Ben. The driver, an ATS girl, happily carried his overnight bag. God knows where his gas mask was but he had a vague recollection he hadn't brought it with him.

The car dropped him outside his billet and fortunately he was able to waylay an orderly to carry his bag as it wouldn't do for the girl to come into an all-male accommodation block.

'Shove this in my room, there's a good chap.'

The young man saluted and vanished with the bag, leaving Ben to swing his way down a couple of side passages and onto a main thoroughfare that led to the admin building.

He knocked on the major's door. There was no call to enter but he heard light footsteps approaching and it swung open.

'Good God – I didn't expect to see you here.'

Eileen didn't salute. If she had done, he would have found it difficult to respond without overbalancing. 'Good morning, sir. Major Bentley has taken a much-needed leave of absence and he's left you to run things for him. I am working as his personal secretary so that means that I'll be working closely with you too.'

He looked around the room and didn't recognise it as the same place he'd been in not so long ago. No overflowing in-trays and empty out-trays, no cigarette ends and ash over the top of the desk, no discarded newspapers and cake crumbs on the floor.

'That should be fun. When I said I'd be happy to help out, I'd no idea he was going to abandon me entirely. There must be a dozen officers more senior than me who could have done this job.'

'He thinks that you're the most able,' Eileen said. 'He doesn't think very highly of your fellow officers and made that abundantly clear on more than one occasion.'

'In that case, Ruffel, let's get started. I hope to God there's no major emergency, no bombs dropped on Baddow whilst I'm in charge.'

'I'm sure that everybody here agrees with you, sir. Now – I'll show you the ropes, shall I?'

Sandwiches and coffee were fetched in for lunch and he munched his way through the lot whilst still getting up to speed on a miscellany of items and events that were mindbogglingly boring.

At four thirty, Ben tossed his fountain pen aside, yawned, stretched and called through the door to the small room in which Eileen was working.

'That's it. We're both done for the day. I'll arrange for a staff car to take you to Chelmsford so you can visit your husband without having to worry about catching a bus.'

She appeared at the door, not looking quite as pleased as she might have done at his offer. 'Thank you, but I saw him yesterday and I don't think he expects me to go every day.'

'I haven't had time to ask you anything personal – how's he getting on?'

'Famously, thank you, sir. The doctors are very pleased with his progress, his stump is infection free and healing up really well. They gave him crutches but he doesn't seem as efficient with them as you are. I expect he'll get the hang of it.'

'I'm sure he will. This is the second time I've had to use them. I suppose he'll be sent away to get his prosthetic leg made and fitted.'

'He'll be going at the end of next week if he continues to improve.' She blinked and he saw the glitter of tears in her eyes.

'You can tell me, Eileen, there's nobody here to disapprove.'

'He won't accept that he's lost a leg. Refuses to discuss anything about leaving the army, where we're going to live, what he's going to do for the rest of his life. I really don't know what to do or how to plan for the future.'

Ben perched himself on the desk. 'Have you found a house?'

'I've not had time to look.'

'Then that staff car won't be wasted. I'll come with you, as any house that I can negotiate with my leg will be fine for him.'

She didn't hesitate. 'Thank you, Ben, that's so kind of you. I suppose as you're temporarily in charge, no one can criticise your behaviour.'

'To be honest, there's nobody here with any gumption and they're only too happy to let me pick up the slack. This is hardly a place any real soldier would want to spend his time. We're basically a place where the dregs of society are sent to be knocked into reasonable shape before joining their permanent regiment.'

'What's taught here will not only keep those soldiers and ATS girls safe, it will also make them useful members of the army, so don't be so hard on Great Baddow's usefulness.'

He'd made sure the ATS driver who'd collected him from hospital a few days ago was driving them as she was unlikely to be bothered about the fact that they were breaking the rules. The car was waiting outside, and Eileen sensibly sat in the front. He was in the back, which meant if anybody happened to see them, they would just assume he was being chauffeured.

'Where are you going to look first, Eileen?' He should have called her Ruffel, but too late to take it back.

'Moulsham Street would be a good place to start

as when we marched into Chelmsford we passed two public houses and at least one inn. Danny will want to be able to go for a drink – that's one thing I am absolutely certain about.' She swivelled in her seat to look at him. 'More importantly, there's St John's Church close by, where I can become an active part of the congregation.'

Ben hadn't appreciated how important her faith was to her, but then she wouldn't be taking her marriage vows so seriously otherwise.

It was a short drive and as soon as they entered Moulsham Street, their driver reduced speed. 'Where do you want me to stop, sir? Shall I turn into Anchor Street? It's the next turning on the left.'

'What do you think, Eileen?'

'Yes, stop as soon as you can. We need to look for a house that's obviously empty and then ask the neighbours who the landlord is. I need to find somewhere close to the shops where I'll have to register, as well as to the pub and to the church.'

The driver wound down her window and stuck her hand out and waved it around in a circle to indicate she was turning left. This was an ancient staff car so didn't have the modern electric indicators – not that they worked particularly well. Hand signals were better, in Ben's opinion, during the day.

The vehicle rocked to a halt and the driver jumped out to open the door for him. He grinned and shuffled across the seat, put his crutches onto the pavement first and then manoeuvred himself out.

'Lance Corporal, we might be some time, so why don't you go and find yourself something to eat?' He already had half a crown in his hand and tossed it across to the driver.

'Thanks, sir, I'll do that. When do you want me back?'

Eileen answered. 'An hour should be enough.'

18

Ben and Eileen didn't have to go very far down Anchor Street before they saw exactly what they wanted. Even better, there was an old man weeding the flower beds, so they had somebody to speak to.

'Excuse me, is this house available to rent?' Eileen asked and the old bloke nodded vigorously.

'It became vacant last week. Mrs Turner passed away and I'm looking for a new tenant. Are you and your husband interested?'

'Good heavens, this is Lieutenant Sawyer, my superior officer. He's been kind enough to accompany me as my husband will also be on crutches and if Lieutenant Sawyer can negotiate the stairs, then that means the house will be suitable for us.'

The old man let them look around. The house was in need of redecoration and new furniture and Ben thought it a miserable sort of place. However, Eileen was overjoyed.

'If I can have the keys as soon as possible, I'll come when I can and start redecorating. I'm also happy to buy whatever's needed. I just want you to clear the house and get somebody in to give it a good clean.'

After that it was straightforward – a reasonable rent was agreed, and they followed the old chap to his own house, which was three doors down. He showed Eileen the rent book but then made it out to her husband, not to herself, but she didn't seem to mind.

'I'll pay the first three months' rent in advance. I just have to draw the money out of my post office account. I'll do that now, Mr Hughes, and return with it as soon as I can.'

'The post office is in Tindal Square. It's no more than a mile from here, I reckon.'

'Yes, I remember seeing it last time I was in Chelmsford.'

When they were back on the pavement and heading towards Moulsham Street, Ben voiced his misgivings. 'Are you quite sure you want to take that depressing place on?'

'It looks awful now because an old lady has been

living there on her own for years. You heard Mr Hughes say she wouldn't let him in to do any maintenance or repairs. It has indoor plumbing, although somewhat antiquated, which is a plus.'

'It's got a WC, cold running water at the kitchen sink but no bathroom and no hot water.'

'There's a good range, a copper in the outhouse for laundry, a decent garden where we can grow vegetables and have a few chickens – using a tin bath in front of the fire will probably be easier for Danny than trying to get into a proper one.' She nodded and continued. 'The best thing about it is the workshop. This will be perfect for when he's ready to start his carpentry again.'

Eileen sounded confident, eager to begin her life with her husband, but Ben saw a sadness in her eyes and guessed she was nervous about this next step. Was she also wishing it was the two of them planning to start a life together?

Ben glanced at his watch. 'The car will be back in a few minutes. There's no need for you to walk.'

'I don't know why you wanted to help me like this, but I really appreciate it.'

'Good God, having you working for me is going to make my life so much easier. This is the least I could do.'

Her eyes widened and she frowned. 'You really are the most extraordinary officer, Ben, anybody else in your position would just issue orders right, left and centre and expect everyone to jump to it. They certainly wouldn't feel obligated to help anyone who followed their orders.'

She was right but he could hardly burden her with the reasons behind his behaviour, why he was potentially damaging his career.

'It just occurred to me that if you resign from the ATS sooner rather than later, you'll have more time to make that dismal hovel into a pleasant home. More importantly, once you're a civilian, I can spend time with you without breaking any rules.' He smiled wryly. 'I do want you to work with me but this might be better for you, don't you think?'

Instead of being shocked by his suggestion, her smile was radiant. 'I hadn't thought of that but you're right. I'm not sure how much use you'll be with decorating when you're on crutches but I'm sure we'll find something you can do.'

* * *

Eileen withdrew the rent money from her post office account and dashed in to Mr Hughes to give it to him whilst Ben remained in the car. The driver expertly did a three-point turn so it was facing in the correct direction when she came out with the precious rent book safely in her pocket.

He leaned across and opened the passenger door so she could jump in. 'I'm so excited, there's nothing I like better than making a home. When I bought our house before we were married, it was very modern, only a few years old, and had a lovely bathroom, but it needed redecorating as the previous owners had painted everything green.'

'I'm glad that's one thing you've got sorted for your future. You just need to get your husband back on his feet and things will fall into place.'

Talking about Danny was like talking about someone she barely knew, not her own husband. Her heart was racing and it wasn't because she was nervous but just from sitting so close to Ben. She'd never felt like this before and was ashamed of herself for being disloyal to her husband.

Ben settled back into the corner of the car; further conversation of a personal nature wasn't wise when there was someone else listening. He had possibly already risked his chances of promotion by coming with her today and she didn't want to jeopardise his career any further.

* * *

The visit to Chelmsford had meant that Eileen missed tea with the others, so she headed straight for the NAAFI. She'd withdrawn a pound extra from the post office so had coins in her purse to pay for things like this.

She was surprised to find Grace and Clara waiting at the counter. Why hadn't they had the tea provided? 'Hello, I've got such exciting news to tell you but I'm curious to know why you've missed your tea.'

'We had a further series of tests this afternoon – such a bore,' Grace said. 'I really think they should know enough about the pair of us after all the endless form filling and test taking that we've done recently.'

Clara took her head and smiled. 'Don't take any notice of her, she's more grumpy than usual – it's her time of the month.'

Eileen nodded sympathetically. 'I sometimes feel it would help if we put a red ribbon in our hair to warn people not to annoy us during those five days.'

Her ridiculous suggestion did the trick and Grace smiled. 'I've taken a couple of aspirins, but what I really want to do is curl up in bed with a hot water bottle, but that's not allowed. Heaven knows how I'm going to manage when I'm fully operational and working with men.'

'One thing you mustn't mention are "women's troubles" when you are,' Eileen said firmly. 'It'll just be an excuse not to have women working alongside men when we know we can do most of the same jobs. We have women driving trains, trams, buses, even flying aeroplanes now.'

'You're preaching to the converted, Eileen. But I still think that there are several things we can't do because most of us aren't as strong as an average male,' Clara said and then moved along as it was her turn to order.

They took their trays to an empty table at the far side of the room.

'Have you noticed, girls, that despite us being allowed to mingle in here we still segregate ourselves?' Grace quite rightly pointed out.

'Personally, I don't want to talk to anyone but ATS, especially after what happened after the dance the other week,' Clara said.

Once they were seated, Eileen proudly got out her rent book and showed it to them. They congratulated her, asked all the right questions, but she detected some hesitation in their comments.

'What's wrong? Why are you both being so peculiar?'

They exchanged a glance and then Clara explained. 'I don't think you realise just how wrong it is that an officer accompanied you on this search. You also call him by his first name, and that's not good.'

Hoping to reassure them they didn't intend to break any further rules, Eileen told them that she was going to resign from the ATS so she could get the house ready and that then it wouldn't be against the rules for Ben to help her out.

Grace was horrified. 'I thought you were the sensible one, yet you can't see what you're getting into. You're halfway to falling in love with him and you're a married woman.'

Eileen gaped at them, for a moment too shocked to form a coherent reply. 'How can you think such a dreadful thing? I'd never be unfaithful to my husband. I said my vows in the sight of God and don't intend to break them.'

'We're not saying you're going to actually sleep with him, but that might well be what your Danny believes if he finds out you've been spending so much time on your own with that Lieutenant Sawyer.'

'I'm disappointed in both of you as I thought you

were my friends. I think it's a good thing that you're both leaving at the weekend.' Eileen stood up, abandoning her meal, and left them, knowing that her anger was more at herself than at them. What they'd said was probably true.

How she wished that Minnie was here and not away on her training course. It was going to be difficult pulling back from her friendship with Ben, but if she didn't want to give Danny any reason to be more distant with her, then it had to be done.

* * *

After Minnie arrived at the barracks where they were to be trained, she'd signed in and been handed a typed itinerary for the three weeks she would be there and had then been allocated her room. She and Sandy would be sharing with two others who'd obviously arrived before them as they'd already unpacked their kit.

'This is a bit of all right, ain't it? A blooming great room for just the four of us. We'll be like pigs in clover, I reckon,' she said as she dropped her kitbag on one of the empty beds.

'It certainly makes a change from sharing with twenty other girls,' Sandy said as she took the last bed. 'We'd better get our kit put away quickly and go in search of everyone else. I wonder what our room-mates are like. I hope neither of them snore.'

'Me, I can sleep through an air-raid siren. I hope my billet's as good as this when I get back.' Minnie had been unpacking her bag as she spoke. 'Mind you, you won't be staying at Great Baddow. I hope you don't get sent the other side of the blooming country as I'd like to see you if we get time off together.'

Sandy didn't misinterpret her suggestion. 'I'd like that too, we've really hit it off, haven't we?' She pushed her gas mask and steel helmet under the bed and stood up. 'There, we even finished putting our stuff away in exactly the same time.'

'Grab your irons, Sandy, if we can find the mess then I reckon we'll be in time to get some scoff.'

They took the stairs at the double, almost col-liding with two girls who were coming in. After laughing apologies were exchanged, these two told them that they'd forgotten to take their irons and had had to come back.

'The mess is the second turning on the left, you can't miss it,' one of them said as she vanished up the stairs.

'Ta, we was about to go looking for it,' Minnie yelled after them. She grinned at Sandy. 'I suppose I shouldn't be yelling but minding me Ps and Qs.'

'You be yourself, Minnie, don't let the army knock your spirit out of you.'

They'd automatically fallen into step and were marching side by side, following the directions they'd been given. They weren't too late as there was still a queue waiting to be served at the counter.

'Like the NAAFI, we don't get served here like what we do at home,' Minnie said.

'Home? It didn't take you long to settle in, did it?' Sandy said as they joined the end of the line.

Minnie introduced herself and Sandy to the eight other girls already seated at the table allocated to them in the large NCOs' mess. 'Has anyone had a dekko at the itinerary? How long have we got to eat before the first thing on the list?'

'We've got precisely thirty minutes to eat tea. I think they should have provided a map of this place as it's vast,' one of the girls at the far end said.

'If we stick together then we'll be late or lost together and they can hardly put all of us on a charge, can they?' Sandy said as she tucked into her dinner.

The last two, the girls who'd forgotten their eating utensils, arrived just as they were about to shut the serving hatch.

'Glad that weren't us, Sandy, I've seen at least two sergeants taking notice.'

'I saw that too. We need to be on top form if we're going to do well.'

'It's going to be exciting learning all this new stuff. I'm a bit nervous but looking forward to it.'

The first meeting was to introduce the two regimental sergeant majors, one of them was an ATS RSM, which surprised Minnie as she didn't know any women had been promoted to this rank. She was RSM Culley and the man was RSM Munson. They both seemed all right, and Minnie was looking forward to starting her training in earnest the next morning.

They now had the remainder of the day to familiarise themselves with the barracks. The ablutions block and latrines were spotless, which was only to be expected on an army base. She and Sandy explored their environment and were suitably impressed. This wasn't just a place to train new recruits like Great Baddow but somewhere that active servicemen lived and trained.

They heard the regular drumming of boots as a platoon approached at the double and hastily stepped to one side to let them pass. Twenty or so fit-looking soldiers ran past in their singlets and shorts, glazed with sweat, but none of them seemed out of breath or particularly red in the face from the effort.

'Blimey, what a difference that lot are to them blokes we've got. I'd like to be able to run like that whilst keeping in step – do you think we're going to be trained to do it?'

'I don't see why not,' Sandy said. 'I begin to see why all of us, including those like me, need to get to grips with all aspects of drill. Being part of the team is what being a soldier is all about, isn't it?'

'King and country – that's who we all serve, it don't matter if we're men or women, do it?' Minnie was impressed. 'I reckon we've passed several dozen ATS so there must be a lot based here.'

'I think we've also saluted a dozen officers – there could be as many as a thousand servicemen living here,' Sandy said.

They naturally gravitated towards the NAAFI, which was twice the size of the one they were used to, but here there were three serving hatches – one for officers, one for other ranks and the third for ATS.

'I'm still stuffed, but I never say no to a cuppa,' Minnie said as she dipped into her pocket for her loose change.

'I'll get these. Don't be offended, Minnie, if you were the wealthy one you would do the same for me.'

There were tables and chairs outside and as the

blue haze from those smoking made Minnie's eyes water, they didn't remain inside.

'This is going to be a doddle after the past four weeks, even with all the lectures and that.'

'I know, no exercise first thing, just a leisurely breakfast and then drill for two hours from nine o'clock until eleven. I'm not too keen on doing five-mile marches, but I suppose it will make a change from hours and hours of lectures.'

'At least we've a spare uniform if we get wet,' Minnie said. 'Even so, I can't think what all them lectures are going to be about. Surely there can't be that much to learn just to go up to corporal?'

'We've got to learn how to give orders and what will now be expected of us. We'll be dealing with sergeants and senior NCOs as well as officers and it's important to understand the protocols. In your case, you've got to know how to train recruits as that's what you're going to be doing. I don't understand why those of us who are going onto something else need to do that part of the course,' Sandy said.

* * *

Minnie clambered into bed that night more than happy with how things were going in her life. She didn't understand why she was so drawn to Sandy, why they'd become such close friends in just a few hours, but she was delighted to have found someone like her. It wasn't quite the same as her friendship with Eileen, but that didn't matter. She wasn't going to think about anything else but this training and intended to enjoy the next three weeks and make sure that she passed out with her corporal's stripes.

19

Ben was having second thoughts about his offer to help Eileen with her redecorating. Even if she was a civilian, she was still out of bounds because she was married. It wasn't like the affair he'd had with Lydia – Eileen was a churchgoer and breaking her marriage vows was something he wouldn't put her in a position of wanting to do.

The next morning, he arrived in his office slightly on edge, still not sure how to restore things to the way they should have been in the first place. Eileen had obviously come to the same decision.

She greeted him by snapping to attention and saluting, he returned the gesture as formally as she.

'Good morning, Ruffel, what's planned for this morning?'

'You have a meeting with the adjutant about the new intake of ATS at nine o'clock. It appears that there might be some problem with the accommodation as the platoons they are replacing will still be in situ, sir.'

'How the hell did that happen?'

'I don't know, sir, but I'm sure somebody's head will roll.'

His had been a rhetorical question but she'd responded, being the epitome of an efficient secretary, not a trace of the Eileen that he'd begun to enjoy the company of rather too much.

'I've filled in your diary for today, sir, and it's on your desk. Would you like me to fetch you a tea or coffee before I return to my desk and get on with my other secretarial duties?'

'Coffee would be splendid. What other duties do you have apart from running this office?'

'The major has asked me to check the finances of several departments. There appear to be discrepancies and I have a bookkeeping and accountancy qualification.' Eileen looked directly at him for the first time.

'I thought you should know, sir, that I'm not going

to resign from the ATS until my husband's actually discharged. Therefore, I'll be here to act as your secretary for the next few weeks.'

'Weeks? I thought the major was only going to be gone for two weeks. Is this something else that he didn't tell me?'

'He hasn't taken any time off for a year so is taking all his entitlement now – that's the next six weeks.'

'He neglected to tell me that. I apologise for occupying your time and you must get on with the work that our commanding officer requires. If I need you for anything, I'll come and find you.'

She half-smiled and saluted again – this time he didn't respond. Her look of relief made him feel uncomfortable. He should never have put her in such a difficult position. He was twenty-three years of age, for God's sake, high time that he grew up and started behaving responsibly.

Eileen had been married for four years, was about to embark on a lifetime of drudgery with a man she didn't love and was the same age as him. He admired her stoicism and was determined from now on things between them would be strictly professional. He would willingly change this but wasn't going to make things more difficult for her.

There was obviously no need to retract his offer to

help with the decorating as she'd made it abundantly clear that in future he was to behave as her officer and not her friend.

She sent one of the other girls in with his coffee and biscuits and he completed the tasks in his diary without needing to speak to her again. He and the adjutant had managed to solve the problem with the new intake by sending the ones that were currently here away a day early to their permanent postings or training.

At five he was finished and stopped by to tell Eileen – he couldn't think of her as Ruffel – that she could go, but her desk was empty. She'd already left.

One of the other clerks saw him coming out of her office. 'Private Ruffel left to catch the bus half an hour ago, sir. She worked through her lunch hour so she's not leaving early.'

'Thank you. If anything urgent crops up, I'll be in the NAAFI.'

He hadn't realised how much he was looking forward to spending more time with Eileen until this possibility had been so summarily removed. Of course, they had to spend some time together but that would have to be strictly formal and professional.

* * *

Eileen had never been so glad to leave her place of work as she was that day. Being so close to Ben – she could only think of him by his first name now – without being able to exchange friendly chat, having to pretend that he was only the officer she was working for, had been all but impossible.

The prospect of being with him every day was going to be torment for both of them. She was sure she hadn't imagined the connection between them but like the gentleman he was, he'd realised they'd both overstepped the mark and had made it so much easier for her to slip back into the role she should never have left.

She was going to see Danny, tell him about the house, explain what she had planned for them both and also speak to his doctors and see when they thought he would be ready to be released. She was dreading that day, but the sooner it came, the better it would be for both her and Ben. If she kept praying for the strength to ignore her growing feelings for him then maybe she'd be able to stay a faithful wife.

The hospital was bustling with visitors, and she threaded her way through to the rear of the building where the servicemen were being nursed. The other beds in this larger ward were occupied and most appeared to have someone with a patient. Danny's bed was closest to the nurses' station and the first as you entered.

He was sitting up in bed watching the door and didn't look at all pleased to see her. Her stomach lurched. Why was he being so difficult? She pinned on a happy smile and crossed the ward to greet him.

'You look so much better, Danny, I expect they'll have you on crutches soon.' She leaned across and kissed the air beside his cheek, making sure her lips didn't touch him.

He didn't smile but snarled at her. 'I was the only one without a visitor yesterday. Why didn't you come and see me?'

'I'm in the army, Danny, I can't just come and go as I please. I'm here now so make the most of it, as I won't be able to come again until the weekend.' She hadn't meant to contradict him so sharply, but his question had upset her.

'That's right, rub it in, why don't you? I know I'm on the rubbish heap now, a cripple and no use to anybody. It's a good thing we're married, and I've got you to take care of me.' He scowled at her, no affection, and certainly no love in his expression. 'I want you out of the ATS right now and that's my final word. It's not right that you should be working when you could be getting a home ready for me like a proper wife.'

She collected the chair placed at the end of the bed for his visitor, smoothed her skirt under her bottom and sat down, giving her a few minutes to gather her thoughts. She put her gas mask on the floor beside her and then looked at the man she'd married so readily four years ago and now disliked.

How could she ever have found this man attractive? He was bad tempered and selfish. He'd always been a bully but until now she'd accepted this and never answered back. Far too late, she understood that she'd made the most disastrous error by marrying him.

'I'm sorry, Danny, but I'm staying in the army until you're discharged. I've already got the matter of our home in hand as I found us the perfect house in Chelmsford. It has...'

He interrupted her. 'Chelmsford? I've got a perfectly good house in St Albans. We'll go back there.'

Eileen took a deep breath. 'No, we won't. I think you're forgetting that it's my house, in my name, and bought with my money. The tenants have a three-year lease and I've no intention of evicting them.' Her hands were clenched, her heart pounding, but she wasn't going to give in to his intimidation. 'Now, do you want to hear about the house we're going to be living in or not?'

'No, I bloody well do not. We live where I say we'll live and I'll hear no more of your nonsense, woman. Being in the ATS has changed you. I never raised a hand to you but if you don't mend your ways when I get out, you'll feel the back of my hand if you dare to speak to me like that again.'

Instead of recoiling, apologising and smoothing things over, Eileen did the opposite and spoke what was in her heart. 'Your behaviour makes what I'm going to say so much easier. I won't be living with you anywhere. I don't love you and don't think that I ever really did. I'm sure that your sister and mother will be only too happy to take care of you because I'm certainly not going to. I won't be coming to see you again. Goodbye, Danny. I'm sorry our marriage has to end like this, but I'm not the only one who's changed.'

As she stood up, Danny moved faster than she'd expected, stretched out and grabbed her wrist. He twisted it viciously and she couldn't bite back her yelp of pain. The hate in his eyes was terrifying. His other hand clenched into a fist. He was going to hit her. There was only one thing she could do. With her free hand, she reached down, snatched up her gas mask and swung it hard at his head.

It connected with a satisfactory thud. He released his grip and clutched at the blood streaming from his nose. She hoped she'd broken it as she was pretty sure he'd broken her wrist.

'My God, come with me, my dear, that wrist needs to be X-rayed.' The speaker was obviously a consultant as he had half a dozen white-coated students, junior doctors and nurses buzzing around him.

Eileen's head was spinning. Her wrist was a very strange shape and the shafts of agony when she moved it left her speechless.

As if from a distance, she listened to this senior medical man take charge. A wheelchair was to be fetched for her. The police were to be called. She thought she heard him say that Danny was to be moved to a side ward.

Tears trickled unheeded down her face – she could scarcely comprehend what had happened. The man that she'd married had never been affectionate, but he'd never been violent either. Was it her fault for answering back?

Someone expertly put a temporary splint on her injured arm and then gently folded it into a sling. This eased the pain a little. She was handed two tablets and a glass of water and with some difficulty she managed to swallow them.

'Private Ruffel, the wheelchair is waiting. We are

going to transfer you into it now. The analgesics you've just taken should take effect quickly.'

She wanted to say that she was quite capable of transferring herself, but her mouth felt as if it was filled with cotton wool and the words wouldn't come. Meekly she allowed them to lift her and put her into the wheelchair.

'Make sure you have a receptacle in case she vomits.' The voice of the senior doctor.

She had only got a four-hour pass to leave the base and would be put on a charge if she didn't return within that time.

She swallowed the bile in her throat, blinked a few times and from somewhere found her voice. 'Excuse me, could somebody please ring Great Baddow and tell them what's happened? I'll be AWOL after eight o'clock.'

'Good, I was hoping that you'd regain your senses.' A large figure, a man about forty, with horn-rimmed glasses and a charming smile appeared in front of her. 'Tell me, my dear, why did your husband assault you?'

'I told him that the marriage was over.'

The man snorted – she wasn't sure if it was in disgust or to hide his amusement. 'Great Scott, that's no way for a chap to behave. If you hadn't clocked him with your gas mask it would have been so much worse. I saw everything from the door but was unable to intervene in time to prevent your injury.' He nodded. 'I'm Jonathan Rhodes, senior surgical consultant here.'

'Thank you for coming to my assistance. I'm glad that you saw I was attacked first, otherwise I'd be the one the police would wish to interview. My husband has always been a taciturn, controlling man but this is the first time – and the last – that he's actually attacked me.'

They arrived at the radiography department. 'I fear, my dear, that your wrist will need pinning. A compound fracture is a nasty business. When did you last eat or drink anything?'

'I had a sandwich and a cup of tea at midday but nothing since.' At least she was now coherent but despite the splint and support of the sling, even the slightest movement made her dizzy with pain. She closed her eyes and took several deep breaths, hoping this would help.

'We won't move you again until the pain subsides.'

She was incapable of answering as her world went black.

* * *

Ben preferred to take his meals in the NAAFI – the Officers' Mess had better food but worse company. As he didn't drink much or smoke at all, he had sufficient to pay for his meals. He had breakfast in the mess but that was all.

He'd got bangers and mash with a decent onion gravy and was happily tucking into this when the ATS clerk he'd spoken to a short while ago hurried up to him.

'Excuse me, sir, I'm sorry to interrupt your meal. I've just taken a telephone call from the hospital. Private Ruffel has been injured and is in theatre. She won't be back today and probably not for a while.'

'Right, thank you for informing me.'

'I'm off duty now, sir, but if there's anything you need me to do tomorrow then I'm a dab hand at figures and so on.'

Ben nodded, with some difficulty keeping his expression bland, thought he'd sounded as if he was unconcerned by this news. As soon as the girl had gone, he abandoned his meal, snatched up his crutches and with remarkable speed for a man on one leg, returned to his office. He grabbed the telephone and ordered a staff car to be outside immediately.

He didn't need permission to leave the base as he was off duty until the morning and officers had more leeway than other ranks. This time it was a different ATS driver, but she was equally efficient and professional.

As before, he travelled in the back. He'd given her instructions to drop him outside the hospital and to then return in an hour.

'I might need to remain here for longer than that, but I'll definitely know more by then.' As he'd not told the girl why he'd come, she would be none the wiser.

He viewed the long flight of steps that led to the main entrance to the hospital with some trepidation – he wasn't sure he could successfully climb them without assistance. A nurse saw his hesitation.

'If you come with me, sir, there's a way in the back that's much safer. You'd do better avoiding those whilst using crutches.'

'Thank you, I've no wish to add to my woes by breaking something else.'

His plaster cast was heavy and it swinging all over the shop was making his leg ache. It wouldn't be removed for another few weeks, so he had to get on with it and stop whining.

The entrance at the rear was used by undertakers to collect the deceased when they were released for burial, but he didn't mind that. Instead of a steep flight of steps to get to the ground floor, there was a lift, which he hopped into gratefully.

As this was rumbling up, he wondered what he was doing there. Eileen had had an accident, but this was absolutely not his concern. In fact, he should have immediately informed her commanding officer, not come rushing into Chelmsford himself.

He made his way to the women's surgical ward. If Eileen had had an accident and needed surgery then this was presumably where she'd be brought afterwards. He hoped the sister in charge of the ward would be able to tell him what had happened and how bad it was.

The hospital was quiet, visiting for the day was over, and he was expecting to be stopped at any moment. Perhaps as an army officer he looked as though he should be there, that he was doing something official for one of the men under his command.

As he approached the women's ward, a staff nurse came out through the double doors. 'Excuse me, I'm looking for Private Ruffel. I believe she had an accident of some sort that required surgery.'

The young woman nodded sympathetically. 'I'd hardly call having her arm broken by her husband an accident. I'm not surprised you've come to investigate. Mr Rhodes called the local constabulary, but they said as the attacker's not yet been discharged from the army, it's a military police matter.'

'Can you tell me how this assault came about?'

The staff nurse filled Ben in with the details and the more he heard, the more horrified he was. Eileen was in recovery but would be on the ward in an hour or two. Both bones in her wrist had been snapped and had required surgical intervention to stabilise them.

'Corporal Ruffel – where is he?'

'He's been moved to a small side ward. I can assure you that as he's only got one leg and no crutches, he won't be going anywhere. Did you wish to speak to him?'

'No, now I've got the facts I'll start the necessary paperwork to have him dishonourably discharged. He will lose his pension, he's also apparently lost his wife. In my opinion, that will be punishment enough. If the local police wish to pursue the matter, then that's their prerogative.'

The staff nurse frowned. 'I don't think they wish to be involved – despite the severity of the injury, they still consider it a domestic matter. Anything between a husband and wife tends to be swept under the carpet.'

'Thank you, I'm going to return to base and set things in motion,' Ben said. 'I'll inform Private Ruffel's commanding officer. I'm sure her CO will arrange for what's needed to be collected and then my driver can return with it. How long is Private Ruffel going to be in here?'

'A week, possibly a bit longer. I hope that she has family to take care of her as doing anything for herself with only one arm working is going to be difficult, especially as it's her left wrist that's broken and she's left-handed.'

'I'm sure something will be arranged. Please give her my best wishes when she comes round from the anaesthetic. I'm Lieutenant Sawyer, by the way. Private Ruffel works for me.'

'Of course, sir, I'll see that she knows you called in.'

Ben had much to think about and, on seeing a vacant chair outside a ward, he collapsed onto it. The only glimmer of positive news in all this was that Eileen had decided to end her marriage. It didn't mean he could step in and take care of her, which was what he'd like to do, but at least things would be simpler if they decided there was something between them.

Going down the steps by the main entrance would be as hazardous as going up, probably more so, so he turned around and took the cadaver lift to the basement a second time. By the time he'd hobbled to the front, the car was there. Having something concrete to do made his worry about Eileen easier to deal with. If that bastard wasn't already in hospital, he'd have put him there himself.

20

Minnie excelled at the practical things but found lectures and written tests more taxing. Sandy was the reverse, therefore they were able to support and help each other and they both were top candidates. There was scarcely a minute to themselves during the day, but they had Friday evening and the following Saturday free. The rest of the cadre had decided to go into the West End.

There'd been an unexpected raid over London and the entire barracks had spent most of the Thursday night in one of the communal shelters, all crammed in higgledy-piggledy with officers, privates and NCOs, both men and women. It was more comfortable than the one Minnie had shared many times with the rest of her street during the heavy bombing last year. She wanted to make sure that her family was safe.

'I ain't keen on going up west but you go with the others if that's what you want to do. I'm going to see me folks.'

'Would you mind if I came with you? I'd much prefer to explore the East End than drink overpriced cocktails in a smoky nightclub,' Sandy said.

'Since the Yanks came over in January it ain't safe to be out on your own as there's dozens of GIs looking for girls to drop their knickers in exchange for a pair of nylons.'

Sandy laughed. 'Tempting, but I think I'd not accept their offer even for something as precious as nylons. I wish we could wear battledress like the men, it would make life so much simpler.'

'Them girls going to join the artillery will be given overalls and trousers – they can't scramble about in the dark moving searchlights and all that in what we've got on.'

'Before I joined up, I always wore slacks, much to the horror of my family and my employers in the city. So much easier than skirts and heeled shoes, don't you think?'

Minnie agreed. 'I ain't ever worn trousers but I

reckon I'd be more comfortable. If I weren't so short, I'd apply to be dispatch rider as they wear battledress.'

* * *

It was quicker and cheaper to go on the underground, even though most of the stations now acted as shelters. Although there'd been hardly any raids since last May, a lot of folk took no chances and still spent the nights down the underground. They'd had bunk beds, latrines of a sort, and the WVS had served drinks and that to the families who stopped there overnight. Minnie had stayed a couple of times and they'd had concerts and even kiddies' birthday parties down there. A regular home from home it was. She doubted it was still like that.

As it was early, the platforms were unoccupied apart from other travellers but everywhere you looked there were piles of blankets, folding chairs, and other personal items. People came to the same place every night and to stake their claim they left things in the space they intended to occupy. Maybe these were folk who'd been bombed out of their homes.

'It's a blooming long way on the District Line from Putney Bridge to Whitechapel,' Minnie said. 'When we get off this underground we can walk down Brady Street, across Bethnal Green Road and Bob's your uncle.'

'I've never been to the East End of London and I'm looking forward to seeing how things are. I do know that during the Blitz they got the worst of the bombs, but everybody just carried on as normal.'

'Hardly normal, climbing over piles of rubble on the way to work, that was no fun, I can tell you. We was lucky in Mansford Street, we never got that many. Plenty of windows and that blown out, but only two houses destroyed.'

'I was almost blown to smithereens just after Christmas,' Sandy said. 'Do you want to hear about it?'

'No, let's talk about something else. The worst of the bombing's over, we ain't got much but we're still alive and that's all that matters.'

'Then I'll tell you a funny story instead. There was an old newspaper vendor who had his stall just outside the underground where I arrived for work. In August last year he lost a leg in a raid and I missed chatting to him every day. We'd always exchanged a few words when I stopped to purchase my daily paper.'

'What's so funny about that, then?' Minnie asked with a smile.

'I was getting to that. I was delighted to see him back at his post a few months later. Of course, I paused to congratulate him and whilst I was doing so, I distinctly heard something playing "Over the Sea to Skye" but couldn't see where this music was coming from. Old Bert watched me for a few minutes and then laughed and said, "It's in me tin leg, lovie. I wind it up before I comes to work and then if I shake me leg, it plays a few bars. Grand, ain't it?"'

'Now that's funny,' Minnie said. 'Barmy old bloke, but salt of the earth. Wish Eileen's old man was taking his amputation like that. I'm worried about her. I hope she's still there when we get back. She might have re-signed if Danny kicked up a fuss.'

'Did you get time to say your farewells to the other two you mentioned, Grace and Clara?'

'I did, as they'll be posted away by now. I hope they got the trade they put in for. They both want to be in the artillery,' Minnie said.

'Do you think you'll stay in touch?'

'Doubt it, I ain't much of a letter writer and to be honest I didn't really take to Grace. Clara's all right, though.'

'I hope you'll make an effort to answer my letters, Minnie, I really want to stay in contact,' Sandy said.

'Course I will. I reckon we've got something a bit special.'

As soon as she spoke, Minnie realised her words could well be misconstrued. Sandy preferred women and Minnie didn't fancy her, but then she didn't fancy Ben either and he was a bit of all right.

'Don't look so worried, Minnie, I'm not going to pounce on you. I do like you and would be delighted if you wanted to be more than a friend but understand if you don't.'

'Then that's okay then. I'm not saying it's never going to be like that for me. I don't like men in that way either. Perhaps, when I've had time to think about it, I might feel a bit differently.'

Sandy's eyes lit up. 'I'll hope for that day, but I'm thrilled to be able to call you my best friend for now.'

Eventually the train rocked to a halt at Whitechapel and they hurried out of the dingy, smelly underground station and up into the warm evening sunshine.

'Blimey, it don't smell much better up here, do it? I'd forgotten how bad the air is in the East End since the bombings. It's nice and clean in Chelmsford.'

Sandy sniffed and smiled. 'You're right, but then I

suppose if you live and work in London, you stop noticing it. After all, it's not called The Smoke for nothing, is it?'

'Come on, if we hurry we can go to the chippy and take some back for the family.'

'My treat, after all, I'm turning up uninvited and unannounced to your family home. The least I can do is bring fish and chips.'

'Crikey, I wasn't going to buy no fish, just chips. They'll be that thrilled to have fish as well as chips they wouldn't care if I bought Hitler himself to tea.'

There was a queue and Minnie knew most of the people in it. She was happy to introduce Sandy and was even happier to discover that her family were all tickety-boo. Each of them had a large hot, vinegary newspaper parcel under an arm and completed the last quarter of a mile at the double so it wouldn't get cold.

* * *

Eileen woke up in a hospital bed with her arm immobilised. It didn't hurt too badly – just a dull ache. Her head was fuzzy, her mouth dry and she felt horribly sick. In fact, the nausea was worse than the broken arm.

Perhaps if she was sitting she'd feel a bit better, as at the moment she was lying flat. Pushing herself upright was going to be difficult with just her right hand as she was the least ambidextrous person in the world. Even putting on her knickers would be problematic whilst her left arm was out of use.

She lay there, her mind whirling, considering how those few moments of madness yesterday had changed her life forever. Despite the fact that she'd probably have to resign immediately from the ATS and move into the house in Chelmsford before it was ready for occupation, that doing anything for herself was going to be really hard, for the first time in years she was looking forward to the future.

A young student nurse in crisp white apron and cap appeared at her side. 'Good, Private Ruffel, Sister was becoming concerned as you've been asleep longer than you should have been.'

'I want to sit up, but I don't think I can do it without assistance,' Eileen replied.

'I'll fetch Brenda, she's another student nurse, we can help you. Would you like a bedpan or a cup of tea?'

'I think I might well need a basin if sitting up doesn't help the nausea.'

The two girls might have been young and only

partially trained but they were good at what they knew. Eileen was soon propped against the pillows, her injured arm relatively comfortable in the sling, and, thank God, her stomach seemed to be settling down.

Using a bedpan wasn't pleasant but she had to get used to these minor embarrassments as one of the nurses had told her she was to remain in bed at least for the next twenty-four hours.

When offered a cup of tea and a piece of toast, she accepted this time. 'Thank you, nurse, I feel much better now I'm sitting up.'

She was wearing a hospital-issue nightie and hated to think how many others had worn this before her. If Minnie had been at Great Baddow then her friend would have come in with Eileen's night things and toilet bag.

She looked around the ward, surprised there were only six beds and that only two others were occupied – she'd thought that women's surgical would have sixteen patients at least. Then she reconsidered; this was probably just for ATS personnel.

There was an empty bed on either side of her and one directly opposite. This meant that the three of them were separated by unoccupied beds, so unless they wanted to raise their voices, they couldn't really chat comfortably together.

The girl in the bed furthest away was obviously sleeping but the one in the other corner was sitting up and tucking into tea and toast like Eileen. This one waved her toast as a greeting before yelling down the ward.

'I'm Vera, had my appendix out yesterday. That's Ange, women's troubles, if you get what I mean.'

'I'm Eileen, broken arm.' She didn't say anything else as her throat was sore and speaking was uncomfortable. The toast had been a bad idea so after the first bite she abandoned it. The tea went down easily, though.

Her precious wristwatch obviously wasn't on her broken arm and she prayed that it was in the locker beside the bed as she'd hate to lose it. She thanked God that she'd not given in to Danny's demands and transferred the money into his name. She hadn't even agreed to open a joint bank account and she wondered if even then she'd had her doubts about him.

To think that just a few days ago she'd been vehement in her denial that she'd ever break her marriage vows and yet now the first thing she intended to do when she was discharged would be to find a solicitor and see if it was possible to divorce him. Getting a divorce wasn't easy, it was expensive, and she wasn't even sure if the fact that he'd broken her arm would be considered sufficient reason by the judge.

Someone she worked with had managed to get one by having an investigator come in and take a photograph of her in bed with another man. Adultery was definitely a reason, but she wasn't quite ready to take that option and smiled at the idea that Ben might be only too happy to step in.

Suddenly a dreadful thought popped into her head. Would a judge insist that she share her savings with Danny? If she was the guilty party, this would be more likely to happen, but until she spoke to a solicitor she couldn't decide if risking her inheritance would be worth being legally free from Danny.

* * *

The doctor who'd operated on her arm said he was happy with the outcome and that he expected her to get the full use of it back eventually. He'd also said it would be in plaster for six weeks at least.

Eileen had no appetite for the dismal hospital lunch and was unsurprised when there were no visitors in the ward that afternoon. By teatime, she was ready to mumble her way through some bread and jam and a very welcome cup of tea.

The bell to announce evening visiting was rung loudly in the corridor and this time, to her surprise, the only person she wanted to see, apart from Minnie, swung into the ward on his crutches.

His smile made her gloom evaporate. Whilst balancing on his good leg, he quickly pulled the curtains around her bed; the noisy rattle of the rings on the metal frame would have alerted Vera. Being cocooned inside the cubicle gave an illusion of privacy. But she was sure his arrival would have been noticed and every word spoken would be avidly listened to.

Ben moved the chair so he could sit close to her on her right side. 'My God, what a bloody awful thing to happen. If that bastard wasn't already incapacitated...' His eyes flashed dangerously. She'd no doubt that Danny had better stay away from her in future if he wanted no further injuries.

'He'll be dishonourably discharged by the end of the day. No disability pension and he's lucky not to be incarcerated in the glasshouse as well.'

'It's what he deserves. I should never have married him and clearly had rose-tinted spectacles on when I did,' Eileen said.

'I know what happened as I was here last night and spoke to the sister on the ward.'

'That was kind of you. It makes it easier as I really don't want to go through it all again. I want to get a divorce but I've no idea if I'll be able to.'

'That's something you can think about when you're back on your feet. It's a shame that you're left-handed as you're going to find things awkward for the next few weeks.'

'I'm going to have to resign from the ATS immediately and move into the house I rented even if it's not ready. I don't know what else to do as I've no family I can go to.'

'There's no need for you to do either of those things,' Ben said. 'I've spoken to Junior Commander Davies and by the time you're ready to be discharged, there will be a place for you at a convalescent home. I'm not exactly sure where that will be, but you'll have transport, you won't have to make your way on the train.'

While Eileen was digesting this news, he leaned down and picked up a smart leather overnight bag and put it beside her on the bed.

'I got one of the clerks in the office to pack what you need. I'm sure you don't want to wear second-hand night clothes any longer than you have to.'

'I can't believe you did all that for me.' Her right hand moved of its own volition and covered his. She wasn't sure who was the most surprised by this, but she knew immediately it had been the right thing to do.

His other hand moved to rest on hers. His expression told her everything she wanted to know about his feelings for her. There was no need for words.

When he spoke, his voice was low, gruff, barely audible. 'I didn't want to fall in love with you, but when I heard that you'd had an accident and were in surgery, I knew if I lost you, I'd be devasted.'

'The same for me. I'd never have spoken to Danny the way I did if I hadn't met you and seen how things could be between a man and a woman.'

'God, this is not how I envisaged it would be when I met the girl I wanted to spend the rest of my life with. What the hell are we going to do?'

'Take one day as it comes. I still think it will be better if I resign. I'm sure if it was discovered there would be a bit of a scandal, but at least you wouldn't be demoted for behaviour unbecoming.'

He smiled a toe-curling smile and for the first time she understood what real love was. Not the lukewarm affection and tolerance for each other that she and Danny had shared, but the exciting, heart-stopping reaction to someone that she was experiencing when all Ben was doing was holding her hand.

'I don't want you living in that dreadful house on your own.'

'It will be a lovely home by the time I'm finished. I'll speak to Sister and see if she can recommend a place I can go to until the plaster comes off this arm.' She'd deliberately ignored his request. This time she wasn't going to be subservient but make her own mind up about things. Being in the ATS had given her the confidence to stand up for what she believed.

* * *

They talked easily, sharing anecdotes and their past history. Ben told her about the muddle with the accommodation, how bored he was being inactive, and how much he was longing to return to his regiment. Eileen listened with growing disquiet. Would getting involved with him when he would be leaving in a few weeks be foolish? They couldn't officially be a couple whilst she was married and she was sure a divorce could take months, if not years.

As she listened to him making plans for their life together, her initial joy began to slip away. She was a practical woman and the more she thought, the more she realised this was the wrong time and the wrong place for them.

Gently she withdrew her hand from between his. 'Ben, I'm so sorry. I do have strong feelings for you but now's not the time to act on them. You'll be posted abroad as soon as your leg's healed and I would really like to remain in the ATS.'

He sat back in the chair and shook his head. 'How can you say that? Half an hour ago you were planning to leave the army to be with me. Have I said something to change your mind?'

21

Ben stared at Eileen, scarcely able to comprehend that despite the fact that they'd declared their love for each other, she'd decided to end things before they'd really begun.

'Look at me, sweetheart, tell me to my face that you don't want to try and make this work.'

She raised her head and when he saw the tears on her cheeks, his anger turned to concern.

'It's breaking my heart, but you must see it just won't do. However much I love you, I won't be intimate with you until we're married. I don't love my husband, but I said my vows in church before God and however much I want to...'

'That doesn't make any sense. If you're so bound by your vows then how can you even contemplate getting a divorce?' He hadn't meant to sound angry, but he was desperate to make her see they belonged together, that what they'd found was too precious to throw aside like this.

'I suppose I'm using my beliefs as an excuse. I'd better be honest with you. Let's say that we get together, spend at the most a few weeks pretending to be man and wife – what then? I might get pregnant; you'll definitely be sent overseas and could be killed. Even though I do love you, I just can't take it any further until we're both free.'

'Free? I don't understand.' Ben frowned. 'Oh, you mean when I'm free of my commitment to the army and the war's over. That could be years.'

Her smile was sad. He wasn't making this easy for either of them. Having a passionate affair would be wrong for someone like Eileen and what she said made sense, however much he disliked it.

'The last thing I want is to leave you in any sort of difficulty. You'll be happier in the ATS than as a civilian, possibly an unmarried mother. I was being selfish – however hard it is for both of us, we must do the right thing.'

'I don't want you to come and see me again. I love you, my darling Ben, and pray that when this ghastly war's over we can find each other again. I'll wait for you, but I'm not holding you to that promise.'

He levered himself onto his good foot, leaned against the bed and put one hand on each side of her beautiful face. He kissed her, knowing it might well be the last time he'd see her, and put all his love into his gesture.

He couldn't speak, blinked away unwanted tears and without another word fought his way out from behind the curtains and walked away from the woman he'd always love, but couldn't be with.

* * *

Ben emerged blinking into the May sunlight, hoping that anyone watching would think it was the brightness and not tears that was causing his eyes to water. Being in love was a damnable business and he wished he hadn't fallen for Eileen.

Physical pain he could endure but emotional hurt was so much worse. He'd heard one of the chaps he'd been in Africa with say that love was like an illness, you either caught it or you didn't. There was nothing you could do but wait for it to pass and hope that you didn't die from a broken heart in the meantime.

He'd been so upset about what had just happened that he'd headed instinctively for the main door of the hospital and now had to face the concrete steps. Ignoring offers of help from a friendly porter and a nurse, he began a slow and dangerous descent, expecting at any moment to pitch forward and break his neck. He almost wished that would happen as then at least he wouldn't be falling apart inside.

All love songs warbled on about its joy, the happiness of the two people involved – nothing had prepared him for the pain. He reached the bottom step without mishap and was just wondering where he should go to wait until his driver came back when the camouflaged staff car pulled up beside him.

The girl was out of the car and opening the rear passenger seat for him whilst he was still gathering his wits and his crutches. He clambered in and she slammed the door behind him.

As they were travelling the short distance from the hospital to the base, Ben couldn't remember if he was supposed to cancel the convalescent home or leave things as they were. Sod it. He didn't care – whatever happened to Eileen next was none of his business. It shouldn't have been anything to do with him in the first place and it served him right that he was now so broken and unhappy because he'd allowed himself to fall in love with someone he shouldn't.

As long as he'd left Baddow before Eileen returned, he'd be able to get on with things, concentrate on his duty and put his personal woes aside.

* * *

Minnie pushed open the front door of her little two up, two down terraced home without knocking. It opened into a dark passageway with the stairs to the right and the door to the front room – rarely used – to the left.

'They'll be in the back, in the kitchen sitting around the table. I reckon they'll be happy to see us.'

She led the way and burst into the kitchen, where her reception was even better than expected. The little ones screamed and flung themselves at her, Dad dropped his Woodbine on his newspaper and Mum flapped her tea towel in the air in excitement.

'We've brought fish and chips for everybody. This is my best mate, Sandy. We're training in Fulham to be corporals.'

The two big parcels were handed to Mum, Minnie dropped to her knees to hug the children and Sandy helped Dad stamp out the flames in his burning newspaper. By the time things were calm, Mum had set chipped plates out on the table and was dishing up the luxury tea.

Fish and chips had never tasted so delicious and by the time every scrap was eaten, fingers were licked, and the newspaper carefully folded up to use to light the fires in the winter, Sandy had slotted in a treat.

'I'll make another pot of tea and I've got a lovely Victoria sponge in the scullery. It was for Sunday, but we'll have it now as this is a special occasion. I can't believe you're already a lance corporal and going to be a corporal, Minnie,' Mum said proudly.

'I'll be bragging about me oldest daughter down the pub tomorrow. None of the nippers will be in the army, thank gawd, as this bleeding war will be over before they're big enough,' Dad said as he resumed his usual seat by the range.

'Mind your language, Dad, we've got company,' Mum said as she lifted the boiling kettle from the range and tipped it into the waiting enamel teapot.

'Don't mind me, Mr Wolton, this is your home, and you can say whatever you like,' Sandy said. 'I promise you I won't be shocked or offended. We hear far worse on the base, don't we, Minnie?'

It would have been nice to stop longer, play more board games with the little ones, catch up on the gossip with her mum, but they had to be back before curfew. If they were spending the night off base it wouldn't matter, they'd have got a pass like the other girls had, but they couldn't stay here as there was no room.

'It was grand seeing you, love, but you get off now as we don't want you to get into no trouble,' Dad said.

In the kerfuffle of getting ready to go, Minnie slipped her dad a ten-bob note and then handed two pounds to her mum. 'Me wages go up when I'm promoted, Mum, so I'll be able to give you a bit more.'

'Are you keeping back a few bob for yourself? Don't you go giving us everything.'

'I don't need much, Mum, everything's paid for. I'm doing all right, I've got me rich friends to help me out, ain't I?'

'You're the best thing what ever happened to me. I ain't got a clue why you came along nine months after me wedding to your dad and then I never fell again for years and then look what I got all in a heap!'

Minnie hugged her mum and then gave each of the kiddies, who ranged in age from ten to four, a tanner each. That left her with one and six to last her until next payday, but it was worth it.

'Cor, Minnie, six whole pennies to spend just for me? Ta ever so,' Tommy, the oldest, said with a gappy grin. 'I don't reckon there'll be no sweets what with rationing and all, but I can buy meself something nice down the shops.'

After further hugging and kissing – everybody smelling of fish, chips and vinegar – she and Sandy escaped to the relative peace of the street.

'Thank you so much for bringing me to meet your family, Minnie, I so enjoyed the visit.'

'They enjoyed your fish and chips and so did I. I ain't keen on walking about in the blackout but I reckon we'll get to the underground station before it's too dark to see.'

They were halfway there when it started to drizzle and they increased their pace. Soon there was a steady downpour and they were both drenched to the skin by the time they rushed into the station, down the staircase and onto the platform to catch the train.

'Blimey, I thought it would be packed, but there ain't that many people down here tonight.' Minnie fidgeted with her skirt, hating the way the thick material clung to her underwear now it was wet.

Sandy seemed less bothered about being wet than

Minnie. 'Would you spend the night down here if you could stay in your own bed? I certainly wouldn't. I'm glad Hitler has turned his attention to Russia and the Luftwaffe only come over occasionally. Our boys in blue seem to have no difficulty keeping those few away.'

'The problem with that, Sandy, is that folk will become complacent, not bother to go into the shelter if the siren goes off. That could be a disaster.'

'Don't be so gloomy, let's look on the bright side. We've had a lovely evening and can get a mug of hot cocoa before we turn in and we have the room to ourselves. We can stay up all night talking, playing cards or doing whatever we want without disturbing the other girls.'

'What about Monopoly? There was one in the rec room and we could borrow that – I ain't never going to own a house nowhere in London so I enjoy playing that game and pretending I'm rich.'

There was nobody using the Monopoly set, so they collected that and their cocoa before bothering to remove their wet clothes. Here they had a wardrobe and actual hangers to put their clothes on so Minnie was sure their uniforms would be dry by the morning. They had their entire kit with them so they could wear the spare if necessary.

Once in nightclothes, they sat on either end of Sandy's bed, the board in between them.

'I'm the top hat, it's always lucky for me,' Minnie said. 'When it come out four years ago, we saved up and brought it as a family treat. Even me dad loves playing as me mum or I read his cards for him.'

'I hate to admit that I've never played and until you mentioned it had never even heard of Monopoly. You were so enthusiastic I wasn't going to disagree with your suggestion.'

'The rules are ever so simple. I'll be the banker and set out the board proper then we can get on with it. I warn you, sometimes it can take blooming hours to get a winner.'

This proved to be the case and it wasn't until the small hours that they declared the game a tie. When they nipped down to the ablutions, the base was quiet, pitch dark, it was strange being the only ones awake.

As Minnie was drifting off to sleep, she was smiling. She couldn't remember ever being so happy – even winning the cup the other day didn't compare. Spending time with her new friend was different to being with anybody else she knew. It was going to be hard seeing Sandy vanish to do something secret and not even know where she was.

* * *

For the next two weeks, Ben was an exemplary commanding officer. The base had never been run so well and when the major returned earlier than expected, having decided he was more than ready to resume his command, he immediately promoted Ben to captain.

'Well done, young man, I didn't think you had the right sort of stuff to make a senior officer, but I was wrong. When's the plaster coming off that damned leg so you can get back to active duty and put your skills to proper use?'

'I have to go to London to see the consultant orthopaedic surgeon next week, sir, and should know more then. He said it would be six weeks and it's not quite four, so it's unlikely I'll be off my crutches for another couple of weeks at least.'

'Bloody bad show, a young man like you sidelined through no fault of your own. I've no idea of the whereabouts of your original regiment but there's plenty going on in Africa at the moment. I'm sure there's work waiting for you.' The major looked rejuvenated – the poor chap had obviously needed a break.

'I can't wait to get back to active duty. Not that I

haven't enjoyed my stay here and particularly since I've been running things for you. I didn't realise administrative work could actually be quite enjoyable.' As soon as he said this, he regretted it – he didn't want to give the impression he preferred desk work to fighting.

'A good officer can turn his hand to anything. You've got natural organisational skills and that's rare. I think you should be at the War Office until you're better, not hobbling around here.'

* * *

The remainder of the course was enjoyable and Minnie and Sandy continued to come out at the top of the group. At the end of the three weeks, only one of the cadre had failed and everyone else was called up in turn to receive their stripes.

After the ceremony, they were asked to go in one by one to speak to the officers in charge and to be given their new postings. They'd been told most wouldn't return to their training bases.

Minnie was relieved that she was returning to Great Baddow, where she would have her own platoon to train. Sandy was quiet when she came out.

'Didn't you get the posting you wanted?'

'I did, thank you, Minnie. For some reason, it no longer seems as exciting as I thought it would be.' She smiled but her eyes were sad. 'To be honest, I'd rather be coming back with you.'

Although they'd become very close, Sandy had never made any physical contact, they'd not hugged or even touched hands inadvertently, which was something she and Eileen often did. The penny dropped – for Sandy, touching her would be too difficult, would mean something more than it did to Minnie.

She knew that if she embraced Sandy, it would be more or less saying that she had the same sort of feelings about women and she wasn't sure that she did.

* * *

Eileen wasn't the sort of girl to mope. She pushed all thoughts of being with the man she loved aside and spent the next few days thinking about her own life. She'd been told she was to go to the convalescent home in two days and a car would take her there. She still didn't know the whereabouts of this place, but it made no difference.

More importantly, she was now able to get up and spend time in the patients' common room as long as she kept her arm in the sling. A junior nurse had to help her dress but after the lack of privacy in the ATS, this no longer bothered her.

'You're a local girl, aren't you, nurse? I don't suppose you happen to know where I can find a solicitor?'

The girl beamed. 'My sister's married to one. I'll get him to come and see you if you like. His firm handles divorces so will be perfect for you.'

'That would be helpful, thank you so much. Please ask him to come as soon as he can, as I'll be leaving here in a couple of days.'

The fact that this student nurse was aware she wanted a divorce wasn't ideal, but then the reason for her being here must have travelled with her.

Sister had told her that Danny was no longer on the services side of the hospital, so Ben had obviously been true to his word and had her husband removed from the army. Eileen thought she should feel guilty that he would now struggle financially, but she hardened her heart and concentrated on doing what she could to make her own life better.

* * *

The following morning, immediately after the doctor's round, a very tall, thin, bespectacled young man appeared at the door of the common room.

'Good morning, Private Ruffel, I am Mr Billings. My sister-in-law, Jenny, said you had need of my services, so here I am. How can I help?'

Fortunately, they had the room to themselves so could talk in privacy. Quickly she explained the circumstances whilst he made notes in a little black book without comment.

'So, Mr Billings, I realise getting a divorce isn't simple and can take a long time, but I'm determined to do it, however difficult it might prove to be.'

He smiled and nodded, which was a good sign. 'In fact, things are not as you thought. Four years ago, the law changed and in addition to adultery by either party, you can now petition for a divorce on the grounds of cruelty, desertion and incurable insanity.'

'Then him breaking my arm and attempting to punch me would count as cruelty?'

'Absolutely. Do you wish me to start the proceedings? I'm afraid it is quite costly.'

'I assumed it would be. Yes, please set things in motion.'

'You will have to appear in court and give an oral

statement under oath. I believe there are several eye-witnesses who are prepared to do the same.'

'Yes, both the sister in charge of my ward and two of the junior nurses saw what happened, as well as the consultant surgeon. How long is this likely to take?'

'It rather depends if your husband wishes to contest your petition,' Mr Billings said. 'If he doesn't, then probably six months. The courts are moving very slowly as you can imagine because of the war.'

'I need you to give me a written estimate of the costs so I can ensure I have sufficient funds to cover the bills as they occur.'

'I shall have my secretary do this on my return to the office. It will be with you by the end of the day. If I don't hear to the contrary, then I'll assume you wish me to begin proceedings.'

'Yes, that seems a sensible way forward. Once my arm's better, I'll either be at Great Baddow or living in Chelmsford. I haven't quite decided what I'm going to do at the moment,' Eileen said.

He already had the address of the house she'd leased for three years so any correspondence could be sent there or to the convalescent home. She hadn't realised that she wasn't sure if she was going to remain in the ATS until she'd mentioned she might be living in Chelmsford.

There was no need for her to make up her mind immediately – she had several weeks of convalescence and physiotherapy in front of her before she had to come to a definite decision.

22

Minnie retuned to Great Baddow feeling unsettled about Sandy. Embarking on a relationship with anyone was risky, but to do so with another woman was even more dangerous. A man loving another man was a criminal offence and both parties could be sent to prison. How could loving anyone be treated in the same way as trying to kill someone or break into their home?

It was a mystery and not one she was ready to think about at the moment. Minnie couldn't contact Sandy, so they'd agreed for the moment not to exchange letters. Sandy had promised to get in touch when she was allowed to and then they'd meet. If this happened, that would be when Minnie would make her decision.

After signing in, Minnie was given the location of her new billet. She was now sharing with another corporal who was on duty and she examined the room to look for clues as to who it might be. Her heart sank. There was a photo on the locker and it was of Endean standing with an ugly bloke in a sailor's uniform.

It was going to be a bit awkward being in the same room as someone who'd been her superior. Experience counted as well as stripes, so she'd be expected to keep her trap shut and do as she was told. She smiled. It could have been worse; it could have been Rigby.

After unpacking her kit, she had the rest of the day and evening free as she wasn't on duty until the following morning. Time to see Eileen.

Minnie knew her friend was working with Ben, so the main admin block was the best place to start. She was surprised that another ATS was in the small office that Eileen had occupied.

Ben must have heard her as he called from next door that she go in and see him. She entered and saluted; he didn't respond.

'Close the door, Corporal Wolton, and take a pew.'

Minnie did as asked but from his haggard expression, she guessed something was wrong. 'Thank you, sir, I called in to see Private Ruffel.'

'Eileen's not here. I'll tell you why.'

Minnie listened in silence, scarcely able to take in what she was being told. She was as shocked about Ben and Eileen being in love as she was about Danny attacking her friend. Where she came from, domestics were common, and it wasn't always the wife who got battered.

'Do you have the address where she is? I'll write to her and go and see her when I get a pass.'

She'd no intention of commenting on his admission that he loved Eileen, it was none of her business. Better to keep things formal too, so she'd not called him Ben, even though he'd called her Minnie.

'I'll give it to you. I won't ask you to give her my love but would like to know how she is if you don't mind telling me when you get back.'

Minnie stood up, saluted again and this time he more or less responded. She smartly about turned and marched out, her head spinning with what she'd just learned. As soon as she was out of the building, she stopped to look at the address and saw Eileen was only in Colchester – no distance at all on the train from Chelmsford.

She marched immediately to the office of Junior

Commander Davies to see if she could somehow wangle a day off. The new recruits were already here and had been allocated their own corporal so she would only be tagging along to gain experience, not actually training her own group of girls.

Her CO was just coming out of the building when she arrived. Minnie halted, snapped her heels together and saluted. Davies did the same.

'Welcome back, Corporal Wolton. I had a glowing report from Fulham. I was told that you are officer material despite your lack of formal education.'

'Thank you, ma'am, that's good to hear. I'm not looking to be an officer but intend to become the highest-ranked NCO.'

'I rather thought you might say that. You'll make an excellent warrant officer but unfortunately, I don't think you'll get that sort of promotion if you remain here.'

'I want to stay at least for a month or two. I was sorry to hear about Eileen and as I don't have my own squad for another two weeks, I was hoping you would give me a day's leave so I can go and see her tomorrow.'

'All ATS are entitled to a weekend free when they finish their training. I've already arranged for you to have a forty-eight-hour pass starting tomorrow morning.'

Minnie was so pleased, she forgot to salute a second time and almost hugged Davies, which would have been entirely the wrong thing to do.

As promised, the necessary paperwork was waiting for her inside. There was no need for her to telephone to the home as Eileen obviously wouldn't be going anywhere. She was glad to have a few hours without official duties to learn more about the differences between being a lance corporal and a corporal. Before she left to begin her investigation, there was something she wanted to know and the clerk on duty in this office was exactly the girl to tell her.

'Did all my platoon get posted where they wanted?'

'Most of them did. I do know that Sinclair was upset Felgate wasn't going with her to join the artillery. I think Felgate changed her mind at the last minute and is going to become a driver and eventually a dispatch rider.'

'Crikey, I never thought Clara would go for that. She's got the education to do something clever. Ta, I wrote their ID numbers down and will write to them. I'm a free agent until Wednesday morning.'

'Lucky you, make the most of it.'

Minnie headed for the NAAFI. Sandy had slipped a ten-shilling note into her pocket so she was flush at the moment. She reckoned it wouldn't cost more than a couple of bob for the train ticket tomorrow so she'd plenty of cash to spare for a cuppa and a bun and maybe something savoury too.

There were very few familiar faces at Great Baddow now all the girls she'd joined up with had moved on.

As it was mid-afternoon, the NAAFI was quiet and Minnie took her food to one of the many empty tables and, as she pulled out a chair, she saw someone had forgotten their newspaper. She might as well give it a read until whoever it was came back to collect it. She opened the paper and was pleased to discover it was the *News Chronicle*. This was a more socialist sort of daily and suited her political views.

After reading a very distressing article about the Nazis gassing Jewish people, she put it aside. Things were going badly in Africa for the Allies and also against the Japanese in the Pacific. Better to avoid the news at the moment as it was all bad. Even the massive bombing raids being sent to Germany made her unhappy. Killing civilians, women and children, didn't seem right to her.

Even bad news didn't spoil her appetite. She was

just biting into her tasty meat pasty when a familiar voice spoke from beside her.

'Excellent. I was looking for you and was also wondering where my paper was. Do you mind if I join you for a moment?'

Minnie looked up, intending to say no, but there was an orderly holding his tray so thought she'd better not.

'Yes, sir, but I'm almost finished.' This was clearly untrue as she'd only just started her meal.

Ben stared at her and his smile became a little less friendly.

'I need to talk to you. I know you're on leave, but when you return, you'll be taking over C Squad from Corporal Fisher. She's broken her leg.'

She laughed, hardly appropriate, but she couldn't help it. 'Blimey, this place ain't safe. Rigby cracked up, Eileen gets her arm broken, you break your ankle again. Now Fisher's had an accident.'

'A string of unfortunate coincidences, Corporal. A male corporal will take over until you're ready to do so.'

'I'll only take a day to see Eileen, sir, so can take charge of the girls the day after tomorrow.'

He nodded. 'I hoped you'd step up. Good show. Did you want to borrow my paper?'

He was now settled opposite her and she wasn't entirely comfortable with this.

'No, ta, too much bad news.' She returned to her pasty, and he munched his sandwich.

'Is it all right for us to be sitting together, sir? Don't want to rock any boats.'

* * *

Ben had been waiting for her to ask this quite legitimate question. 'As we are sitting in full view of everybody else, and all formalities are being observed, I think it's perfectly acceptable. After all, this is the one place where we're allowed to fraternise.'

'In Fulham, where I got trained, they have three separate hatches – no mixing at all. I enjoyed being on an active base, I reckon there must have been more than a thousand soldiers and that living there.'

'I spent a couple of months at Fulham myself before joining my regiment. We had a jolly time as it was so close to the West End and the war hadn't really got started.'

She nodded towards his folded newspaper. 'Horrible things in there that don't bear thinking about. I knew the Nazis were cruel and that but what they're doing in those camps...'

Minnie couldn't continue and he wasn't surprised. He hastily changed the subject.

'Do you know who you're bunking with?'

She pulled a face. 'Corporal Endean. It's going to be tricky sharing a room with someone who was training me a couple of weeks ago.'

'If anyone is going to overcome that small difficulty, it's you, Corporal Wolton.' She was an observant young woman but didn't appear to have noticed he was now a captain. He touched his new pips and raised an eyebrow. He now had three on his epaulette instead of two and three silver stripes on his arm.

'I'm not daft, Captain Sawyer, I saw you'd been promoted. We're both going up in the world, ain't we?'

'We certainly are. Actually, what I really wanted to tell you was that I'm being posted to the War Office until such time as I'm fit for active duty.' He cleared his throat, not sure how to continue without embarrassing them both. 'Well, in case anybody needs to know where I am, will you tell them?'

'I certainly will. You're wasted here, Captain, I reckon you'll find things a lot easier in London. I doubt you'll have time for any regrets.' Minnie drained her mug, brushed a few crumbs from her immaculate uniform, and with a sympathetic smile she left him to finish his belated lunch.

She was right – but then she usually was – if he was busier and doing something more useful then he wouldn't have time to mope about thinking about what might have been. His duty was to fight in whatever way he could to defeat the Nazis. There wasn't room in his life for love. Eileen had said she would wait for him, and he smiled. A lot of chaps would have been away for the entire war by the time they were demobbed, so what did it matter if he and the woman he loved were separated the same length of time?

Anyone watching would have thought he was deranged, grinning and nodding to himself. His spirits lifted and things began to fall into place. If he survived this bloody war, then he'd come back and claim Eileen for himself.

* * *

Eileen wasn't exactly enjoying her enforced stay at the convalescent home but as she had to be somewhere, it was preferable to be as far away from Ben as possible. Mr Billings was proceeding with the divorce petition and would keep her informed. It was going to be prohibitively expensive but wouldn't take all her savings, thank goodness. The rent from the middle-aged couple who were living in her house hadn't been touched, as she'd opened a separate post office account for the money to be deposited every week.

A doctor had called in from the military hospital to check on her wrist and told her that it was healing well and she could start using it as long as she returned it to the sling afterwards. She was now able to dress herself, wash and clean her teeth but far more importantly was able to use the WC without assistance.

While she was here, she wasn't wearing her uniform but a mismatch of borrowed clothes provided by the home. They were obviously clean and fresh, but she really didn't like second-hand clothes and couldn't wait to be back in her uniform or in her own civvies if she decided to leave the ATS. Thousands of families had to rely entirely on donations of everything after having been bombed out during the Blitz last year and yet here she was complaining about her lot. She frowned, feeling ashamed of her selfishness.

She was pretending to read an Agatha Christie mystery when, to her surprise and delight, Minnie walked in.

'Hello, I'm so pleased to see you, Eileen. We've got such a lot to talk about.'

They hugged and kissed and then sat down on the comfortable, if rather saggy, sofa.

'You've lost ever so much weight, ain't they feeding you properly here?'

'The food's quite good but I've lost my appetite. I always wanted to be thin but didn't expect to achieve my dream because of a broken heart.'

Instead of sympathising, Minnie laughed. 'Blimey, you and Ben need your heads knocking together. Why are you making each other so miserable? Nobody cares apart from you if you get together. Anyway, he said to tell you he's moving to the War Office so you can contact him there if you want to.'

'We agreed it was over, at least for now. Why would he say that?'

'Well, to be honest, he didn't say exactly that. I've just interpreted his words. He looks as miserable as you.'

'It's not just Ben making me unhappy,' Eileen said. 'I've always been someone decisive, able to make decisions and stick with them even if they happen to be the wrong ones, like marrying Danny. Now I can't decide whether to leave the ATS and return to book-keeping and accounting during the day and something war related and useful in the evening. Do you think I should resign?'

'Ask yourself where you'd be happiest. Even if you and Ben were together, you'd still be apart. You won't be able to really be with him until this blooming war's over. Are you worried that your broken arm won't be able to do the things you want as a PT instructor?'

Eileen thought for a moment. 'That's one of the reasons. Look what happened to Ben and he wasn't even doing anything vigorous when his leg gave way. I'm going to have to be able to swing dumbbells, do press-ups and somehow I don't think I'm ever going to be able to do that without the risk of it giving way.'

'Then that's your answer. You could leave the ATS, find a job what paid you more but in a reserved occupation. Don't work in one of them munitions factories. It was all over the papers last week, weren't it, about some girls being killed when something blew up in the factory.'

Eileen was about to agree but Minnie hadn't finished.

'Or you can stay in the ATS like what you want to and do something else. You could become a trainer like me or with your education do something clever. There's ever so much choice in that booklet and they won't want to lose you, that's for sure.'

'Golly, I can't believe I didn't consider that option. I'll definitely stay. I could be a kinetheodolite operator – not exactly sure what that is but I've got the qualifications and the lecture we had on joining the anti-aircraft sites did sound interesting.'

'There you are then, all tickety-boo. I'll speak to Davies when I get back this evening, let her know what you've decided. By the time your arm's out of plaster, there'll be another lot of recruits going off to do that training and you can join them. I reckon you'll be promoted to lance corporal immediately and sent away to be a corporal as well.'

'I'm so glad you've come, Minnie, I'd never have come to a decision on my own. Now, tell me what's been happening in your life. What's it like being a corporal?'

'Smashing. I'm sharing with Endean but she's all right, not bossy nor nothing. We'll get on okay, I reckon.'

'That's good. Are you still intending to stay at Baddow?'

'For a few weeks, then I'll apply for something else. I want to end up a WO2 by the end of this lot.' She paused and looked a bit self-conscious, not like Minnie at all.

'I met someone I really like, but it ain't a bloke, if you see what I mean.'

'Good heavens, you've rather taken me by surprise. I didn't know you were that way inclined,' Eileen said.

'I'm not sure that I am. Never thought about it before I met Sandy. She's not made any advances, she respects my reluctance, but it could explain why I've never wanted to go out with no man nor nothing.'

'To be honest, I'm dreadfully shocked. I'm just not comfortable with that sort of thing.' As soon as she saw the look of disappointment on her best friend's face, Eileen regretted what she'd said.

'Fair enough. Not everyone's broadminded.'

Eileen took exception to this. 'Come on, Minnie, I bet there's no one on the base that's "broadminded", as you call it, about women being with women or men being with men. In fact, I think you'll find that if it was known then you'd be dishonourably discharged.'

'I'm sure I would be. Are you intending to tell them? Not that I've made up my mind or done anything anyone, even you, could be offended by.'

Eileen didn't know what to say to put things right. She didn't want to lose her best friend as well as the man she loved, but it was against the teachings of her faith and there was nothing she could do to change that.

'I'd better be getting off; I don't want to miss me

train. I don't reckon I'll be at Baddow when you come back, so I'll say goodbye and wish you luck.'

Eileen sat silent, too upset to speak, but knowing if she didn't she'd not see Minnie again. 'Don't go like this, please, Minnie. Can't we just pretend you didn't tell me?'

Sadly, Minnie shook her head. 'Too late, Eileen. I thought I could tell you anything and you'd under-stand, but I were wrong. I ain't a believer as you know, but I reckon I'm more forgiving, more loving and more understanding than you or most of your lot.'

Minnie had to dash into the ladies' room as she didn't want anyone to see her crying. She'd thought better of Eileen, but then you never knew what a person was really like until something like this happened.

Eileen was right, though; she'd be chucked out if she decided to become involved with Sandy. She blew her nose, splashed her face with cold water and was ready to face the world. She knew now that she didn't want to give up her career in the ATS for anyone, not a man or a woman. Maybe after the war was over it would be different. Two friends could live together without raising any eyebrows. What went on behind a closed door was nobody else's business.

When she emerged, Eileen was outside the door,

her face tear-streaked and without a second thought, Minnie rushed forward and put her arms around her.

'I ain't going to lose my best friend because of something we don't agree on. What a pair of silly moos we are, crying and that.'

'Please don't move away from Baddow because of me. I'll go somewhere else if you want me to. I'm so very sorry for being judgemental and tactless.'

'Don't worry about it. Water under the bridge. I'm not going nowhere and neither are you.' She still had hold of Eileen's good arm as she stepped back. 'Are you allowed out? We could go into Colchester and have a look round and get ourselves something to eat.'

Eileen sniffed and blew her nose on a lovely clean hanky. 'This isn't a prison. If you give me a hand, I'll get back into uniform as I'm certainly not going out in these horrible things.'

'Righto. I did wonder why you were wearing them things – not your usual style – not that I know much about you when you were a civilian.'

Twenty minutes later, they were marching briskly into the town centre, enjoying the admiring looks they got from other pedestrians. This was a garrison town and they weren't the only ones in khaki, but Minnie reckoned they were the best.

'There's a castle here somewhere, I'd love to go

and see it if we have time. When do you have to be back?'

'I ain't on duty until seven tomorrow so whenever I like. I've been to the Tower a couple of times but I never went inside. We'll definitely go to see this castle after dinner.'

Colchester was full of narrow streets of old houses covered in beams. They found a nice little café tucked away down Trinity Street and ordered a fry-up – no bacon, but the sausages looked good.

Eileen insisted she was paying and Minnie didn't argue. She explained to her friend that whatever her inclinations, she wasn't going to act on them while she was in the army.

'You did tell me that you'd never give up your career for a man, so it makes sense that you'd make the same decision now. Will you still speak to Junior Commander Davies for me?'

'Course I will. She told me I'd never get the promotion I want if I stayed put, so I'm going to do a couple of months' training where I am and then go somewhere else. It looks a bit of all right here, and it's certainly big enough.'

The elderly waitress overheard them talking and as the café wasn't busy, she stopped for a chat.

'There's half a dozen RAF airfields around Colchester to protect our garrison as it's so important. There's a cavalry barracks as well where they train the horses and the soldiers that ride them.' The woman pointed to Eileen's arm. 'You recuperating near the military hospital then?'

'I am and very comfortable it is too. We want to see the castle – is it far from here?'

'No, very close. You just carry on down Trinity Street, turn right into Culver Street and follow it to the end. Then turn left and you'll be in the main street, called the High Street. Go across the road and it's on your left, you can't miss it.'

'Ta, we'll have a look. Me, I like a bit of history,' Minnie said.

'There's been a museum since 1850, not sure it's open now, though.' The waitress turned to go. 'Colchester was a Roman city, ever so old it is.'

* * *

The visit to the ancient castle was worth the short walk and Minnie was disappointed the museum was closed. 'Let's walk back up the High Street and then I can go down North Hill to the station and you can walk back to your home.' It was only four o'clock, but she wanted to go and Eileen didn't protest.

'I'm ready for a lie down. I've not had so much exercise since my arm was broken,' Eileen said.

'Do you want me to come back with you?'

'No, I'll be tickety-boo. Come and see me again if you get the chance. Your visit has cheered me up.'

When they reached the corner of High Street and Head Street where Minnie had to turn down North Hill, they embraced and she walked away. Minnie didn't look back.

It was about a mile to the station and didn't take her long to get there. After three weeks of five-mile marches, and hours of drill, Minnie was fitter than she'd ever been. She had half an hour to wait for the next train and found a bench on the platform and sat down.

There was a lot to get straight in her head and she wanted to have it all sorted before she got back to base. One thing she did know was that although Eileen would always be a good friend, something had been broken by what had been said. Minnie knew if Eileen hadn't been outside the ladies' room then she wouldn't have gone to see her.

On the surface, things were the same as before, but they weren't. She sat up straighter and squared her shoulders. From now on, she was on her own. She'd continue to help her family out but, despite saying she wasn't looking to move from Baddow, she was going to apply for a new posting as soon as she got back.

Not Colchester, nor London, but somewhere she could start afresh, forget about Eileen, Ben and especially Sandy. She did feel differently about her but pursuing this would be stupid. She was needed in the ATS, intended to concentrate on doing her duty and in her own small way help Britain to eventually defeat Germany.

* * *

Minnie was lucky and there was a bus waiting when she emerged from the station. She hopped on and happily paid her pennies to the conductor. On arriving at the barracks, she marched straight to the ATS building. She was lucky, Davies was still there and happy to speak to Minnie.

'I didn't expect you back so early, Wolton. Also, giving up your leave is appreciated.'

'Thank you, ma'am.' She remained at ease and ignored the gesture to sit. Easier to say what she had to standing up.

'Private Ruffel has asked me to tell you that she

wants to train as a kinetheodolite operator. She's not going to leave the ATS.'

'Excellent. We don't want to lose her. Was there something else?'

'Yes, ma'am. I want to put in for a posting as soon as I've finished with this squad. On an active garrison where I've got more to do and more opportunity to be promoted. I'm eager to learn and you told me I'll not progress if I stay here.'

'True enough,' Davies said. 'I'll be sorry to see you move on but understand why you want to. You are, as you know, obliged to go or stay as needed. However, I'll put your name forward for something more interesting. I can't promise that you'll get the posting you want, good trainers are hard to find and it might be decided that you're needed here.'

Minnie saluted. 'Thank you, ma'am. I'll do my best wherever I am.'

There wasn't anything else she could do. Until she was told otherwise, she'd be the best blooming trainer at Great Baddow. A couple of months ago, she'd been a seamstress living in a cramped house in the East End, and look at her now.

She was a soldier in the ATS, a corporal, and knew that if she worked hard and kept out of trouble then she'd be a sergeant before the summer was done. She might not have a special someone in her life right now but one day she'd find Sandy and maybe there would be.

* * *

Ben was driven to London in a staff car as he couldn't manoeuvre crutches and his heavy navy-blue kit bag himself. Everything he owned was either rammed into this bag or in his pack. When he'd been in Africa last year and living in a tent, he'd had to empty his boots every morning to make sure no unwanted scorpion had taken residence overnight. He couldn't wait to be back there in the desert, doing his bit.

Officers working at Horse Guards in Westminster had a decent per diem to pay for the lodgings they found for themselves. He needed somewhere within half a mile maximum from his workplace and had a few recommendations. The first was in Tothill Street, a small hotel which took in long-term residents.

The duty manager escorted Ben up to the second floor in the antiquated lift and into a suite of rooms that looked out over the rooftops. He could see Westminster Abbey and Parliament, which was good.

'Captain Sawyer, the last officer who lived here has just been posted overseas and I can assure you these rooms will be taken by this evening. You're fortunate that you've come this morning. You have a small kitchen with a table for dining, a comfortable sitting room, a bedroom with shower and WC.'

Ben didn't need to look round. These rooms were ideal and the amount he was paid each day would more than cover the cost and any meals he ate here.

'Thank you, I'll take them. I'll be here until I'm fit for active duty. Probably about six weeks.'

'They are yours for as long as you need them, sir. If you'd care to look around, I'll have your driver bring up your belongings. I'll send a chambermaid to unpack for you.'

'That would be kind. Can I have meals sent up? Laundry service?'

'Laundry and housekeeping are included and room service is available at extra cost. The bar and restaurant are open from seven until midnight.'

'Even better. As long as the lift's always working, I'll be fine. I can't manage three flights of stairs.'

'We have a small service lift that would be made available to you if that happened, Captain, so everything is catered for.'

'Do you need any paperwork signed? Advance payment?'

'No, sir, that won't be necessary. Weekly payment

will suffice. The invoice will be brought to you every Monday. Would you like luncheon served here or will you come down?'

'If my things are being fetched and unpacked for me then I'll come down,' Ben said.

The manager glanced at the somewhat grubby white cast fully visible as an orderly had had to cut one leg off a pair of trousers to accommodate it.

'We have an excellent seamstress employed here. I'm sure she could alter a pair of your trousers to fit.'

'That would be good. I get a few disapproving looks from my superiors for being improperly dressed.'

'Then I'll arrange for that to be done as soon as a girl has unpacked. When that plaster comes off, things can be put back as they were.'

Ben followed this helpful chap to the ground floor and followed the noise of cutlery and glassware into the well-appointed dining room. This was a small, select establishment that catered, it seemed, solely to army officers if the occupants of the dining room were any indication.

A decrepit waiter ushered him to one of the two remaining tables. He bowed. 'Vegetable soup, lamb chops, followed by fruit salad and cream. Would sir like a beverage to go with his luncheon?'

Obviously no choice, but the meal sounded fine. 'A carafe of water, thank you.'

The other tables were occupied by singletons like him. All were eating and none were talking. This suited him as the last thing he wanted was to strike up any transitory friendships during his brief sojourn in London.

The water arrived at once, the soup followed soon after. He had been the last to arrive but was one of the first to depart. It was warm and stuffy in the dining room and Ben wanted to wander about London and get his bearings. He had a forty-eight-hour pass so wasn't expected at Horse Guards.

He was saddened by how much London had changed since he'd been here just before the outbreak of war. There were so many boarded-up houses in Tothill Street, and a couple missing altogether. Even if the houses weren't demolished by a bomb, they were often rendered unusable because of the force of the explosion.

Everywhere piles of sandbags, taped-up windows, virtually the only pedestrians he saw were in uniform of one sort or another. The loud voices of the brash GIs grated, and he made a point of avoiding them. They walked about as though they owned the place – which he supposed they did as they were Americans.

He doubted Britain would ever be able to repay the massive amount of money borrowed to finance the war.

He wasn't the only one he passed using crutches or walking sticks, but he was the only one in uniform. Presumably the other poor sods had been discharged with an invalidity pension. He was lucky his superior officers had wanted to keep him, as not only was he highly trained, had already won a couple of gongs for bravery, but he was regular army and not a conscript or a volunteer.

He'd signed on for ten years, which meant he couldn't leave for another six years, whatever happened. He hoped the war would be over before then, but the way things were going it didn't seem likely. Now the Yanks had joined in, there was plenty of manpower, hardware, aircraft – both bombers and fighters – to take the fight to Hitler, but making a successful landing on the French coast wasn't going to be easy. After all, the Germans would have invaded Britain if they'd been able to cross the Channel safely.

It was a reasonable trek to the Mall and from there down Regent Street to Piccadilly Circus, where there were a dozen cinemas to choose from. Ben settled for the Plaza where a film with Rex Harrison called *Ten Days in Paris* was showing. He came out when the main film finished as he didn't want to see the cartoon or the news and thought it was a few shillings well spent. The film had been entertaining, although the plot had been somewhat convoluted and unlikely.

The streets were busier now as those that worked in the city, or Parliament perhaps, were heading for home and twice he was almost knocked off his feet by a swinging briefcase and an uncaring, black-suited businessman.

Ben was relieved to return to the relative sanctuary of his new accommodation. He informed the man on duty at the desk that he would be dining in and was told that a table would be reserved for him for seven o'clock.

* * *

It didn't take Ben long to settle into his new routine and, for the first time in months, he believed he was doing a valuable job again. After three weeks, his consultant decided to remove the plaster cast and was satisfied that the leg had healed perfectly this time.

'You'll need to use a walking stick initially, Captain Sawyer, to allow your leg to regain its strength. Do the exercises on the sheet that I've given you and I'll see you in three weeks. I'm hoping to be able to sign you off then as fit for active duty.'

'That's the best news I've had in months. Thank you, I promise I'll follow these instructions to the letter as I don't want a repeat of last time.'

'That won't happen, young man, I did a proper job, if I say so myself.'

They shook hands and Ben limped out, shocked at how much weight he needed to put on the stick in order to stay upright. Major Collins, who he was working for, had provided him with a staff car so Ben could be back at his desk quickly.

The major was waiting for him. 'Good man. I've just heard that the Americans have beaten Japan at the Battle of Midway.'

'Good news at last. I'm going to be using this stick for three weeks and then should be given the all-clear by the quack. Do you have any idea where I'm going to be sent? What regiment I'll be joining?'

'Sit down, Captain, we need to talk.'

Ben didn't like the sound of this and had a sinking feeling he might be forced to remain in London as he was doing such a good job.

'As you know, preparations for the invasion of France are underway, but it's going to be a year or two before we're ready to move. The arrangements that need to be made are massive and complicated and you seem to have a head for that sort of thing.'

'I do, sir, but I desperately need to get back to active service. I'm a skilled tactician, an excellent leader of men, and with all due respect, I think I'll be more use to the war effort leading from the front.'

Collins nodded and half-smiled. 'We expected you to say that and although we'd like you to remain with us at Horse Guards until the Allied invasion, when you're declared fit for duty you can decide where you want to go. Plenty of action with Rommel in the desert, and things are pretty hairy in Burma, so you can take your pick.'

'If at all possible, sir, I'd like to rejoin my regiment. I'm not exactly sure where they are as it's been more than six months since I was with them, but I'm sure it wouldn't be too hard to find them.'

The major chuckled. 'On paper perhaps, my boy, but you might find it a little harder to do it in person. That said, if that's what you want to do, then that's what will happen.'

'Thank you, I never thought I'd be in a position to fight again but now that I am almost there, I can't wait to leave,' Ben said.

'I suggest you get your affairs in order, Sawyer, you never know when you'll be back or even if you will.

Bloody horrible in the desert and in the jungle and we're losing as many men because of the climate as we are through fighting.'

'I understand that, but I'm ready to go. There's someone I need to speak to but there's no urgency as I've got at least three more weeks of recuperation before I'm declared fit.'

24

Eileen had letters to write and decided to train her right hand to do what her left hand normally did. It took a week but by then she thought her handwriting was reasonably legible and she could return the rent book to the landlord with apologies. She'd paid three months in advance and was hopeful that he'd refund four weeks' rent at least.

Next, she wrote to Junior Commander Davies to confirm her request to be sent to train to operate the complicated rangefinder that would be part of an artillery site. As she was now able to use the fingers of her left hand without any pain, she spoke to the doctor when he called to see another recuperating ATS.

'Please could I have my cast removed before the six weeks? I need to be back on duty, not malingering here doing nothing.'

'Five weeks is the absolute minimum, Private Ruffel, so I'll take it off then, but you'll have to have it strapped for at least another week.'

'Thank you, sir, I can't return to duty until the plaster's off.'

'And neither should you – the army doesn't want soldiers of any sort on duty unless they're fully fit. Recipe for disaster that would be.'

The days dragged and she kept busy by continuing to practise using her unfamiliar hand and was pleasantly surprised that she'd been able to train herself to be quite ambidextrous. She went for long walks around the parade ground and the cavalry barracks, where she spent hours watching the horses being trained and exercised.

She was disappointed that Minnie had been unable to visit again but being a corporal now, she would be far busier than she'd been before.

Four weeks after her incarceration at the convalescent home, Eileen received two letters, both of which were very welcome news. The first was from Davies. In this she was told that she was now Lance Corporal Ruffel and would be on the permanent staff working in the main admin building when she returned to duty.

The second was a large, overfilled letter from her solicitor, Mr Billings.

Dear Private Ruffel,

I hope that you are making a good recovery and that my news will help with this.

The solicitor acting for Mr Ruffel has informed me that your husband is not contesting the divorce.

You are now legally separated. This means that things can be expedited and the decree nisi could well be issued within three months. The decree absolute will follow sometime later and then you will be free to remarry if you so wish.

Could I ask you to please sign the enclosed forms, have them witnessed, and return them to me as soon as you can.

I remain your obedient servant,

Eileen read the letter a second time. There was no mention of sending him a money order, but she would settle his bill as soon as she was back in Chelmsford. This was certainly the best possible news, but she had a moment of regret that her marriage was going to be ended so easily.

She wondered why Danny had agreed to the divorce, especially as he was now without resources. His violence was unforgivable, but she couldn't live with the thought that he would be destitute whilst she was doing well financially.

Matron was happy to witness the documents and Eileen replied to Mr Billings saying that she wanted to make a settlement of £300 on her husband, even though it wasn't necessary.

On her daily walk, she posted the letter in Colchester and treated herself to afternoon tea. Did the fact that she would be a free woman later this year change anything between her and Ben? As she was now 'legally separated', she rather thought that it did.

On her return to Baddow, she would write to him, update him on her status and suggest that they might meet before he was posted overseas. He had had his leg repaired more than a week before her arm had been broken, so he would be out of plaster before her.

She was quite sure that as soon he was declared fit for duty, he would leave his temporary post in London and rejoin his regiment. She was a realist and knew it was quite likely he wouldn't return, so it was imperative he left knowing that she loved him, would wait for him, and happily marry him when he next got leave.

The three elderly ladies drinking tea and eating cake at the table next to her smiled. One of them spoke to her directly. 'You look happy, love. Thinking of your hubby?'

'I'm thinking of the man I love. Things haven't been officially settled between us. He's got a broken leg and is waiting to have his cast removed too. I'm hoping we'll come to an understanding before he rejoins his regiment in a few weeks.'

'That's the ticket. Good luck – I admire you girls joining the army and doing your bit.'

Eileen returned to her tea and cake, making it clear she didn't wish to continue the conversation. Talking about her feelings for Ben to strangers had made it seem real somehow, that maybe against all the odds the two of them could be together. Not now, but sometime in the future.

* * *

The cast on her arm was removed at her insistence a week earlier than had initially been planned. The arm looked thinner and was certainly weaker than before, but apart from that it worked perfectly well, even with the strapping on.

'Keep this on for another week and don't lift anything heavy or do anything silly in the meantime,' the doctor told her firmly. 'I'm not happy about taking the cast off so soon but I can hardly stand in the way of a young lady determined to do her duty.'

'Thank you, sir, I give you my word that I will not take any chances. I'll do the exercises and be cautious.'

She didn't have her kitbag, just the clothes she'd come in and her personal items. She'd expected her things to be sent on, but they hadn't arrived. She sincerely hoped they weren't languishing somewhere else and she'd have to buy another set of uniform. Heaven knows where her gas mask and tin hat were – no doubt she'd have to pay for them if they didn't turn up by the time she had her next kit inspection.

This time, Eileen made her own way to the station, but at least she had a travel warrant. On arriving outside Chelmsford Station, she was delighted there was a bus waiting. In less than three hours from leaving the home she'd been living in for the past five weeks, she was walking smartly up to the guard at Great Baddow and showing her ID papers.

He barely glanced at them – after all, she was now

a lance corporal and he was a lowly private, so he could hardly interrogate her.

The letter she'd received from Junior Commander Davies had told her where she was now to be billeted and that her belongings were already in situ. This was a relief as she'd feared they had been lost. The first thing she needed to do was put on her spare uniform and everything that could be washed would go into the laundry. Her skirt and jacket must be sponged and pressed, but she'd do that herself.

She'd missed lunch but was too excited to worry about food. She was sharing with a Lance Corporal Simmons – not somebody she knew but they would soon become acquainted, as the room was barely big enough for two beds. It would be impossible to be formal or have any privacy in such a confined space.

Her next task was to find out where Minnie had her accommodation. Eileen knew she was lucky not to be in with twenty other girls, as someone of her lowly rank didn't usually warrant a separate billet. However, corporals and above just shared with two or three others, so she supposed she was the lucky one having only one roommate.

To say the room was cosy was an understatement, as even with the iron bedsteads against each wall there was still only room for one locker between them. This was already being used by Simmons. The locker for her was at the foot of her bed and there was no wardrobe, just half a dozen hooks each by the door.

Now smartly dressed and feeling much more professional, Eileen headed for the ATS admin block, where one of the clerks who worked in the offices was bound to know where Minnie was billeted.

The girl she asked was puzzled by the question. 'Corporal Wolton isn't here. She was posted to Putney Barracks last week. Sorry, Lance Corporal, but I thought you knew as you and she were good friends.'

'Never mind, I knew she was hoping to move somewhere busier. I expect to be leaving here in a few weeks too.'

She hurried out, more upset than she should be that Minnie had vanished without a word. She'd thought that things had been restored to normal after their disagreement, but obviously not.

This setback made her even more determined to contact Ben and she rushed back to her billet in order to write this important, hopefully life-changing letter.

* * *

Ben worked hard on building up the muscles in his slightly withered leg but didn't overdo it. He thought that perhaps him starting to jog around the parade ground had contributed to the catastrophic collapse of his ankle last time.

He'd settled in well in his new billet and particularly liked the fact that none of the other residents had made any effort to get to know him, so he remained anonymous, as did they. The war in Africa continued to cause logistical problems for the British Army and Rommel seemed to be getting the best of it.

As an infantry commander, Ben had been in the thick of it in Libya. He'd been in charge of a company of Waltzing Matilda tanks, twenty-eight-tonne heavy fighting and assault tanks, and these vehicles were ably designed to attack dug-in enemy positions. He and his men had proved successful in attacking the Germans. He hoped he would be put in command of these again as the smaller tanks, in his opinion, might be faster but were not as effective.

He was still concerned that he might be kept in Britain to oversee training of the infantry who would be crucial in an Allied victory when they landed in France in a year or two. Would he be tempting fate to start collecting his tropical uniform? He didn't want to be told when he eventually got a clean bill of health that he was on the next ship out to Africa and be obliged to leave in his heavy woollen khakis.

He got little free time and that suited him – he was using his tactical skills to help with the planning for the day they started to take back Europe from the Nazis. The RAF were carpet bombing German cities, ports, factories and airbases so it was only a matter of time before Hitler was sufficiently weakened for an invasion to be possible.

Rommel was a formidable enemy and he needed to be defeated by whatever means possible if the allies were going to reclaim Europe and be victorious.

After two weeks, Ben's leg was sufficiently strong for him to abandon his walking stick. He had an appointment with the orthopaedic surgeon in ten days and would then get embarkation leave and be told where he was being posted – that still seemed to be in the lap of the gods at the moment.

He'd still not written to Eileen and thought that it was the possibility of rejection that was holding him back. Better to leave to fight thinking she still loved him, would be waiting for him, than to find out the reverse was true.

He'd been busy all day in meetings, missed lunch, and had half an hour to grab a bite at the canteen downstairs before the final one of the day. He could send someone down to purchase food, but he wanted to stretch his legs so headed for the door of the conference room where all the meetings had been held.

A pretty red-headed ATS, who reminded him of Eileen, pounced on him as he walked past his usual office. 'A letter came for you, sir, I thought you might like to read it whilst you eat your lunch.'

He held out his hand and she dropped a letter into it. His heart jumped when he saw the postmark. It had come from Chelmsford, was handwritten, and he could think of only one person who would be writing to him.

'Thank you.' He tucked it into his inside pocket as if it was of no particular importance and instead of going to the canteen for much-needed sustenance, he headed outside, where he could read the letter without being overlooked or disturbed.

His hands were shaking as he tore it open. He scarcely dared to start reading in case it wasn't what he was hoping to hear.

Dear Ben,

I expect that you have also had your cast re-moved and that you are now almost ready to be deployed overseas. I don't want you to go without knowing that things have changed for me.

I'm staying in the ATS and going to train as a kinetheodolite operator if I'm accepted on the next training course. Therefore, I've handed back the keys to that dear little house – I must say I'm quite relieved if I'm honest, as I didn't want to live there on my own.

Danny isn't contesting the divorce, so everything is going smoothly and my solicitor thinks that I will be free of him by the autumn. I am now legally separated, which as far as I'm concerned is almost the same thing as being unmarried.

I haven't changed my mind. I told you when we parted I would always love you, that I would wait for you and wasn't going to hold you to that promise.

I still love you – more than I can say – and would like to see you before you leave if that's possible and you still want to meet up.

If you've changed your mind and no longer want to be involved with someone who comes with so much unhappy baggage, I'll understand.

I'm working in the office again, the major

hasn't quite reverted to his old ways but still needs me to keep him organised.

You can contact me here if you want to. If I don't hear from you then I'll know there is no future for us.

I love you,

Ben wanted to punch the air, grab the nearest person and shake them vigorously by the hand but wisely contained his joy. He read the letter quickly a second time and then stuffed it into the envelope and put it back in his pocket. This was the first letter Eileen had sent him and he would always treasure it – he knew now it wouldn't be the last.

He just had time to grab a mug of indifferent coffee and the last sandwich and race back upstairs with both. He stood at his desk to eat and drink and then, feeling invincible, he returned to the conference room, knowing it was going to be hard to concentrate when all he wanted to do was reply to that so important letter.

After what seemed an interminable two hours, he was finished for the day. If he wrote his letter at his desk, it could go in the pouch and she'd get it first thing tomorrow.

My darling Eileen,

I've never been happier to receive a letter in my life. Of course I love you, want to spend the rest of my life with you if I can. I'll get a week's embarkation leave when I'm declared fit for active duty next week.

Where shall we meet? I can't take you to the hotel where I'm staying as it's full of stuffy officers, but there are plenty of decent hotels. Do I book one room or two? Whatever you prefer – as long as I can spend as much time with you as possible, getting to know you better, planning our future, then I'll be happy.

Reply by return and it should reach me in good time. As soon as I know your preferences, I'll book a hotel. We can go to the theatre, cinema, walk in the park, dine out, whatever you want, my darling.

I know you won't be free to marry me before I leave but would you be my fiancée, wear my ring, so when I come back we can be married immediately?

I'll put you down as my next-of-kin so if anything happens you will be informed. Yesterday I thought I might well die in the desert, but now I've got too much to live for to let that happen.

*I've so much to say to you, but want to say it
in person,
I love you,*

He scrawled his name, blotted the paper and shoved it into the envelope. He descended the stairs more quickly than was sensible but he could see the clerk about to empty the post box.

'Hang on, another one to go tonight.'

If the private saluted, Ben didn't notice as he was already on his way out of the building. Tonight, London looked bright and welcoming, the pedestrians both civilian and in uniform seemed happier and everywhere he looked he was met with smiles.

Only as he entered his hotel did he realise he'd been grinning like an idiot all the way there. It didn't matter that in a few weeks' time he might be blown to smithereens in his tank, because today he'd never been happier.

This evening called for a celebration and he decided not to dine in but go somewhere where people talked and were smiling and he might be able to share his good news with somebody.

Over the past few weeks, he'd become familiar with his surroundings and he'd heard a couple of chaps talking about a hotel they'd stayed at with their fiancées just off Park Lane, near Marble Arch. It was called the Mount Royal Hotel and was in Brynston Street and he thought this was far enough away from anyone who might know him to be exactly what he wanted.

The main problem was that both he and Eileen had to remain in uniform so would be easy enough to identify if anybody wished to do so. If they were to share a room – God, he hoped they were – then he'd have to register them as a married couple but obviously couldn't use his actual name.

It would be easier for them to have separate rooms in some ways, as neither of them would have to lie, but he hoped she would want to sleep with him. There were prophylactics he could use to ensure she didn't get pregnant.

He frowned and then smiled. Hadn't Eileen told him how different things would have been if she'd been able to have children? Obviously, one day he'd have liked to have a family of his own but wouldn't be too bothered if he didn't.

No – he wasn't going to risk putting his beloved Eileen at risk. Why was he obsessing about sex? She was more likely to ask for a separate room as he was quite sure that, being a religious girl, she wouldn't want to do anything so beyond the pale as committing what would effectively be adultery.

Time enough to worry about the details when he'd had her reply. Then he'd telephone the hotel and make whatever reservations were necessary.

25

Eileen was astonished to receive a reply to her letter the next day and tore it open immediately, regardless of the interested faces of the clerks working in the office next door who were watching her do it.

She devoured the contents of Ben's letter and at the end was crying unashamedly. She was touched when one of the girls quietly closed the door, giving her some much-needed privacy.

She sniffed, dried her eyes, and wrote her reply. If she'd stopped to think, she wouldn't have made the same response. She agreed to share a room with him, told him she would meet him whenever and wherever he wanted, even if it meant being AWOL. She posted the letter immediately so she wouldn't have second thoughts.

After her narrowminded reaction to Minnie's revelation, which had cost her the friendship, she wasn't going to risk losing Ben by being a prude. They might only have these precious few days together, he might not return to her at the end of the war, and even if she wasn't officially his wife, the fact that they were engaged would have to do.

Major Bentley would be more sympathetic to her request for a leave of absence as he was the senior officer here. If he gave his permission, then it didn't matter what her CO thought about the matter.

There was a secret stash of biscuits in her desk drawer saved for just such an occasion. The major had a sweet tooth and she would give him three bourbon biscuits instead of his usual rich tea. Hopefully, he'd sign her slip so she could be with Ben because she didn't think she had the courage to actually be absent without leave.

'Here is your morning tea, sir, I've got you a special treat.'

He smiled benevolently and winked. 'What favour do you want from me, my dear?'

This made it so much easier. She explained in a rush about Ben, her words tumbling over each other as she tried to make him understand just how important it was that she was able to spend Ben's last leave with him.

'Good God, how did I not guess that the two of you were involved? It's a great shame you can't be married before he leaves but his intentions are honourable and it's quite obvious even to an old duffer like me that the two of you are meant to be together.'

'Until I hear back, I don't know the days I need to be away. I feel really guilty asking, especially as I was on sick leave for five weeks.'

'Just fill in the form with the appropriate dates and times when you know them and I'll sign it. I'd like to ask you a favour in return.'

'What would you like me to do?'

'I want you to stay here and not go off and train to be one of those technical girls – this place has never run so smoothly since you took charge of the office.' He grinned and continued. 'That's not exactly true, is it? Captain Sawyer did sterling work whilst you were gone. The army needs you here, not gallivanting all over the country with the ack-ack boys.'

Eileen didn't hesitate. 'I haven't actually handed in my request to apply for the training, sir, I was going to do so next week when this batch of new recruits give in their forms. I'll tear it up and happily stay as long as you want me to.'

'Good girl, as recompense for giving up your chosen career path, I'll have you sent on the next cadre to train to be a corporal. How does that sound?'

She returned his smile. 'Absolutely perfect, sir. Private Jennings managed very well in my absence and I'm sure she'll do the same again for these few days.'

This was the best possible result, as if she was sent to Putney to train then she'd be able to seek out her erstwhile friend Minnie and try and put things right.

***

Two days after sending her hasty reply, Ben wrote a second time, giving her the dates of his embarkation leave. He'd been given clearance to return to his regiment somewhere in Africa and was due to depart on a troop ship leaving from Liverpool at the end of the month.

They would have five days together in London and then she would accompany him to Liverpool and hopefully be able to wave him off. As he was a solo passenger, tagging along with a different regiment of soldiers, he was making his own arrangements.

Eileen had never recovered her gas mask, but

she'd not been asked to replace it. Her tin hat was another matter but luckily she hadn't had to pay for that either as it turned up in the stores. Permanent staff at the barracks only had occasional kit inspections, unlike the trainees.

She'd been to see Mr Billings and settled his account to date and he'd assured her that because he had sworn affidavits from three witnesses, there would be no need for any of them to appear in court in person. Eileen had been dreading that, so this was a relief.

She scarcely slept the night before she left for London and got up at dawn to have an illegal bath, wash her hair and make sure she was fragrant from top to toe.

'Good luck, I hope everything goes all right,' her roommate, Sybil, said from her bed as Eileen was tiptoeing out, trying not to wake her up.

'Thank you, I won't be telling you *all* about it, but I promise to give you the general gist when I get back.'

Her aim was to catch the first train into London, even though it meant paying more for the ticket and travelling in the rush hour with pinstripe-suited businessmen holding briefcases and furled umbrellas.

As she stepped out of the base, her eyes widened and her mouth rounded. Parked by the kerb was the unforgettable bright red MG with her beloved Ben leaning nonchalantly against it – she'd forgotten he still owned this dashing sports car.

In three strides, he was at her side. He swept her into his arms and kissed her, regardless of the gawping spectators enjoying every moment of their reunion. She was breathless when he finally released her. His eyes blazed down at her and he pulled a ring box from his pocket, flipped it open and then slid the magnificent diamond onto her finger. She was glad that she'd removed her unwanted wedding ring weeks ago.

'My darling, I guessed you'd leave at the crack of dawn so came to meet you. My car's been in a local garage waiting for me to collect it. I've cancelled the hotel booking in London and thought we could take a road trip together and make our way slowly to Liverpool.'

'That sounds even better than staying in Town and will give us an extra day. I've brought my old wedding band so if I put it on, nobody will know that we're not what we appear to be.'

'You'll do no such thing. Throw the bloody thing away or sell it if you must. I bought your wedding ring at the same time as I bought this.'

Carefully she removed the ring he'd just put on

her finger, and he slipped the plain gold band on first and she was thrilled the other one fitted snugly against it.

'How did you know what size my ring finger is? They could have been too big or too small.'

'When I was in the jewellers there was a young couple buying the same things and she looked to be your size. I asked her and she told me what to get,' Ben said.

'I think we'd better go; we've got an interested audience gathered by the bus stop. My reputation will be in shreds.'

'You're my fiancée, I'm entitled to kiss you in public if I wish to.'

He grabbed her bag and tossed it into the back seat. 'I love you so much, as far as I'm concerned you're already my wife in everything but name. Let's get going, shall we?'

He opened the passenger door for her and kissed her a second time before she settled into the leather seat. He vaulted over his door and seconds later engaged the gears and they roared off.

Eileen looked across at him – he'd never looked so handsome or so happy. She could scarcely believe that this wonderful man was now hers. It hadn't been like this when she married Danny and she'd never really understood the fuss people made about a wedding.

Today she did. Being with the man you loved, and who loved you, made the world a place of wonder. She relaxed into the seat, putting her right hand on his knee. He glanced across at her and his smile made her heart pound.

The roof was down, the sky was blue, and the future, despite the war, had never looked brighter.

BIBLIOGRAPHY

Girls in Khaki by Barbara Green
Sergeant Elsie by M. Crossley
Sister in Arms by Vee Robinson
Army Girls by Tessa Dunlop
Farming, Fighting and Family by Miranda McCormick
The Girls Who Went to War by Duncan Barrett and Nuala Green
Wartime Women by Dorothy Sheridan
The Girls Behind the Guns by Dorothy Brewer Kent
The Women's Royal Army Corps by Shelford Bidwell
A to Z Atlas Guide to London by Alexander Gross F. R. G. S.
Wartime Britain 1939–1945 by Juliet Gardiner
How We Lived Then by Norman Longmate
The War Illustrated News edited by Sir John Hammerton
BBC History Archives
It's a Long Way to Tooting Broadway by Reginald Cambridge
The War Diaries of Colin Dunford Wood edited by James Dunford Wood
An Englishman at War: The Wartime Diaries of Stanley Christopher DSO, MC, TD, 1939–45 edited by James Holland

ACKNOWLEDGMENTS

I wish to thank my husband's niece Brenda Bensley for giving me an almost complete set of *The War Illustrated News*. To have primary source material like this is invaluable for a historical fiction writer.

facebook.com/fenella miller
to her.com/novelistwriter

ABOUT THE AUTHOR

Fenella J. Miller is a bestselling writer of historical sagas. She also has a passion for Regency romantic adventures and has published over fifty to great acclaim.

Sign up to Fenella J. Miller's mailing list for news, competitions and updates on future books.

Visit Fenella's website: www.fenellajmiller.co.uk

Follow Fenella on social media here:

facebook.com/fenella.miller

twitter.com/fenellawriter

ALSO BY FENELLA J. MILLER

Goodwill House Series

The War Girls of Goodwill House

New Recruits at Goodwill House

Duty Calls at Goodwill House

The Land Girls of Goodwill House

A Wartime Reunion at Goodwill House

Wedding Bells at Goodwill House

A Christmas Baby at Goodwill House

The Army Girls Series

Army Girls Reporting For Duty

Standalone

The Land Girl's Secret

Sixpence Stories

Introducing Sixpence Stories!

Discover page-turning historical novels from your favourite authors, meet new friends and be transported back in time.

Join our book club Facebook group

https://bit.ly/SixpenceGroup

Sign up to our newsletter

https://bit.ly/SixpenceNews

Boldwood

Boldwood Books is an award-winning fiction publishing company seeking out the best stories from around the world.

Find out more at www.boldwoodbooks.com

Join our reader community for brilliant books, competitions and offers!

Follow us
@BoldwoodBooks
@TheBoldBookClub

Sign up to our weekly deals newsletter

https://bit.ly/BoldwoodBNewsletter

www.ingramcontent.com/pod-product-compliance
Lightning Source LLC
Chambersburg PA
CBHW010659100726
47900CB00010B/2731